Laura Martin writes historical romances
with an adventurous undercurrent. When
not writing she spends her time working
as a doctor in Cambridgeshire, where
she lives with her husband. In her spare
moments Laura loves to lose herself in a
book, and has been known to read from
cover to cover in a single day when the story
is particularly gripping. She also loves to
travel—especially visiting historical sites
and far-flung shores.

AN EARL TO SAVE HER REPUTATION

Laura Martin

MILLS & BOON

First published in Great Britain 2018
by Mills & Boon, an imprint of HarperCollins*Publishers*
1 London Bridge Street, London, SE1 9GF

Large Print edition 2018

ISBN: 978-0-263-07494-9

MIX
Paper from
responsible sources
FSC® C007454

This book is produced from independently certified
FSC™ paper to ensure responsible forest management. For
more information visit www.harpercollins.co.uk/green.

Printed and bound in Great Britain
by CPI Group (UK) Ltd, Croydon, CR0 4YY

For my family, all of you.
Together you make me stronger.

Chapter One

'Three husbands in six years. If I didn't know it to be true, I wouldn't think it possible.'

'And the rumours of how those poor men died…'

'She might have a pretty face, but I wouldn't want any relative of mine becoming embroiled with her. One can only guess what will happen to husband number four.'

'It's nothing short of scandalous how she's swanning around this ballroom. Hardly out of mourning and she's all smiles and laughter.'

'And insisting she continue to run that grubby little business of her second husband. It's not lady-like and it's not proper.'

Anna closed her eyes for a moment before pressing herself further into the recess of the ballroom. The two women who were gossiping openly and maliciously were shielded from view by a tall, lush potted plant. But one of them only needed to move a few inches to their right or left and they would catch sight of Anna desperately trying to avoid them.

The words themselves didn't hurt. She had been married three times and all three husbands had died within a year of their marriage. Anna was well aware of the less-than-complimentary names she was called by the spiteful matrons and wide-eyed debutantes. *Murderer, husband killer, black widow.* It didn't seem to matter to them that it just wasn't true and Anna had learnt long ago that it was better to let people speculate than to fuel the gossip with denials and pleas to be left alone.

Despite becoming hardened to the infamy, Anna hated the sort of situation she found herself in right now. She wished she could just slink away without anyone noticing her presence.

'Lady Fortescue, how pleasant to see you again after so long,' a man Anna vaguely recognised called out in a voice that seemed to echo off the walls. From her position behind the plant pot Anna saw the two gossips turning to look her way. There was no escaping their line of sight.

Straightening her back, dropping her shoulders and lifting her chin, adopting the posture that made her look more confident even if she didn't feel it, Anna stepped out of the recess and into the ballroom. She acknowledged the man with a polite incline of her head, then turned to fix the two women with a glacial stare.

'Give my regards to your brother, Mrs Weston. Such a darling man,' Anna said, before gliding away as if she didn't have a care in the world. Anna wasn't sure if Mrs Weston even had a brother, they'd certainly never been introduced, but the small deception was worth it for the look of abject horror on both women's faces.

Anna needed to get away. With a quick glance across the ballroom she saw Beatrice, her young cousin who she had agreed to chaperon for the Season, dancing a lively cotillion, her face lit up by a sunny smile and her chest heaving from the exertion. Beatrice would be unlikely to require Anna's attention for a few minutes at least, so quickly Anna slipped out of the ballroom.

It was noticeably cooler in the hallway and there was a scent of freshly cut flowers mixed with the smell of hundreds of burning candles. Even out here small groups gathered, glad to be away from the heat and crowds in the ballroom for a few minutes, and Anna had to force herself to walk calmly past them rather than pick up her skirts and run. She just wanted some privacy, or even better anonymity, to be able to enjoy the music and dancing without everyone talking about her behind their hands.

As she ventured further from the ballroom the hallway became quieter. Anna felt her heart beginning to slow and the panic that had seized her only moments before start to subside. She tried one door handle, then another, finding an unlocked door on her third attempt. Quickly she slipped into the room, closing the door softly behind her.

It took a few minutes for her eyes to adjust to the darkness after the brilliantly lit hallway, but after a while Anna could make out the lines of bookshelves against the walls and the shapes of a few comfortable chairs with a desk at one end. This was some sort of study or library, the perfect retreat for a few moments' peace. Before long she would have to steel herself for another round of sideways looks and malicious gossip in the ballroom, but right now she would just enjoy the solitude.

Anna lowered herself into a high-backed chair, her posture rigid even though no one else would see her. Her late husband, her *latest* late husband, had been a stickler for good posture and impeccable manners. Anna had learnt quickly to glide slowly around the house, sit with a straight back and never let any emotion show on her face. The punishment for breaking these rules was unmerciful, like many of Lord Fortescue's whims.

Closing her eyes, she listened to the distant hum of conversation from the ballroom and the first faint notes of a waltz. Even through the background noise Anna noticed the sound of hurried footsteps getting closer, but before she could move the door to the study opened and two people slipped inside. It was apparent immediately that Anna's unwanted companions were a man and a woman, and by the excited whispers and scent of champagne she could only assume they were here for some secret assignation.

'Your husband won't miss you?' the man said, as Anna heard the rustle of silk.

'Old fool is at the gaming tables—he wouldn't notice a stampede of wild horses.'

Anna wondered if she should stand and make her presence known. The last thing she wanted was to become embroiled in this couple's illicit affair, but she didn't much desire to be witness to their intimacy either.

She'd just gripped the armrests, ready to push herself up, when the door opened for a second time. Anna heard the couple freeze, then spring apart in a rustle of fabric and clatter of shoes.

The light of a candle illuminated the room, causing the shadows to lengthen around her. She sank back into the chair, fervently hoping that the new guest would scare away the couple and then leave her in peace.

'My apologies,' a deep, slightly amused voice said. Anna analysed the tone and intonation, but was sure she had never met this newcomer before. Even after being removed from society for the past couple of years she still was familiar with most of the aristocratic gentlemen who frequented these balls, but this man she did not think she recognised.

The young woman gasped theatrically and ran from the room.

'Edgerton.'

'Wilbraham.'

The two men greeted each other with just a single word which suggested they knew one another at least passably well. The silence stretched out uncomfortably as Anna in her hidden position held her breath and willed both men to leave.

'You won't say anything, old chap?'

'No. Not my place.'

Footsteps and the closing of the door followed, but the candlelight still illuminated the room and

Anna could hear the light breathing of one of the gentlemen.

Wondering whether to make a dash for the door, Anna shifted in her chair just as the newcomer came into view.

'Good evening,' he said, no trace of surprise at finding her sitting in the high-back chair evident in either his face or his voice.

'Good evening.' Despite her thumping heart Anna managed to sound poised and calm. Years of practice at maintaining a serene façade came in useful sometimes.

'Looking for a little peace?'

'Yes.' Anna kept her voice clipped and icy, hoping the gentleman would understand she wanted to be left alone.

She watched as he sauntered around the study, opening cupboards and cabinets until he came across what he was looking for: a bottle of whisky and two short glasses.

'Can't abide champagne,' the gentleman said, pouring out two generous measures of the caramel-coloured liquid. 'And punch is even worse.'

He held out one of the glasses, waiting for Anna to take it before he sat down in the chair next to hers. Taking a gulp, he examined the liquid thoughtfully before chuckling softly.

'What's so funny?' Anna asked, regretting the question as soon as it passed her lips. She knew better than to engage.

'Prendy's servants are watering down his whisky,' he said, raising the glass to his lips for another taste.

'Prendy's?'

'Lord Prenderson. Our host.'

'You know him well?'

'Doesn't everyone know everyone else?'

Anna was just about to bid her companion farewell when he fixed her with a penetrating stare.

'Although I don't think we've ever met.' He regarded her, letting his eyes sweep from the top of her head, across her features and down over her body. 'I'm sure I'd remember.'

The polite thing would be to introduce herself, yet Anna stood abruptly, set her untouched glass on the table and took a step towards the door.

'I wouldn't go out there just yet if I were you.'

She took another step forward.

'Bad idea.'

Two more steps. In another few seconds she would be out of the study and heading back towards the crowds.

'It's your choice, of course, but the gossips would be delighted to find you in here unchaperoned.'

Anna stiffened, closing her eyes for a brief few seconds before turning slowly and facing her companion.

'Gossips?'

'A group of middle-aged matrons are recovering from the heat of the ballroom out in the hall. I'm sure it would not escape their notice that you were in here with Lord Wilbraham and Mrs Featherstone.' He frowned as if something had just occurred to him. 'What were you planning on doing if they'd decided to further their intimacy?'

'In the study? So close to the ballroom? I hardly think that was likely,' Anna said, her voice dry and her face serene.

'I understand some people find the danger exciting.'

Anna knew he was teasing her now, but instead of rising to the bait she changed the subject.

'When will it be safe to exit, Mr Edgerton?'

'Lord Edgerton,' he corrected absently. 'And now you have me at a disadvantage.'

'Lady Fortescue,' Anna supplied reluctantly.

He fixed her with a curious gaze that told her he'd heard the rumours. *All* the rumours.

'The notorious Lady Fortescue,' he murmured.

'You're not meant to say that,' Anna said, adding under her breath, 'At least not to my face.'

'It is a pleasure to meet you, Lady Fortescue,' Edgerton said, standing and taking her hand, bringing it to his lips after a few seconds.

This close Anna could appreciate his physical size. He was at least a foot taller than her and sported broad shoulders that filled his jacket perfectly. For the first time since he'd entered, Anna realised the folly of being alone with this man. It wasn't just the scandal that could occur if they were discovered, but the risk he might take advantage. Slowly she stepped back. He didn't look as though he were about to pounce on her, but history had shown her to be a poor judge of character. Kind eyes and a relaxed manner didn't mean a man was trustworthy.

Harry saw the flash of fear in Lady Fortescue's eyes before the stony façade once again concealed her emotions. Quickly he stepped back, realising it was him she was afraid of. That had never been his intention, to scare the poor woman—he'd been called many things in his life, but frightening was not one of them.

'Let me check the hallway,' he said, summoning his friendliest smile.

Crossing to the doorway, he opened the door a crack and peered out. The group of meddling matrons still stood fanning themselves and chattering ten feet away. There was no way past them, at least not without being seen.

'Still there. I'm sure they will return to the ballroom shortly.'

Harry returned to his chair and sat, watching Lady Fortescue out of the corner of his eye. When she'd introduced herself he'd been unable to stop from staring. Normally so in control of his reactions, he'd been thrown by her identity. She was notorious, perhaps the most notorious widow in society at the present time. Married three times before the age of twenty-five, her latest husband, Lord Fortescue, in the ground for twelve months now. He'd expected her to look different somehow, perhaps more exotic. Instead a perfectly pleasant-looking young woman stood before him. She was pretty, but not any more so than most of the young debutantes. He couldn't deny she had poise and grace, but there was a coolness about her that hinted at a reserved character and a tendency to shun company. Her most intriguing feature were her eyes. Cool and grey, they seemed impenetrable. Normally a young woman's eyes gave away her emotions, but not Lady Fortescue's. If eyes were the window to the soul, then Lady Fortescue's were shuttered and barred against intruders.

They remained silent for some minutes, Harry reclining in the armchair, Lady Fortescue standing in the middle of the room, her hands folded together in front of her abdomen, the perfect picture of demure womanhood.

'So tell me,' Harry said when he could bear the silence no longer, 'are the rumours true?'

His companion sighed, a deep and heartfelt sound that hinted that she'd rather be anywhere but here.

'I find rumours rarely are,' she said evasively.

'Very true,' Harry murmured. He knew better than most the damage malicious gossip could cause. 'How do you bear it? People talking about you, speculating?'

Lady Fortescue shrugged, an instinctive movement that she seemed to try to suppress at the last moment. 'People will always talk. It doesn't matter what they say if you don't listen.'

Although she was younger than he, and undoubtedly hadn't been exposed to as much of the world as he, she had a quiet wisdom about her that suggested she'd had more important things to cope with than a little gossip in her time.

'Most women would not feel comfortable leaving the ballroom on their own, let alone wandering about a strange house,' Harry said, changing the focus of the conversation. He was curious as to why she had put herself in this position in the first place. Although the *ton* were meant to be respectable, the cream of society, some of the men still got uncontrollably drunk at functions such as this and thought it their right to take advantage of any unchaperoned woman. From a young age the future debutantes were cautioned about wandering away from crowds if they wanted to keep their virtue intact. A necessary requirement Harry was painfully aware of.

Again that almost imperceptible shrug. Lady Fortescue might be intriguing, but she certainly wasn't the easiest woman to make conversation with.

'Sometimes a little peace is worth a considered risk.' Moving gracefully, as if she were gliding across the floor instead of walking, Lady Fortescue crossed to the window. 'This leads out on to the terrace,' she said, turning her neck to look in one direction and then the other. 'It would be an easy way back to the ballroom.'

'Surely my company isn't so intolerable you have to contemplate climbing out a window?'

A grimace and then a reluctant smile flitted across Lady Fortescue's face. Although the smile was barely more than an upturning of the corner of her lips, it transformed her face and Harry caught a glimpse of what her three husbands must have been so enamoured with.

'I am supposed to be chaperoning my young cousin,' she said by way of explanation, still eyeing up the window as if it were a valid option.

'You're far too young to be relegated to the role of chaperon,' Harry said, without thinking the words through. It was a compliment, in a roundabout way, and he had the feeling Lady Fortescue was not comfortable with receiving compliments.

'Three times a widow,' Lady Fortescue said, adding so quietly Harry was sure he wasn't meant to hear, 'and happy to never have to dance a waltz again.'

She'd just stepped away from the window when the faint hum of voices out in the hallway became a little louder. Both Harry and his companion stiffened, and Harry realised he was holding his breath waiting to see if the doorknob started to turn.

'We can't be found together,' Harry whispered, standing quickly and crossing to the window. Normally he wouldn't worry for his own reputation in this sort of situation. As a titled and wealthy gentleman he could generally withstand being found in a compromising position with a young lady, even one as notorious as Lady Fortescue. However, following his sister's unfortunate liaison with the dishonourable Captain Mountfield last year and the ensuing scandal, the Edgerton family was not in a position to be embarrassed again. Added to that the look of pure fear in Lady Fortescue's eyes at the thought of giving the gossips of London society something to really get their teeth into, the window escape was looking more appealing every second that passed.

Quickly he unbolted the window, slid it up and motioned for Lady Fortescue to join him. She was at his side in an instant, nodding as he motioned for her to go first. With more grace than should have been possible in this situation Lady Fortescue gathered up her skirts, giving Harry a fleeting glimpse of a slender, stockinged leg, and allowed him to steady her as she stepped up to the windowsill.

Behind them the voices were getting louder still and now Harry had no doubt they were heading for the study. If he could just get Lady Fortescue out of the window he would be able to distract whoever came into the room until she had managed to move out of sight.

She stepped up as the doorknob began to turn. One foot was through the window, balancing on the sill outside as the door began to open. Then Lady Fortescue gave a quiet cry of pain, lost her footing and came careening back into the room. Harry instinctively caught her, spinning round with the impact of her body into his and ending up with her chest pressed against his, one arm looped around her waist and the other resting between her shoulder blades.

At that very instant the door opened fully.

'Merciful Lord,' Mrs Winter, one of the worst gossips in the whole of London, exclaimed loudly.

Quietly Lady Fortescue groaned.

All in all there were four women standing on the other side of the study door. Each and every one looked thrilled to be at the centre of such a scandal.

Slowly, aware his every movement was being observed and mentally recorded for later dissection and discussion, Harry ensured Lady Fortescue had her balance before removing his arms and stepping away.

'Ladies,' he said with a polite bow.

'Lord Edgerton,' Mrs Winter gushed breathlessly, 'and Lady Fortescue.'

Muscling a path through her companions, a well-built lady in her late forties stepped into the room. Harry closed his eyes momentarily, wondering how he'd sinned to be punished this badly.

'Lord Edgerton, this really won't do,' Lady Prenderson, their hostess for this evening, said, her eyes burning with righteous indignation. 'This behaviour is unacceptable—having *relations* with this woman in my husband's study.'

Harry wasn't sure what she objected to the most: the supposed relations between him and Lady Fortescue or the fact that it had occurred in her husband's study.

'I expect this behaviour from certain people,' Lady Prenderson said, giving Lady Fortescue a disdainful look, 'but after the scandal your sister has caused your family I would have thought you would know better.'

Harry had been all ready to apologise, but the mention of his sister made a red curtain descend over his normally cool head. Lady Fortescue must have sensed this change in him and calmly stepped forward.

'Please excuse me, ladies, I have a duty to my cousin.' Her voice was cool and her demeanour poised and collected. Harry supposed she had endured all manner of gossip over the last few years—she must have had practice at dealing with staying calm when faced with further notoriety.

He knew she was just as bothered as he by the position they'd been discovered in—her eagerness to climb out the window to avoid exactly this situation was testament to that fact—but the face she showed the world was one of complete indifference.

None of the ladies in the doorway moved, blocking the escape route to the more populated ballroom. With a tremendous effort Harry managed to regain control of his emotions and stepped forward, taking Lady Fortescue's arm. There was only one thing to be done. He took a deep breath, quelled the doubts clamouring for attention in his mind and spoke.

'Ladies, may I present my fiancée,' Harry said with a confident and winning smile. 'Lady Fortescue has just agreed to marry me.'

Shock blossomed on the four faces gawping at them from the study door. Lady Fortescue barely reacted, the only sign she'd heard what he'd just said the subtle stiffening of the muscles Harry could feel where their arms interlinked. She was certainly difficult to shock.

'Surely not, Lord Edgerton,' Mrs Winter said, a hint of disappointment in her voice. Harry remembered she had two unmarried daughters and had to suppress a smile. The work of the meddling matron was never done.

'Now if you would excuse us, I wish to get my new fiancée a glass of champagne to celebrate.'

The crowd of gossips parted silently and Harry led Lady Fortescue through them and down the hallway. Only once they were back in the ballroom did they pause, with Lady Fortescue turning to him with a raised eyebrow.

'Fiancée?' she asked.

'It will save us both from the scandal.' It wasn't exactly true, but it would at least delay the moment of scandal until a point when they were both prepared for it.

'You've just engaged yourself to the most notorious woman in this ballroom. I hardly think you've saved yourself from scandal.'

Harry felt the heat begin to rise in his body. Surely she didn't think this a real engagement. He'd meant for it to be a simple ruse, an engagement that would last a few weeks, perhaps a month until something else noteworthy occurred in society, and then they would quietly go their separate ways. The *ton* would still gossip, but it would not be the most scandalous thing to happen all year.

'Being found together in the Prendersons' study will be all over London by breakfast tomorrow morning. This way we are an unlikely engaged couple, not a disgraced earl and a widow.'

'I thank you for your consideration,' Lady Fortescue said, her grey eyes latching on to Harry's and making him shiver with the intensity, 'but I think it better we dispense with this pretence and ride out the scandal.' Leaning in, she whispered in his ear, 'Trust me, a little gossip isn't the worst thing in the world.'

Chapter Two

'I really wouldn't read that, my dear,' Mr Tenby, Anna's kindly uncle, said, a look of concern in his eyes.

Anna's hand stilled on top of the folded gossip sheets. She'd hoped the news from the Prendersons' ball would not be reported for another couple of days. It was a miracle how quickly they seemed to be able to publish the latest intrigue and style faux pas.

'Words cannot hurt me,' Anna said brightly, picking up the paper and scanning the text, trying to ignore the concerned looks coming across the breakfast table from her uncle and her cousin Beatrice.

'"*Congratulations are due to Lady Fortescue on her engagement to Lord Edgerton at Lord and Lady Prenderson's ball two days ago. Recently out of mourning for her third husband, Lady For-*

tescue will no doubt be keen to legalise her tie to one of London's most eligible bachelors."'

Anna read the offending paragraph out loud, wondering how many other people were doing the same thing at breakfast tables across London.

'What did happen, Anna?' Beatrice asked.

Ever since the Prenderson ball Anna had kept herself distant from the rest of the household and steadfastly refused any visitors. Even her sweet younger cousin had been kept in the dark.

'A misunderstanding, nothing more.'

'This Edgerton chap has called on you twice,' Mr Tenby said. 'Seems keen to see you.'

'He was merely trying to save an impossible situation.'

'Decent young man by all accounts.'

'Uncle,' Anna said kindly, 'I do not care if he takes in waifs and strays off the streets and gives half his income to the poor, I will never marry again.'

'He's very handsome, in a rugged sort of way,' Beatrice said.

Anna supposed he had been handsome. Sparkling blue eyes contrasting with hair so dark it was almost black, and a toned and muscular physique. She could see why he was dubbed one of

London's most eligible bachelors even without the title and the income that went with it.

'He could look like a wild boar for all that it matters,' Anna said.

'And he proposed to you to save you from scandal. He's clearly a gentleman of honour,' Beatrice said, her voice dreamy and distant.

Remembering what it was like to be eighteen and innocent, Anna ignored this last statement entirely, biting back the retort that was on her tongue.

'Anna dear, you know you will always have a home here with me,' her uncle said, 'no matter what happens with your settlement from Lord Fortescue. I enjoy your company and dare say will even more so when my little Beatrice has left for a life with a husband of her own.' Mr Tenby paused, as if considering whether to say more. 'But more than your company, I wish for your happiness. One day you may want to marry again. You're still young, you may want children, a home of your own. Don't rule out anything yet.'

'Of course, Uncle.' Anna smiled at the kindly man who had taken her in after her husband had died. Lord Fortescue had three children from his first marriage. Two brutish sons and a spiteful daughter who had turned Anna out of her home less than thirty minutes after her husband's death. They'd taken everything, left her with nothing but the clothes she was wearing, and even now were contesting the settlements she was due from her late husband's estate. Anna's uncle had travelled halfway across the country when he'd heard of her plight, swept her up into his carriage and brought her back to his home. He'd reminded her that there was kindness in the world and that not everyone was cruel and selfish.

Patting her on the hand, Mr Tenby rose from his seat and made his way towards the door.

'Whatever your feelings for this gentleman, he deserves an audience,' he said softly, 'even if it is just to end this *engagement* between you.'

'Yes, Uncle.'

Anna knew he was right. It had been rude and cowardly to refuse to see Lord Edgerton the past two days. If he came to call on her today, she would see him briefly and clear up any misunderstanding between them.

Harry whistled as he strode up the stairs two at a time. The sun was shining and it was impossible to feel anything but positive on such a day. Today he would insist on an audience with Lady Fortescue and no one would stand in his way.

The door opened before he could raise the polished doorknocker and an elderly butler opened the door.

'Lady Fortescue is in the music room, Lord Edgerton. She will see you directly.'

Perhaps this was going to be easier than he had anticipated.

Looking around him with interest, Harry followed the butler up the sweeping staircase to the first floor. As they climbed Harry could hear an exquisitely played piece of piano music getting louder, as if the pianist was growing in confidence with every note.

'Lord Edgerton,' the butler announced as he showed Harry into a sunny room. The piano music stopped abruptly and Lady Fortescue stood to greet him, her expression as inscrutable as it had been at the Prendersons' ball.

'A pleasure to see you again, Lady Fortescue. I do hope you have not been unwell,' Harry said pointedly, reminding the woman who stood before him he'd tried to visit twice in the last two days. He wondered if she would lie, if she would pretend to have been stricken down with a bad chest or a headache, but instead Lady Fortescue regarded him for a few seconds before speaking.

'I must confess I was hoping to put all this nonsense behind us,' she said quietly.

Harry waited for her to step out from behind the piano and glide towards him before he took her hand and bent over it formally. He felt her flinch ever so slightly at his touch, but her expression did not change.

'Please have a seat.' She motioned to one of two upright chairs positioned a few feet apart.

'The world thinks we are engaged,' Harry said, getting straight to the point. Lady Fortescue's cool grey eyes were disconcerting when she fixed them so intently on his.

'It would seem so.' There was no reproach in her voice, just an air of mild uninterest.

'I suppose that is preferable to the alternative.'

'Which is?'

'The rumours of us being found together in a compromising position.'

Tilting her head to one side, Lady Fortescue appeared to consider this for a moment.

'You're probably correct,' she conceded.

'Forgive me for my bluntness, but you seem wildly unconcerned about the gossip attached to our names,' Harry said.

The situation was feeling rather surreal. Normally if a man and a woman had been found in a compromising position it would be the woman who was eager to save her reputation. Gentlemen, especially titled ones, were forgiven all manner of indiscretions. Gently bred ladies were not. It was perhaps unfair, but it was the way society worked.

Harry watched Lady Fortescue carefully and detected a tiny twitch in the muscles of her fore-head. It could mean anything, but he wondered if it was yet another sign that Lady Fortescue was unnaturally good at hiding her emotions.

'Lord Edgerton,' she said with a sigh, 'before you met me what had you heard?'

Harry opened his mouth to answer and then closed it again. He'd heard plenty. The ballrooms and gentlemen's clubs had been rife with rumours and speculation about Lady Fortescue and her three deceased husbands.

'I take it from your silence the rumours were not complimentary...' She paused, smiling to re-veal a perfect set of white teeth. 'Ever since my second husband passed away people have talked about me, not to my face, of course, but they have picked and prodded at my life as if it were nothing more than an episode for public entertainment.'

'That cannot be pleasant.'

'It isn't, of course it isn't, but I'm still here. A little gossip isn't the worst thing in the world.' It was the second time she'd made that statement, the second time she'd brushed off the damage unkind words could do, and Harry began to wonder what Lady Fortescue *did* think was the worst thing in the world.

'A scandal can ruin lives,' Harry said resolutely. 'Even end lives,' he added too quietly for Lady Fortescue to hear.

'It depends on the person and the nature of the scandal, I suppose.'

Harry thought of his sister. She'd always been strong, vivacious, until the fateful night when her reputation had been dashed by a scoundrel of a young man and a few malicious onlookers. Before it had happened Harry would have said his sister could withstand anything; now he knew how fragile people could be.

'I am grateful for your concern,' Lady Fortescue said softly, the coolness of her demeanour lifting slightly. 'You want to do the honourable thing and I'm sure any other young woman would be delighted to continue with a sham engagement until the rumours were lessened, if not forgotten.'

'But not you?'

Every word she uttered was considered and carefully chosen, every movement precise. And every moment that passed by Harry found himself becoming more and more intrigued by the notorious Lady Fortescue.

'People already say the worst about me—another rumour is not going to make much difference.'

Harry wasn't so sure. Sometimes even the weakest of gossip could be turned into something hurtful and malicious.

Sitting up even straighter in her seat, Lady Fortescue fixed Harry with an assessing gaze. 'Unless you have a reason to want to avoid the scandal.'

Of course he did. The Edgerton family name had been dragged through the dirt after his sister's disgrace, but Harry was titled and reasonably wealthy and his reputation wouldn't suffer overly much by being caught in a compromising position with Lady Fortescue. Especially if he married a nice, respectable young woman in a few months' time. No, his reason for being here today wasn't for himself or the rest of the Edgertons— in fact, he knew by embroiling himself with such a notorious widow he was opening himself up for more gossip and scandal than if he just stayed away. The real reason for him being here today was a sense of wanting to do the right thing by a young woman who might have a bad reputation, but seemed decent and vulnerable in Harry's assessment. Perhaps he wouldn't have been so insistent a year ago, but seeing his sister go through just such a scandal had awakened him to the hurt a woman could suffer at the hands of an unscrupulous man.

'Not at all,' Harry said. Lady Fortescue did not need to hear the dark, intimate Edgerton family secrets. 'There is simply the matter of our supposed engagement to deal with.'

For the first time today Lady Fortescue smiled, her eyes sparkling with repressed humour. 'You can throw me over, I really don't mind.'

'Shall I say I caught you in the arms of another man?' Harry couldn't help himself, he wanted to see how far he could push her before she cracked.

There was a beat of silence, then Lady Fortescue's shoulders sagged a little, the perfect posture disappearing and with it some of the formality she exuded.

'I've been rude,' she said, her voice softer, less clipped. 'Inexcusably so. I apologise. I suppose I'm not used to talking to people.'

The door opened before Harry could answer, the elderly butler followed closely by a young maid.

'I thought you might like to offer your guest some tea, my lady,' the butler said.

The maid set down a tray with two teacups, a

pot, a jug of milk and a plate of crumbly biscuits before hurriedly leaving the room. The butler hesitated for a moment at the door.

'Perhaps the gentleman will be staying for lunch?' he asked, almost hopefully.

Lady Fortescue laughed, exuding warmth towards the elderly servant, her grey eyes glittering as she turned back to Harry.

'I'm sure you're far too busy.'

He inclined his head. There was always work to be done running his country estate and looking over the accounts, but he could of course have made time for lunch.

The butler left, muttering something about a proper invitation before closing the door behind him.

'Your uncle's butler seems very keen to have guests to wait upon.'

'I expect my cousin, Beatrice, put him up to asking. He is completely devoted to her, probably would jump in front of a horse if she asked him to without a second's thought.'

'Your cousin is playing matchmaker?'

Lady Fortescue grimaced, a reaction that would have normally dented Harry's pride, but he was quickly learning this young widow was strongly opposed to any future romantic link.

'Forgive me for not ordering tea sooner,' she said. 'I am not used to entertaining guests.'

Most wives of titled gentlemen were exemplary hosts, their main role to welcome guests into a well-looked-after home, but perhaps during her mourning period Lady Fortescue had locked herself away out of devotion to her late husband and forgotten the basics of hospitality.

Harry sipped his tea, selected a biscuit and munched on it. All in all it had been a strange morning. He'd expected to come away with an engagement, at least in name, to Lady Fortescue. Instead he'd been more or less dismissed, despite the young widow's softening in the last part of their interview.

Standing, Harry was just about to take his leave when the door opened again and the doddery butler entered.

'A package for you, my lady.'

He'd never seen the blood drain from someone's face as quickly as it did from Lady Fortescue's. Quietly she thanked the butler, who placed the package on the table in front of her before leaving the room.

Her hands were shaking as she stood, an unnaturally sunny smile plastered on her face.

'Thank you for visiting.' Her words came out as a choked whisper, and a hand flew to her mouth as if to claw them back in.

Chapter Three

The world was spinning, or that was how it seemed to Anna. Everything in the room had gone blurry and she felt herself stagger uncoordinatedly a few steps to one side. Before she could get her panic under control strong arms had looped around her waist and were guiding her back to the armchair, pressing her firmly, insistently, into the seat.

'Take deep, slow breaths.' Lord Edgerton's voice was quiet and calm in her ear.

Silently Anna cursed. Two minutes later and Lord Edgerton would have left. Now there would be questions, enquiries about her health, probably even a follow-up visit. At least the rules of politeness meant he would not enquire what was in the package.

'What on earth is in that package?' Lord Edgerton murmured, more to himself than to her.

'That's it, long, deep breaths, you'll feel recovered in a moment.'

Thankfully he didn't seem inclined to call for a servant or her cousin to come and attend her; he seemed perfectly content to deal with this himself. Anna had to admire a man who could deal calmly with a panicking near-stranger—most would just step back and convince themselves it wasn't their problem.

Opening her eyes, she saw the room had come back into focus. In front of her she could see her hands gripping the arms of the chair so firmly her knuckles had turned white, and a few feet further away was the offending package.

'Have some tea,' Lord Edgerton suggested, backing away and sitting down in the other armchair, his demeanour remarkably relaxed.

She declined with a shake of her head. The teacup would only rattle in the saucer and give away quite how discomposed she was, if the attack of panic hadn't done that enough already.

'Tell me it is none of my concern,' Lord Edgerton said, his eyes fixed on hers, 'but what could be so awful about this package on the table?'

'It is none of your concern,' Anna said, trying to inject some haughtiness into her voice, but failing miserably—the squeak that came forth from her mouth was more adolescent girl than woman of the world.

Lord Edgerton actually grinned. 'The gossips say you are unreadable, Lady Fortescue. Unreadable and superior, but I think they've got you all wrong. Right now I can read you as easily as I read the morning papers.' He paused, catching her eye and holding it until Anna was forced to look away. 'You're petrified of whatever is inside that box.'

Slowly she inclined her head; there was no point denying it. He'd witnessed her reaction first-hand.

'What do you think is inside?'

'Truly, I have no idea,' she said honestly. It could be a bloodied rag, a pile of excrement, a particularly graphic and threatening letter. All of these things she'd received in similar packages over the last few weeks. 'But it won't be anything pleasant.'

'There's no markings to say where or who it is from. How can you be so sure it will be something unpleasant?'

Instead of answering Anna stood, steeling herself mentally before raising her hands and starting to open the package. Her fingers were shaking so badly that she fumbled with the string that held the box closed. Quickly Lord Edgerton rose to his feet and placed a cool hand on top of hers, stilling her fingers.

'Allow me,' he said, not waiting for her to reply before unfastening the string and opening the box.

The sharp inhalation of surprise told Anna that he hadn't been prepared for whatever was inside. She stepped forward, but Lord Edgerton moved in front of her, blocking her view. As he raised his hands to her arms she flinched, as she always did whenever anyone touched her, but he gripped her gently but insistently, moving her away from the table.

'What was inside?' Anna asked.

'A dead animal.'

Anna felt the bile rise up in her throat. The vendetta against her was escalating. In a few short weeks it had gone from threatening letters to a dead animal in a box.

'What sort of animal?'

'A cat, I think.'

Anna stiffened, torn between breaking free from Lord Edgerton's grip and seeing for herself, and burying her head in his shoulder and crying for the animal she knew instinctively was in that box.

'A ginger cat? Small?'

Lord Edgerton nodded. 'Was it yours?'

Morosely Anna nodded. Beatrice had bought her the animal soon after Anna had come to live in London. It had been her younger cousin's attempt to brighten Anna's days and in a strange and unexpected way it had worked. At least until a few days ago when the lovely creature had gone missing.

Lord Edgerton turned to her, his face fixed in an expression of determination. 'You need to tell me what is going on here.'

She needed to do nothing of the sort. He was little more than a stranger, albeit a chivalrous one. For a moment she avoided his eyes, trying to work out exactly what she could say to make Lord Edgerton go away and forget what he had seen here. It was a deep instinct, this need to deal with her problems with no help from anyone else. For so long she'd been on her own—even through her marriages she'd never found a true companion, someone to share the difficulties of daily life with.

'I think you should leave,' Anna said quietly, knowing he would protest, but trying all the same.

'Not a chance.'

'This really is none of your concern.'

'Would you rather I called your uncle in here? Or your cousin?'

Silently Anna shook her head.

'I thought not. You haven't told them, have you?' he asked.

'There is no need. I am dealing with it.'

'You've had similar packages before?'

Closing her eyes for a moment, Anna assessed her options. Either she could confide a little in Lord Edgerton, just enough to satisfy his curiosity, or she could insist he leave and risk him informing her uncle of what was happening.

'Can we go for a walk?' she asked, eyeing the package from a distance.

'Of course. What would you like done with the box?'

Anna felt the tears building in her eyes. Although she'd always insisted she wasn't an animal lover, her little cat had brought her happiness in a time of fear and uncertainty.

'Perhaps you would like to bury the cat discreetly?'

Before she could answer he picked up the box, folded the lid over to shield the dead animal from her eyes and tucked it under his arm.

'I will meet you on the front steps.'

Anna watched in amazement as he left the room, crossed the hallway and quickly descended the stairs to the basement, no doubt in search of a servant to help him with whatever it was he had in mind. Although she prized her independence, in this situation it was rather pleasant to have someone else take charge and make the decisions.

Lady Fortescue had just emerged into the hallway when Harry came striding up the stairs from the basement kitchen, taking them two at a time. He'd found a footman and paid him a generous sum to store the package somewhere discreet, warning the man against looking inside. To ensure he would comply, Harry had tied the string in a complicated knot which meant he would know if it had been tampered with. Later he would organise for the box to be buried in the garden and for the gardener to mark the spot with a rose or some other flower of Lady Fortescue's choice.

'Shall we take a walk to the park?' he suggested, offering Lady Fortescue his arm.

She nodded, her face still ashen from the surprise of finding out what was in the parcel.

They left the house and walked in silence for a few minutes, Harry content to let his companion gather her thoughts before pressing her for answers. He wasn't sure what she'd got herself mixed up in, but his curiosity had been piqued and some deep-seated instinct meant he couldn't abandon a woman in distress even if on the surface she didn't want his help.

'I'm not sure how much you know about me,' Lady Fortescue said quietly as they entered Hyde Park. It was a sunny day, but still chilly for April, and there weren't many people out taking the air at this hour.

'Not all that much,' Harry said, realising it was the truth. He'd heard many rumours, but none of them had included any information of substance.

'I've been married three times,' Lady Fortescue said, looking straight ahead as she spoke. 'My first husband was elderly and infirm, wealthy, of course, with a title. My father arranged the marriage and it was assumed it would not be a long-lasting union. He died seven months after we were married.'

'Lord Humphries,' Harry said. He remembered the announcement now and his mother sympathising with the young debutante who'd been forced into marrying such an elderly man.

'I was in mourning for a year and then I met Captain Trevels. I was a widow of some means and independent enough to make my own decisions, so I married Captain Trevels against my father's wishes.'

This union Harry had been unaware of. No doubt Lady Fortescue's family had wanted to hush up what they saw as an inferior match for their daughter.

'Soon after we married my husband was sent to India for a year. On his return he was dreadfully unwell and died only four weeks after our reunion.'

Two dead husbands in the space of a couple of years, but despite the society gossip there seemed nothing untoward about the deaths. Elderly men and officers of the army died all too often.

'Unfortunately my second husband had been a little too free with my inheritance and after my mourning period was complete I was dependent again on my father.'

'He chose your third husband?'

'I managed to hold out for two whole months before I agreed to marry Lord Fortescue,' she said with a grimace, 'but even at the very beginning I knew I had no choice. Eventually I would end up as Lady Fortescue.'

For such a private person Lady Fortescue was being remarkably open and honest about her past. Harry wondered if she found it easier talking to him, a relative stranger, than someone who was close to her. If he probed too much, got too close, he was sure it would be easy for her to push him away.

'Lord Fortescue had three children from his first marriage, all grown adults now. They resented our marriage from the very start. My husband was fifty-eight when we married, in good health and very physically active.'

'And then he died,' Harry summarised.

'And then he died. Of course his children tried to blame me. They threw me out of the house, have contested the settlements I am entitled to from the estate and even asked the local magistrate to investigate my husband's death.'

'So they're the ones sending you these horrible packages?'

'I don't know.' The words sounded so pitiful that Harry wondered just how much this young woman was having to deal with all on her own. 'The packages only started arriving when I came out of mourning. I wonder if the Fortescue children would have waited so long.'

'How many have there been?'

'Four packages, and two letters.'

'What was in the other packages?'

Lady Fortescue shuddered, her fingers tightening their grip on his arm involuntarily.

'One was full of excrement, from a horse, I think. One had a bloodied scarf and another an animal's heart.'

'And the content of the letters?'

'Vile words, threats, profanities.'

'But no clue as to the author?'

She shook her head. They walked on in silence for a few minutes, Harry trying to take in everything he'd just been told.

'Have you told anyone?'

She turned to him, her large grey eyes wide, and shook her head. 'Only you.'

Harry felt his pulse quicken as she regarded him with an expression of reluctant hopefulness. Even though their acquaintance was only a brief one already he felt a desire building not to disappoint her. Swallowing, he realised his mouth was dry and his tongue felt heavy behind his lips. Lady Fortescue might not be an exotic beauty, but she possessed a quiet, mesmerising quality that made it difficult to walk away.

'Lord Edgerton, what a delight,' a middle-aged woman called from some distance away and Harry had to search his memory for her name and the circumstances of their acquaintance. 'I'd heard rumours you and Lady Fortescue were engaged, and here you are walking out together. How lovely.'

'Mrs Henderson,' Harry said, taking the woman's proffered hand. 'It has been too long.'

'You must tell me,' Mrs Henderson said, flashing a smile at Lady Fortescue, 'how you managed to catch such a fine man as Lord Edgerton. I have an unmarried daughter and the best offer we've had so far is from the local vicar.'

From many women there would have been at least a hint of envy, but Mrs Henderson was a cheerful, unjudgemental soul who wouldn't begrudge a young couple's happiness.

'I have to confess I have no idea how it happened,' Lady Fortescue said softly.

At least she wasn't denying their engagement to anyone who would listen now. It would work out much better if they could pretend to be promised to one another for a month or two and then quietly break off the engagement. Harry was under no illusion that they would be able to avoid a scandal completely, but at least it would be at a moment of their own choosing.

'I will leave you to continue your walk,' Mrs

Henderson said, 'without the interruptions of a nosy old lady.'

'It is always a pleasure, Mrs Henderson.'

'The entirety of London society will know we have been out walking together by the end of the evening,' Lady Fortescue said with a shake of her head, following Mrs Henderson's departure with her solemn grey eyes. 'I don't understand why people are so interested in the lives of others.'

'Boredom and human nature,' Harry said with a shrug. Gently he guided Lady Fortescue over to a bench situated just in front of a small pond. 'Let me help you.'

'How? Why?'

'You're not very trusting.' It was said in jest, but he felt his companion stiffen next to him. 'Let me help you get to the bottom of who is sending you those packages, who is threatening you,' he ploughed on quickly.

'I'm sure you have much better things to be doing with your time.'

'Give me six weeks. If I haven't found out who is behind the threats by then, I will admit defeat.'

Six weeks should be plenty of time to find the culprit. Harry had spent five years in the army and, although he had fought in his share of skirmishes, most of the time he had been deployed to gather information, to blend in with the locals and uncover any plots and plans. Those were skills you never lost once acquired and it had been a while since Harry had been given a challenge like this.

'Why would you?' Lady Fortescue asked, turning those searching grey eyes on Harry and making him feel as though she were staring past his face and into his mind.

'No one should have to live in fear. No one should have to endure what you are enduring every single day.'

There was more to it than that, but Harry couldn't tell Lady Fortescue he'd seen the same desperate expression she'd had on her face when the package had arrived before. That in the weeks after his sister had been humiliated and shamed he'd seen that *emptiness*, that desperation. He had failed Lydia in her time of need and the results had been almost fatal—he would not let another woman suffer alone.

'Let me consider the idea,' she said.

'Shall I call on you tomorrow?'

'I have some business to conduct in the morning, but perhaps you would care to dine with us at lunchtime.'

'Perfect. I will look forward to it.'

Instinctively he raised her hand to his lips, brushing a kiss over the knuckles. Although she concealed it well, Harry sensed her discomfort at even this most innocent of contact. Moving away, he wondered just what had happened to Lady Fortescue to make her so averse to human touch.

Chapter Four

'There's been a problem, ma'am,' Billy Godden said as he rapped on the door and strode into the office, his face grim.

'Tell me, Billy.'

'Reports of a storm off the coast of Portugal. The Tildenhall Shipping Company have lost three ships, the London Shipping Company two and there are rumours many more have gone down.'

Anna closed her eyes for a few seconds, trying to digest this newest disaster that had befallen the company since she had taken over managing it.

'Both the *Lady Magdalene* and the *Norfolk* were scheduled to be sailing along the coast of Portugal.' Anna stood and crossed to the shelving unit on the opposite wall, running her fingers along the handwritten labels until she came to the correct one. Quickly she pulled out a large map, unrolled it and laid it on her desk. 'Where did the storm hit?'

Billy took his time, consulting a small note-book and tracing his fingers over the map before pointing out an area just to the south of the city of Porto.

Trying to keep calm, Anna opened the ledgers that contained the details of the routes and cargos of the two ships.

'If on schedule, the *Norfolk* should be out of danger—it is due to round the Cabo de Roca to-morrow.'

'And the *Lady Magdalene*?'

Tracing the predicted route with her finger, Anna grimaced.

'There have been no sightings?' she asked. 'No reports of it docking in Lisbon for repairs?' she asked hopefully.

'Nothing, ma'am.'

Resisting the urge to sink to the floor in de-spair, Anna rolled up the map and then focused on the details in the ledger. Twenty-four sailors were aboard the *Lady Magdalene*—she just hoped they were unharmed.

'Send out messages to anyone who might have information and see if you can persuade one of your men they might like a trip to Portugal to investigate if there are no sightings within the week. I will deal with the clients.'

'Yes, ma'am.'

Once she was alone Anna allowed her body to sag. The loss of a ship was devastating for any shipping company, but many of the larger outfits could withstand one loss here and there. The Trevels Shipping Company was still in its infancy. After the death of Lord Fortescue, the only thing his children had not contested was her ownership of the small shipping company her second husband had owned and run into the ground. When Anna had revived it she'd barely hoped that they would survive a year, but slowly they were emerging from the piles of debts and starting to make a small and hard-won profit. A disaster like this could cripple them.

Straightening up, Anna closed the ledger. She would not overreact. As yet there was no evidence the *Lady Magdalene* had sunk. The captain was experienced and knew how to handle a ship in a storm, and the ship itself was one of their newer vessels.

With a glance at the clock that hung above the fireplace Anna grimaced. Already she was late for lunch and now she had to compile a list of the clients whose goods were aboard the *Lady Magdalene* and decide when to contact them. Quickly she scribbled a note, explaining the delay to her uncle. Uncle Phillip had never tried to control her movements, never quibbled when she was called out to attend to business or missed the odd meal here or there, but he did worry if she didn't inform him that she would be delayed. The office for the shipping company was situated in the docks, not the most salubrious of areas, and although Anna had become used to most of the more colourful characters, she still ensured she never walked alone outside the office.

'Lady Fortescue, hard at work as usual, I see.' A large man burst through the door without knocking.

Anna forced a smile. Roger Maltravers ran the biggest and most profitable shipping company in London and had his office situated on the other side of the docks, the more prosperous side, but that didn't stop his frequent visits to the offices of the Trevels Shipping Company.

'I've said it a thousand times and I'll say it again, not proper work for a woman, this shipping business. And certainly not one as lovely as you.' As he spoke he wandered around the office, fingering charts and ledgers, peering at the maps on the walls.

Anna clenched her teeth together to try to hide her irritation. It wasn't that she disliked Roger Maltravers, but she didn't particularly like him either. He was too effusive, too sure of himself, and ever since her company had started to have a modicum of success he'd been trying to persuade her to join her company with his.

'Awful storm off Portugal, I hear,' he said casually.

'So I am told,' Anna said, wondering if he didn't notice the coolness in her voice or if he just ignored it.

'Could be devastating if you lost one of your ships.'

'We have insurance.'

'Crafty scoundrels, you'll never see a penny back.' He paused and Anna knew what was coming next. It was the same every week, had been for the past six months. 'You wouldn't have to worry your pretty head about issues like this if you married me. I would look after you.'

Anna stood, smoothing down her skirts.

'A very kind offer, Mr Maltravers, but I am a

widow three times over and have resolved not to marry again.'

'Dastardly shame.'

'My mind is made up.'

'You need a man to look after you.'

'I have my uncle.'

'You need a husband.'

Anna felt the irritation bubbling inside, straining for release. She'd had three husbands and not one of them had looked after her, not really. The only person she could truly rely on was herself.

'It doesn't sit well with me the idea of a vulnerable young woman alone in the world. There are bad people out there, people ready to take advantage. I only want to protect you, Lady Fortescue.'

'I have a lot of work to do today, Mr Maltravers, please excuse me.'

She crossed to the door and opened it for him.

'I shall call on you tomorrow,' Mr Maltravers said as he left reluctantly, calling over his shoulder, 'Think about what I've said.'

Anna resisted the urge to slam the door behind him, instead closing it softly and resting her forehead on the cool wood. She knew it was beyond unusual for a woman to run a business, let alone a shipping company. She was one woman in a world full of men, but there was absolutely no way she would ever give up her freedom and her independence again.

Harry frowned as he strolled through the docks, keeping his wits sharp and his pace brisk. The area wasn't the worst in London, but it wasn't far off. Surely he must have the address wrong, surely Lady Fortescue's uncle hadn't meant to send him here?

He'd arrived for lunch at Mr Tenby's residence at the agreed time, only to find Lady Fortescue hadn't returned home. Her uncle wasn't overly concerned and Harry got the impression this was a regular occurrence.

Rather than dine without his fiancée, Harry had offered to go and find her and escort her home, hence his trip to the docks. When he'd made the offer he had assumed she was out shopping, or perhaps taking tea with a friend, not running a business in one of the most notorious parts of London. Lady Fortescue was becoming more interesting with every snippet of information he picked up about her.

Glancing at the piece of paper with the address, Harry started to ascend a rickety set of wooden stairs, having to pause on the way up to let a large man pass him on his way back to ground level.

Harry knocked on the door and was surprised when it was flung open immediately, with some force.

'Mr Maltravers, I must insist…' Lady Fortescue trailed off, her eyes widening in surprise. 'Lord Edgerton,' she managed after a few seconds.

'Lady Fortescue.' Harry bowed, trying to conceal a smile. He found he rather liked surprising his so-called fiancée.

'I invited you to lunch,' she said softly, a hand covering her lips. 'And then didn't turn up.'

'A more sensitive man might be offended,' Harry said, following her into the office and looking around him with interest.

'You're not offended?'

'Your uncle tells me it happens all the time. Not forgetting guests, but forgetting meals.'

'I don't often have guests,' Lady Fortescue said quietly.

He'd been in such offices before, when organising shipments or booking passage to the Continent, but usually they were run by weathered old men, men who looked like the sea had chewed them up and spat them out. They were not run by gently bred young ladies, even notorious widows.

'This is your business?' he asked eventually, studying a detailed map of the English Channel.

'My late husband...' Lady Fortescue paused and corrected herself, 'My second late husband, Captain Trevels, owned this business. It came to me on his death and it was one of the few things I was allowed to keep possession of throughout my last marriage.'

'It is an unusual business for a woman,' Harry said bluntly.

Lady Fortescue smiled, not the usual, polite up-turning of the corner of her lips, but a proper, full on smile of amusement.

'You're very direct, Lord Edgerton.'

'Perhaps you should call me Harry. We are engaged after all.'

'We're pretending to be engaged,' Lady Fortescue corrected, just in case he forgot. 'Harry,' she said his name quietly as if trying it out on her tongue. He saw the faintest of blushes blossom on her cheeks, gone before he could even be sure it was truly there.

He waited for her to offer her given name. He waited so long he began to wonder if she might insist he call her Lady Fortescue for the rest of their acquaintance.

'My name is Anna.'

'It is a very unusual business for a woman, Anna,' Harry repeated.

She shrugged, that small movement that Harry was beginning to associate with his fiancée, and smiled. 'Most men would say any business is a strange one for a woman.'

'That's very true.' He saw her stiffen a little and leaned in closer. 'But most men are fools,' he said quietly. 'Now, your uncle promised to save us some lunch, if you can spare an hour or two.'

She glanced at the pile of papers on the huge wooden desk and hesitated.

'You'll work more efficiently on a full stomach.'

'A quick lunch,' Anna conceded.

'And you can tell me about the world of shipping.'

Chapter Five

As the music in the ballroom swelled above the chatter Anna found herself looking around in anticipation. Against her better judgement she had agreed to attend the Carmichael ball this evening, a ball that Lord Edgerton, Harry, would be making an appearance at, too.

She had been doing a lot of things against her better judgement these past few days: agreeing to this sham engagement just to avoid a little scandal, allowing Harry into her life and confiding in him about the malicious parcels she'd been receiving. After a long time spent being a meek and mild wife, Anna didn't usually give in to anyone easily now she had her much wished-for freedom and independence, but Harry seemed to be able to get her to agree to anything with his confident persistence.

'You're thinking about him,' Beatrice said breathlessly, sitting down beside her and taking a large gulp from the glass of lemonade Anna had been holding.

'Who?'

'Who?' Beatrice laughed. 'Your fiancé, who else?'

'Fiancé in name only,' Anna said, lowering her voice. She didn't want her cousin to get carried away in a romantic fantasy.

'For now. Admit you were thinking about him.'

'Shouldn't you find your partner for the next dance?'

'Hah, I knew it. You were daydreaming about him.'

'Beatrice Tenby, don't be so ridiculous. I haven't daydreamed about anything or anyone in the past five years.'

Handing the glass of lemonade back to her, Beatrice stood.

'I don't think you're half as prim and proper as you make out.' Beatrice flounced off, swishing her skirts and fluttering her eyelashes at any young man who glanced in her direction.

'I do hope not,' a low voice said in her ear.

Anna stood abruptly, using all her self-control not to exclaim out loud. Lord Edgerton—*Harry*, she reminded herself—was standing directly behind her. He took her hand, bowing over it before straightening and giving her a wink.

'It would seem we're the centre of attention,' Harry said quietly.

Nonchalantly Anna glanced to the left and right. Everyone around them was deeply engrossed in conversation. Too deeply engrossed. Behind the uninterested façade they were watching every move Harry and Anna made.

'I trust you are well, Lord Edgerton,' she said loud enough for the gossips to hear.

'Very well, Lady Fortescue. Perhaps you will do me the honour of granting me this dance.'

Anna stiffened. She didn't dance, at least not any more. Her role here was purely that of chaperon to Beatrice. She was expected to sit on the periphery of the ballroom, watch the young women dance and laugh and be merry, and hold the lemonade whenever her cousin retreated to the edges for a rest.

'I'd wager you are a fabulous dancer.'

Once. Once she'd been as carefree and happy as Beatrice. She'd whirled across ballroom after ballroom, content to let her partner of the moment guide her, happy to trust a man she barely knew completely for those few minutes of the dance.

'I don't dance.'

Harry stepped back and regarded her. 'I don't believe you,' he said finally.

'You don't believe me?'

'I don't believe you. You have more grace than a dancer in the ballet.'

He held out his hand, waiting for her to take it. There was no way she could refuse and a part of her felt a spark of excitement at the thought of dancing again.

Slowly she placed her hand in his and stood, allowing Harry to lead her to the dance floor. The last dance was just finishing, the dancers breathless and flushed from the quick steps to a lively tempo. There was a brief pause before the musicians struck up again, this time with the unmistakable first notes of a waltz.

'My lucky night,' Harry murmured.

He gripped her lightly, guiding her to a space on the dance floor and smiling before leading her across the room. As the seconds passed Anna felt herself relaxing, Harry was a good dancer and despite her years spent away from balls and ballrooms Anna felt the steps returning like long-lost friends. As they twirled past the other couples Anna could feel her spirits soaring. There was a freedom in dancing, a wonderful feeling that you might take flight, and she couldn't believe she had gone so long without experiencing it.

They didn't speak while they danced and Anna found herself sneaking the odd glance at her companion. Beatrice was right, he *was* handsome, although maybe not in the conventional sense. Most men of the *ton* followed fashion closely. They wore intricately decorated waistcoats and spent time and money styling their hair as well as their clothes. Harry stood out in the ballroom exactly because he didn't do those things. His hair was cut short and his clothes were no doubt expensive and finely made, but lacked the excessive pomp of the other men in the ballroom. What he did have was presence. He was tall, with broad shoulders and a muscular build, but more than physical size he exuded a confidence that could not be imitated— you were either born with it or not.

As the dance drew to a close Anna found herself disappointed. For a moment she had been transported back to the carefree days when she'd been a debutante. Before the marriages and the husbands, when the only reprimand she would get if she laughed too loud or danced too merrily was a stern word from her father.

'Do you care for a breath of air?' Harry asked as he escorted her from the dance floor. He picked up two glasses of champagne as they passed a table lined with sparkling flutes and offered her one.

'I'm doing all the things I cautioned Beatrice against,' Anna said, still allowing Harry to lead her out on to the terrace.

The raised patio stretched the whole length of the back of the house and was well illuminated with lanterns. Coy young women strolled arm in arm with swaggering young men, while the more daring of couples whispered in darkened corners. Steps led from the raised terrace into the garden, with only the first few feet visible in the moonlight. Every debutante with hopes of a good match would have been warned from straying any further from the ballroom, but inevitably someone would be caught where they shouldn't tonight.

'Did you enjoy our waltz?' Harry asked as he led her to the stone balustrade. They leaned on the smooth stone and gazed out into the garden, their forearms almost touching.

There was no point in denying it. Anna knew her love of dancing had been rekindled and any onlooker would have been able to tell with a single glance how much she enjoyed her first waltz for many years.

'I did, thank you.'

'Your late husband wasn't much of a dancer?' Harry asked.

Anna shook her head, not trusting herself to speak. Early in the marriage they had attended various balls and functions together and Anna had made the mistake of accepting a young man's invitation to dance after Lord Fortescue had made it clear he would not be making an appearance on the dance floor. Her husband had seen the dance as a betrayal and Anna had paid a high price for her few minutes of merriment.

'I thought you didn't like champagne,' Anna said, motioning to the half-empty glass in Harry's hand, latching on to the first thing she'd seen to try to steer the topic of conversation away from her disastrous marriage.

'I thought it best we didn't sneak through the house in search of something more palatable and get caught in a compromising position a second time within two weeks.'

'Probably for the best,' Anna murmured.

'Tell me,' Harry said, turning to her, 'what made you agree to be a chaperon for your cousin?'

'My uncle asked.'

'That was all?'

'I owe him a lot, not that he would ever ask anything I wasn't comfortable with.'

'He took you in after the death of Lord Fortescue?'

'Among other things.'

He'd done so much more than take her in. Anna had been broken, barely surviving when Uncle Phillip came and swept her into his loving home. He'd given her space to heal and provided gentle reminders that not everyone was a monster.

'I think he is the only person to ever love me unconditionally,' Anna said quietly.

'What about your parents?'

She shrugged before she could stop herself. Shrugging was a habit she'd always had, but Lord Fortescue had hated the miniscule movement of her shoulder. This past year she still repressed many of her natural reactions, but slowly they were creeping back.

'My mother died when I was a young child, I barely remember her. My father...' She paused, wondering how best to describe him. 'I'm sure he *did* care, he just didn't think a gentleman should be affectionate, so most of the time I had no idea what he was thinking.'

'I'm glad you have someone to care for you.' There was a softness to Harry's voice that made her turn and look at him. He was smiling at her, a smile filled with warmth that crinkled the skin around his eyes and suddenly Anna was aware of just how attractive her companion actually was. As her pulse quickened she tried to gain control of herself with a sharp reprimand, but found her body swaying towards Harry before she could stop herself.

Their arms touched, just a sliver of contact, but enough to cause a spark of excitement to jump through Anna's body. Here in the moonlight, with the beautiful music from the ballroom drifting on the evening breeze, Anna felt the first surge of hopeful anticipation.

Shaking herself, she managed to look away and as soon as she did the spell was broken. Quickly she took a step back, pretending to adjust her skirts to cover her confusion. It was the warm evening's air, and perhaps a touch too much champagne, that had caused her momentary lapse in sanity, nothing more.

Harry was looking at her with an amused expression and she wondered how much he'd been able to read on her face.

'You should be ashamed,' a low voice hissed behind them.

Quickly Anna spun around, stepping back as

she recognised the woman striding towards them. Before she had time to react Miss Antonia Fortescue, her spiteful stepdaughter, had stepped much closer than Anna was comfortable with, only stopping when their noses were almost touching.

'Miss Fortescue,' Anna said, her voice devoid of emotion, 'I did not expect to see you here.' It was the politest thing Anna could bring herself to say.

'Look at you, making merry with my father barely in the ground.'

'Your father died over a year ago, Miss Fortescue. My mourning period has finished.'

Anna thought her stepdaughter might reach out and strike her at that comment, but her disdain was limited to a narrowing of the eyes.

'Miss Fortescue?' Harry asked, stepping between the two women.

'Yes?' Miss Fortescue snapped, glancing at Harry before returning her unwavering gaze to Anna.

'I don't think we've had the pleasure of being introduced. I am Lord Edgerton.'

His title, and no doubt his reputation, earned him another glance from Miss Fortescue. Anna prayed he would keep silent about their sham engagement. The last thing she needed was for her late husband's family to find out she'd become engaged again.

'I hope you know what company you keep, Lord Edgerton.'

'Lady Fortescue is the most amenable of companions,' Harry said.

Antonia snorted, an unladylike sound that required her to screw up her nose and turn an already unattractive face into something pinched and malicious.

'Your stepmother was just explaining how she gained an entire family when she married into the Fortescue clan,' Harry said, without a hint of sarcasm in his voice. Anna looked at him appraisingly—he might come across as easy-going and mild-mannered, but her companion was sharp and intelligent along with it.

'She is no stepmother of mine.'

Silence followed. There wasn't really much else to say, but Antonia seemed reluctant to move on.

'I understand you haven't seen much of Lady Fortescue since your father's passing,' Harry said, his voice suitably sombre. 'Perhaps we should remedy that.'

Anna felt her jaw clench as she turned slowly towards Harry. She tried to communicate how much she would like him to be silent with just a dramatic widening of her eyes, but he flashed her a smile and wilfully ignored her, pushing on with his invitation.

'I'm having a little house party, the weekend after next. It's at my country estate, just south of Sevenoaks. We'd be delighted if you could attend. And your brothers, of course.'

Anna didn't know who was more shocked, her or Antonia, but they both stood with mouths slightly opened, unable to utter a word.

'Fantastic,' Harry said. 'We look forward to seeing you there.'

Anna felt him grip her arm and guide her along the terrace, no doubt planning on escaping before she or Antonia had a chance to collect themselves and protest at the idea of spending more than a few seconds in each other's company.

Harry was feeling rather pleased with himself. The evening was going well, exceedingly well. He'd managed to claim a dance from his initially reluctant fiancée, watch her eyes light up as he whisked her around the ballroom and see some of her legendary composure slip as they stood side by side on the terrace. To top it all, he'd furthered his little investigation into the horrible packages

Anna was receiving by inviting his main suspect to a country house party.

Next to him Anna walked with her head held high, but her fingers were digging into his arm through his jacket. He hadn't warned her of his plan, there hadn't been the opportunity, but he was sure once she'd recovered from the shock she would see it was the sensible thing to do: gather all the possible culprits in one place and wait for them to strike.

They'd just reached the end of the terrace when he felt Anna's grip on his arm tighten even more. Before he knew what was happening she'd whisked him around the corner and down a short set of stone steps to the shadowy lawn below. In ten quick paces she'd pressed him into an alcove, hidden from view from the terrace above.

'Lady Fortescue,' he murmured, 'I thought we were going to try our best to behave this evening.'

She was standing close to him, so close he could smell the lavender scent of her hair and before he could stop himself he reached out and tucked a stray, coppery strand behind her ear.

'What do you think you are doing?' Anna asked, her voice barely more than a whisper, but managing to convey the depth of her fury all the same.

'A strand of hair…'

'Up on the terrace, with Miss Fortescue.'

'Being polite.'

'To a woman who might be sending me—' She broke off, her voice faltering at the memory of what was in the last package.

'We're never going to get to the bottom of what's happening if we avoid the people who might be responsible. We need to observe them, confront them, push them into making a mistake.'

'By inviting them to stay under the same roof as us?'

'I'll be there to look out for you.'

Anna closed her eyes and shook her head. 'I barely know you,' she said quietly.

'That's not true.' Although they had only met for the first time a little over a week ago Harry felt as though they'd known each other for much longer.

'You do not get to make decisions about my life,' Anna said, her voice low but firm. 'No one gets to make decisions about my life.'

There was such conviction as she spoke, such determination, that Harry wondered what had happened to drive her to this point. She didn't trust anyone and clung to her independence more than any woman he had ever encountered. It should be annoying, but Harry found himself admiring her more for her strength.

'I'm sorry,' Harry said, knowing when to take a step back and regroup. 'I should have discussed my idea about the house party with you first.'

The apology seemed to disarm her and Harry watched as some of the fury seeped from her body. Without thinking he raised a hand and smoothed the furrow between her eyebrows. She stiffened at his touch, but did not jerk away, instead slowly raising her eyes to meet his own.

For an instant Harry wanted nothing more in the world than to kiss her. He wanted to cover her lips with his own, gather her to his body and kiss her until she forgot whatever it was that was making her frown.

'Perhaps we should discuss it tomorrow,' Anna said, taking a step back.

'Good idea.'

Anna looked around her as if only just realising where they were. A sardonic smile crossed her lips.

'Thankfully the world thinks we are engaged,' she said, 'or this would be an even bigger scandal than us being discovered together at the Prendersons' ball.'

All the same she peered out into the darkness carefully, judging her moment to return to the ballroom. Just as she was about to dash out from the alcove Harry caught her hand.

'Dance with me,' he said.

'Here? Don't be silly.'

'No one can see us.'

'People will be wondering where we are.'

'Let them wonder.'

'This whole engagement is to try to minimise the scandal attached to our names, not increase it.'

'Dance with me.'

He saw her hesitate, torn between returning to the safety of the ballroom and sharing another wonderful waltz. The music from the ballroom was audible down here, muffled by the chatter of people on the terrace, but still good enough to dance to.

For an instant he thought she would and he felt his heart leap in his chest, then she was gone, her dress swishing behind her, her head bent low as she fled back to the safety of the ballroom.

Chapter Six

Distractedly Anna handed her bonnet to Grace, her maid, and patted her hair with both hands to tame any stray strands. She'd been unable to sleep after the ball and early that morning she'd headed to the shipping company offices to try to catch up on paperwork. It had been a gruelling day, with the *Lady Magdalene* still missing and the clients who had their goods aboard the ship getting restless.

'Lady Fortescue would like some tea,' Mr Maltravers said, ushering Grace away with a shake of his hand.

'Grace,' Anna said sharply, 'I have a headache. I think I will lie down.'

Her effusive business rival had insisted on escorting her home after turning up uninvited at the shipping company office earlier in the afternoon. Anna had argued, strongly enough that anyone else would consider her rude, but Mr Maltravers had been unaffected by her protests and escorted her home anyway.

'A cup of tea will cure that,' Mr Maltravers said, taking her by the arm and leading her into the drawing room.

As always Anna stiffened at his touch, visibly shuddering at the feel of his clammy palm on her arm.

'Thank you very much for your escort, Mr Maltravers,' Anna said firmly, 'but I am weary and feel unwell. You will have to forgive me for being a terrible host and not offering you any refreshment before you leave.' Despite her conciliatory words Anna kept her tone and manner as cold as possible. Mr Maltravers was irking her, making her feel uncomfortable in the one place she normally felt safe.

'I could wait.'

'No.' She wasn't above begging him to go, but instead placed a hand on his arm and guided him back to the front door, even opening it herself.

'I shall call on you tomorrow to check you have recovered. I worry about you, Lady Fortescue.'

'Please do not trouble yourself.'

She hadn't once encouraged him, hadn't ever been anything more than polite and most of the time had been downright frosty towards him, but still Mr Maltravers insisted on popping up in every aspect of her life.

Anna shut the door while he was still on the top step, closing her eyes and leaning her head against the wood.

'Shall I bring you a cold compress for your head, my lady?' Grace asked, a mischievous glint in her eyes.

'It is a miracle I do not truly have a headache after spending close to an hour in Mr Maltravers's carriage with him puffing away on that disgusting pipe.'

'Lady Fortescue, you have a guest,' Williams, the elderly butler, announced. He grimaced. 'He is in the garden.'

Uncle Phillip's town house was large and well proportioned, but like many houses in the city it didn't have much of a garden. A small patio with a stretch of grass beyond it, it took less than five minutes to stroll around the whole perimeter.

'The garden?' It was a strange place to put a guest.

'With Mr Tenby and Miss Tenby.' Williams paused and Anna could sense there was more to be said. 'They are playing shuttlecock.'

Of course Harry would come to call today. He

came to call most days, but for some reason today seemed more significant than any other. Anna wondered if he'd felt it too, that spark, that flare of attraction as they stood together in the Carmichaels' garden. For a moment she'd wanted to kiss him, wanted to fall into his arms and feel his lips on hers. It was ridiculous, worse than ridiculous, and now Anna could feel the butterflies in her stomach as she walked slowly towards the doors to the garden.

For a few seconds she stood and watched the scene outside. Harry and Beatrice had expressions of furious concentration on their faces as they hit the shuttlecock backwards and forward. Uncle Phillip was seated in the sun, shouting out words of encouragement. It looked like an idyllic family scene.

Harry was in good spirits as usual, his shirt-sleeves rolled up to expose strong forearms and his eyes sparkling in the sunshine. He was a good-looking man, there was no denying it, but Anna knew that wasn't the only reason she felt a tightening inside her as she watched him. There was more to him than a desirable exterior. There was a drive in Harry to look after people, to ensure they came to no harm. He quietly got on and made the important decisions without causing too much fuss.

Of course there was a bad side, too. Yesterday on the terrace he'd assumed control, taken over and made decisions that weren't his to make. That was why she had to stop this reaction she had to him before it went any further. Never again would she give up her autonomy, not for anyone.

Pushing open the door, she stepped out into the sunshine.

'Anna,' Harry called as soon as he caught sight of her, 'come join us.'

She hesitated, just for a moment, and then stepped off the patio and on to the grass, picking up a spare racket as she went.

'Our record is twenty,' Beatrice said, her eyes shining. 'Lord Edgerton is rather good.'

Anna regarded her cousin out of the corner of her eye. If she wasn't much mistaken, Beatrice was developing a little affection for Harry.

'I hope you're ready,' Harry said, swinging his racket. 'Whoever misses the shuttlecock first has to do a forfeit.'

'What's the forfeit?' Anna asked.

Beatrice laughed and Harry hit the shuttlecock, powering it towards her. It had been years since Anna had picked up a racket, but she swung it instinctively, hearing the satisfying *ping* as the small shuttlecock bounced off the strings. It looped through the air towards Beatrice who hit it easily. Round and round the shuttlecock flew, faster and faster until Anna had to dive to reach it. The shuttlecock spun off the edge of her racket with a dull *thunk*, losing momentum and heading for the ground. Both Beatrice and Harry jumped forward, angling their rackets towards the small, tumbling object, but, before either of them could reach it, it hit the ground.

'Congratulations,' Harry said. 'You won.'

'What's my prize?'

Harry stepped towards her, his eyes fixed on hers, took her hand and raised it to his lips. Anna shivered as he brushed the lightest of kisses against her knuckles. For a moment the rest of the world faded into the background and it was just the two of them on this patch of lawn. Then reality came tumbling back as Harry let go of her hand and stepped away.

'An evening of entertainment. How do you ladies feel about the opera?'

Anna felt her heart sink. She hated the opera. All those people watching each other, their eyes fixed on the other spectators rather than the stage. It felt as though you were an exhibit in a museum.

'I love the opera,' Beatrice enthused. Anna had a sneaking suspicion her cousin would profess her love for any activity Harry suggested right now, even something as horrible as bear-baiting. There was a hint of adoration on Beatrice's face every time she looked at Anna's fake fiancé.

'Anna?'

She almost lied, almost found herself professing a love for something that in truth she found disagreeable, but then she paused. After Lord Fortescue had died, after she had recovered from the rawest emotional and physical wounds she'd acquired in that marriage, she'd promised herself she would start to be true to herself. There was no need to do anything to please other people now; she could accept or decline invitations as she desired. No one could cajole or force her to do anything.

'I am not keen on the opera,' she said.

'Anna,' Beatrice said, her voice shocked and admonishing.

Anna shrugged. 'I'm not. I see no reason to lie to Lord Edgerton.'

'Harry,' Harry corrected her. 'And you're right, there is no reason to lie to me.'

'I would be delighted to accompany you to the opera, Lord Edgerton,' Beatrice said.

Harry smiled indulgently, the smile of a big brother to a younger sister. 'As much as I would enjoy that, we must find something that Anna enjoys, too.' He turned to her, eyes narrowing. 'What is it about the opera you dislike? The singing? The impenetrable language? The garish costumes?'

'I find all that quite enjoyable. It is the audience I dislike, the feeling of being on display.'

Lord Fortescue had enjoyed the opera, often journeying to London for a performance. As always he'd required Anna to be exquisitely turned out for the trip, cataloguing any imperfection to punish her for later. Then he would spend most of the performance looking for signs Anna was flirting with other men. Of course it never happened, Anna wasn't foolish—she kept her eyes fixed on either the stage or her husband—but the lack of evidence never deterred Lord Fortescue. It meant the opera had gone from a pleasant excursion to a place of fear and horror.

Harry regarded her, his blue eyes seeming to pierce through her protective layer.

'Let me surprise you,' he said eventually.

'As you wish.'

'Beatrice my dear, help your decrepit father inside,' Anna's uncle called from his spot at the edge of the patio.

Beatrice eyed her father reluctantly before bobbing a curtsy to Harry and gliding off to do as she was bid.

'My cousin seems to adore you after just a few hours,' Anna said as they were left alone.

'She is a young woman of good taste,' Harry said.

'She is foolish and impulsive.'

'Like all girls of eighteen.' It was spoken as if he had personal experience with a foolish young girl.

'You have a sister,' Anna said as she slipped her hand through his arm.

'I do.'

'Is she the same age as Beatrice?'

'She's eighteen.'

'Is she making her debut this year?'

Harry shook his head. Normally so easy to talk to, he was not forthcoming when it came to his family.

'Next year, then?'

'Perhaps.'

'Are you her guardian?'

'In a sense. My mother is still alive, but she leaves most of the decisions surrounding Lydia to me.'

'That must be difficult for you. The minds of young girls are impenetrable.'

Harry smiled stiffly, but didn't answer, then, swiftly changing the subject, he said, 'I thought we should discuss this house party I am arranging.'

'Perhaps we should abandon the idea.'

'No. It is the only way to get all of our suspects in one place.'

'They won't accept an invitation from me.'

'But they will from me.'

'How can you be sure?'

'I'm an earl, people always accept my invitations. Who should we invite? Who might want to cause you harm?'

'*If* we agree to have this party, we should invite my late husband's three children, Miss Antonia Fortescue, the new Lord Fortescue and Mr Ronald Fortescue. Also probably my late husband's brother, Mr Lionel Fortescue.'

'Anyone else?'

'Anyone else dislike me enough to murder my cat?' Anna asked. 'No, I don't think so.'

'I'll draw up a guest list, include some old friends to keep it civil, then we can decide on a date.'

'I haven't decided whether I want to do this yet or not,' Anna said.

'Nonsense, it's the best way. I'll organise everything. All you need to do is turn up.'

'I need more time to think.'

'There's nothing to think about. I have it all in hand. This is for the best.'

Anna stiffened, withdrawing her hand from his arm. 'Do not presume to tell me what is best for me,' she said icily. 'You do not know me.'

'Anna…' Harry started to say, but Anna held up a hand.

'I make my own decisions. I do not need any man to make them for me.'

'I wasn't trying to make any decisions for you.'

'And yet that was the end result. I thank you for calling on me today, Lord Edgerton, but perhaps we should end our acquaintance here.' Before Harry could protest Anna turned and swept away, her heart hammering in her chest. She was inside before he'd moved and safely upstairs before she heard his footsteps in the hallway.

'Anna…' she heard him call, followed by the polite, muted tones from the butler. A minute later the door opened and closed as no doubt Harry was shown out. Anna risked a peek through the curtains at her window, drawing back as Harry stood back from the house and looked up directly at her. She was angry. Angry at the presumptive way he'd tried to make such a major decision for her and angry at herself for allowing him to get so close. Independent and single, that was how she would spend the rest of her life, even if the idea of never seeing Harry again hurt more than it should.

Chapter Seven

'So you're not at risk of being the Black Widow's fourth victim?' Mr James Rifield asked, laying down a card as he spoke.

'Don't call her that. And, no, the engagement is purely a sham, a way to avoid a little scandal.'

'I did hear a whisper you were caught in a rather compromising position, one where neither of you was wearing many clothes.'

Harry grimaced—here was the rumour mill at its very worst. He and Anna had been doing nothing more than conversing, albeit unchaperoned, and now half of London thought they had been caught midway through an evening of passion.

'We were caught alone in a room together, nothing more.'

'And you proposed to save her reputation. Little old-fashioned, isn't it?'

'There is nothing more damaging in this world than malicious gossip.'

Rifield's expression hardened. 'How is Lydia?'

Harry shook his head. 'Just the same.'

'She'll get there, old chap.'

Sometimes Harry wondered if the miraculous improvement he was hoping for would ever happen. It had been over a year since his sister's disgrace, over a year since the scandal had become too much for her. Now she sequestered herself away at Halstead Hall, refusing to come out of her room for days on end. It wasn't the life he wanted for her.

'So what happened?' Rifield asked.

Harry shrugged. It was difficult to know. One minute they had been strolling through the garden, the next Anna had gone very pale and said that she had wanted to end their acquaintance. She'd been angry, although she'd not once raised her voice and her face had remained impassive, but Harry wasn't entirely sure what had upset her.

'Lady Fortescue is very independent. I think she felt I was trying to impose my ideas on her.'

Perhaps he had been a little forceful, ploughing on with the idea of a country house party without stopping to consider her views, but he'd been doing it for her. He hated the idea of her receiving any more unpleasant packages and worried that someone might actually try to do her harm.

'Maybe it's for the best. This engagement had to end at some point and now you don't have to be the one to make the break.'

Harry nodded absently. It didn't feel for the best. He'd promised he would help find whoever was terrorising her and now it looked like he wouldn't even get the chance to look the main suspects in the eye.

'Unless there was more to it than a temporary arrangement of convenience,' Rifield said shrewdly. 'I've never met her myself, but I'm told Lady Fortescue is very attractive.'

'No more so than most of the other young women,' Harry said. Strictly it was true—she had pleasant features, a slender physique and just the right amount of womanly curves in all the right places. What it was more difficult to explain was how he struggled to look away from her cool grey eyes or how her coppery hair reflected the sunlight on a bright day. There was something enthralling about Anna, something that was difficult to put into words.

'She's not like I expected,' Harry said slowly.

'So there is something more?'

'No. No, I *like* her. I didn't expect that, but she's

not exactly a suitable wife for a man who wants to settle down with a quiet and scandal-free wife.'

'In a couple of years people will have forgotten the scandal with Lydia. And then you'll be stuck with a dull wife you care nothing for.'

'You're a romantic at heart, Rifield,' Harry teased and then became serious again. 'I failed her, I failed Lydia. I should have seen how low the whole affair brought her, should have anticipated...' He paused, closing his eyes for a second while trying to block out the awful night he'd found his sister trying to take her own life. 'Anyway, this engagement to Lady Fortescue is temporary. We shall break off our betrothal within a few months and I can go back to looking for an amiable, respectable young woman to be my wife.'

'But what about love, Edgerton? What about passion?'

Harry grunted, flicking open his hand of cards and focusing on the numbers. He didn't believe in love, or at least he didn't believe it was a good idea to base an entire marriage on it.

'Love has no place in a marriage,' he said.

The two men played on in silence for a few minutes. They'd had this argument many times before, although not of course with the complication of Lady Fortescue. Rifield was a rare man among the titled and wealthy—he believed marriage should be to someone you loved. Harry had no such beliefs. Marriage was about a lot of things—money, titles, land, reputations—but the one thing it wasn't about was love.

'You're nothing but an old sceptic,' Rifield said as he laid down two cards.

'I'd rather a quiet, straightforward companionship with a woman I admire than a marriage filled with destructive passion any day.'

He'd seen what a marriage based on love could be like. His own parents had been madly in love and their union had been anything but content. By the time his father had died, his mother had become a husk of her former self and he wouldn't want to inflict that on anyone. No, he planned on doing his duty by Anna, helping her find whoever was terrorising her and then he would return to his search for a companion he could envisage himself spending a quiet and passionless marriage with.

'Will you try to salvage things with Lady Fortescue?' Rifield asked as he frowned at his cards.

'I must. She needs me, even if she's too stubborn to admit it.'

'So a bouquet of flowers and a trip to the opera?'

Grimacing, Harry shook his head. He knew it would take a lot more than that to win round his reluctant fiancée.

Chapter Eight

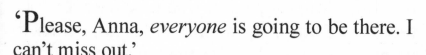

'Please, Anna, *everyone* is going to be there. I can't miss out.'

'I thought your father was going to take you.'

'He has one of his headaches, he can't get out of bed.'

'There will be other operas, Beatrice.'

'But what if tonight is the night I'm destined to meet my future husband? If I'm not there, I might be condemned to the life of a spinster.'

Anna fought the urge to roll her eyes. She'd been young and romantically inclined once, too, although possibly not this naïve.

'Who will we be sitting with?' Anna asked reluctantly.

'Thank you, thank you, thank you,' Beatrice gushed, throwing her arms around her cousin. 'Mrs Towertrap and her three daughters.'

Anna wished she could take back her agreement. Mrs Towertrap was pleasant enough, but Anna had met Anastasia, the eldest of the Towertrap daughters before. The young woman had been rude, verging on cruel, and Anna had no desire to renew their acquaintance.

'Will you come home with me now to get ready?' Beatrice asked.

Looking down at the mound of paperwork on her desk, Anna sighed. It would be there tomorrow. The *Lady Magdalene* still hadn't turned up nearly two weeks after the big storm and the losses looked to be catastrophic. Still, there was no point worrying about that now, tomorrow was another day.

'Do you have your carriage?'

'Of course. Father has forbidden me from coming to see you here,' Beatrice said, looking around her in barely concealed excitement, 'but Smith, the coachman, knows I would just find another way to get here if he didn't bring me.'

'You really should listen to your father. The docks are no place for a well-bred young woman.'

'*You* spend all your time here,' Beatrice said.

'That's different.'

'Because you're a widow?'

'Because I know a bit more about the cruel realities of the world.'

Beatrice rolled her eyes. Quickly Anna tidied away the papers she'd been working on and followed her cousin out of the office and down the stairs to the street below.

'What happened between you and Lord Edgerton?' Beatrice asked as the carriage wove its way through the busy docks.

'Nothing.'

'You're refusing to see him because of nothing?'

'I should never have agreed to this sham engagement in the first place,' Anna said. 'I just came to my senses, nothing more.'

'I liked him.'

'He is a very likeable man. That doesn't change the fact that I do not wish to have any man in my life.'

'Not even the perfect man? One who would bring you a lifetime of happiness.'

'No such person exists. Everyone is flawed.'

'You might be lucky with your fourth marriage,' Beatrice said, looking out the window.

'It's not worth the risk,' Anna murmured, too quiet for her cousin to hear her.

Of course she sometimes wondered if she was making the right decision, embracing her widowhood in such a manner. The future stretched out before her, years full of solitude. One day Beatrice would marry and at some time in the distant future her uncle would pass away. She'd have friends, but they would have their own husbands, their own children. Still, a lifetime of loneliness was better than one of misery and that would be what she was risking if she married again. You couldn't truly know a man until you shared a life with him.

'Perhaps I might ask Lord Edgerton to call on me,' Beatrice said, her voice light, her gaze fixed out of the window.

Suppressing a smile, Anna nodded. 'He would be a fine match for you,' she said.

Anna knew her cousin was only trying to bait her, although there had been a hint of infatuation in her eyes the afternoon they had all played shuttlecock together.

The carriage pulled up in front of the opera house and Anna waited for the door to open before stepping down, turning to wait for Beatrice. Theirs was not the only carriage arriving, in front and behind the ladies and gentlemen of the *ton* were eagerly alighting from their coaches and carriages, ready for an evening of people watching and passing judgement.

Linking her arm through Beatrice's, Anna ascended the steps, smiling politely at the gaggle of young women going through the door ahead of them.

'I hear the Duke of Westfield is going to be in attendance tonight,' Beatrice whispered, her face aglow with excitement.

If going on title and wealth alone the Duke of Westfield was considered the most eligible bachelor in society at the present time. Unfortunately he also had a rapidly receding hairline, a pot belly to rival a pig and a voice that could send a listener to sleep in a matter of seconds. Anna had been introduced to him a few years ago and had spent a dull half an hour listening to the intricacies of numismatics, which she had learnt at length meant rare coin collecting. Despite his dull personality he would have his pick of the debutantes when he decided to tear himself away from his coin collection to choose a wife.

As they entered the foyer Beatrice spotted a couple of her friends and rushed over, no doubt ready to discuss the young men in attendance.

'You look ravishing,' a low voice said in her ear.

Anna spun so quickly she almost lost her balance, but Harry placed a steadying hand on her arm.

'Beatrice engineered this,' she said flatly.

'I did enlist her help,' Harry admitted.

'I should go.'

'Please let me apologise.'

Anna hesitated. As usual people were looking at them, but she was still tempted to turn and flee from the opera house. Beatrice was safely ensconced with the three Towertrap girls under the watchful eye of their mother; there was no need for her to stay.

'You know how much I dislike the opera, yet you bring me here to apologise,' Anna said, her voice low.

'I can see that it looks as if I haven't learnt anything, but please give me a chance. Come with me.'

Part of her wanted to. It would be easy to forgive him, easy to return to the pleasant companionship they had shared the last few weeks, but she knew she had to be careful. More than once she'd found herself wondering what it would be like to kiss Harry, how it would feel to have his arms pull her close. Dangerous thoughts, thoughts that could lead somewhere Anna most certainly did not want to go.

'Lord Edgerton,' Anna said with a sigh, 'everything we have done in the past few weeks has been working towards trying to minimise the scandal that surrounds us and now you want me to sneak off and sully my reputation even further?'

'Harry,' he said. 'Last week you called me Harry.'

'Last week was a mistake.'

'Which part?'

'Let's just say everything I have done since meeting you was a mistake.'

'You don't mean that.'

She thought of the glorious waltz they'd shared and the almost magical moment on the terrace afterwards.

'Almost everything,' she conceded. 'Lord Edgerton…'

'Harry.'

'Lord Edgerton,' Anna said firmly, 'you are a kind man with good intentions, but I am perfectly capable of looking after myself.'

'I disagree.'

Anna felt herself stiffen. He was doing it again, speaking in a completely aristocratic, completely *male* way, making statements with such confidence it bordered on arrogance and presuming he knew best.

'You are capable,' Harry said quickly. 'You're the most capable woman I've ever known, but no one, man or woman, should have to deal with the persecution you are suffering alone.'

'Truly, it does not bother me.'

'Don't lie to me, Anna. I was there when you received the last parcel, remember.'

A shiver ran down her spine at the memory, but she managed to suppress it.

Taking her arm, Harry gently led her to one side of the foyer. Multiple sets of eyes followed their every move, no doubt cataloguing their expressions and body language.

'I'm sorry. I was overbearing and controlling. I shouldn't have ploughed on with my plan without consulting you first. It's your life, you deserve to be involved in every decision.'

Anna felt herself softening. It wasn't often anyone had apologised to her and meant it, but, seeing the sincerity in Harry's eyes, she knew he truly did regret how he'd handled the situation.

'Thank you,' she said quietly.

'Forgive me?'

She hesitated for only a second before nodding.

People were starting to move upstairs and find their boxes and Anna knew she would have to rejoin Beatrice for the duration of the performance.

'Stay for the first act and then plead a headache,' Harry said.

'Why?'

'I have a surprise for you.'

Despite her hardest efforts at self-control, Anna felt a spark of anticipation.

'We cannot both leave midway through. It'll look too suspicious.'

'It was a pleasure to see you this evening, Lady Fortescue,' Harry said loudly, bending over her hand as he raised it to his lips. 'Alas, I have a prior engagement, but I did not want to go an entire day without setting eyes on my beautiful fiancée.'

'A bit much,' Anna murmured, trying to suppress a smile. Harry might be too assertive sometimes, but he made her smile more than anyone else ever had. 'Good night, Lord Edgerton,' Anna replied, turning to join her cousin and their companions.

Harry stepped out into the crisp evening air, whistling to himself. It had been easier than he'd envisaged to apologise to Anna. Despite her frosty exterior she was forgiving and Harry had the sense that she hadn't wanted to stay mad at him. Anna might protest that she liked her solitude and privacy, but he suspected underneath that initial private layer there was a lonely young woman just crying to be rescued.

'Not your place,' he murmured to himself. He would help her with the anonymous packages, try to save her from a little scandal, but then they would have to go their separate ways. No matter how much he liked her, she wasn't the right choice of wife for him in the long term. She wouldn't bring the stability and respectability needed to the Edgerton family and he feared after spending a few months in her company he would find it a little difficult to play the role of the distant husband he had planned for himself. There was something enthralling about Anna, something that drew you in.

'Lord Edgerton, isn't it?'

Harry spun around to find himself looking into the face of a vaguely familiar man.

'You have me at a disadvantage, Mr...'

'Mr Maltravers. I'm a close personal friend of Lady Fortescue.'

'That's right, we bumped into each other at the docks.' Harry remembered the brief encounter on the steps up to Anna's shipping office.

'I hear you are engaged to Lady Fortescue.'

'Yes.'

'May I offer my congratulations. Lady Fortescue is a fine woman. I have admired her ever since she took over her husband's company,' Mr Maltravers said.

'Thank you.'

'I have often advised Lady Fortescue she needs a protector. The world is such a dangerous and cruel place.'

Harry murmured in general agreement, wondering how Anna knew Mr Maltravers. He was well dressed, but had an air of desperation about him and kept looking around furtively as if he expected to be thrown out at any moment.

'Please don't take this the wrong way. I have been a close friend to Lady Fortescue for quite some time. She is a vulnerable young woman despite her efforts to seem strong. I trust you will not hurt her.'

Harry frowned. It was an odd thing to say, especially from a man he'd just met.

'Of course not.'

'Good,' Mr Maltravers said, nodding his head once and then again. 'She deserves to be cherished. I'd hoped...' He trailed off. 'Never mind. I must excuse myself, I'm heading to the opera and already I am late.'

'Good evening,' Harry said, inclining his head.

He watched as Mr Maltravers hurried up the steps and through the doors of the opera house, throwing a glance back over his shoulder to where Harry was standing. An odd man, certainly one he couldn't see Anna having much time for.

* * *

The first act was not as long as some and Harry found himself waiting with anticipation to see if Anna would emerge early from one of the boxes. There was a chance she would decide not to come, sit through the first interval ensconced safely in the box with her companions, but Harry had seen the spark in her eyes and knew at least a little part of her wanted to see what he had planned.

Just as the crescendo of the first act was being reached Harry slipped back into the foyer of the opera house. It would be difficult to explain his presence if Anna did not emerge and he was instead seen by another member of the *ton*, but it was a risk worth taking. From here in the richly decorated foyer he could hear the impressive vocal talents of Giuditta Felini, the Italian opera singer who was the talk of London at the moment. Just as the audience broke into spontaneous applause a door upstairs opened and Harry saw Anna slip out.

Despite the risk she was taking in coming to meet him she moved slowly, gracefully, gliding down the stairs as if on her way to take tea with a friend. As she reached Harry he had an overwhelming urge to reach out, pull her to him and kiss her, but before he could even smile a greeting other doors began opening and Anna's eyes widened in panic.

'This way,' he whispered, grasping her by the hand and pulling her through a nondescript door, closing off the view of the foyer which would soon be busy with other audience members socialising during the interval.

He'd paid one of the opera-house employees handsomely to leave this particular door unlocked and provide a burning candle to light their way, and the young man hadn't disappointed. Sitting on a ledge at the bottom of a narrow staircase was a flickering candle.

'Where are we going?' Anna asked. She sounded a little nervous and he wondered if she were afraid of the dark.

'Up.' Gently he took her hand again and guided her up the stairs. 'You said the other day that you enjoyed the actual opera performance—it was the rest of the audience that put you off attending the opera.'

'Everyone is looking at everyone else, judging them.'

'Well, I thought you might like to enjoy the rest of this performance without anyone looking at you.' *Except me*, he added to himself.

They climbed in the darkness, flight after flight,

until they came to the very top of the staircase. In front of them was a door that Harry pushed open and then they were on a small platform at the very top of the opera house.

'Where are we?' Anna asked.

'This building has so many nooks and crannies I'm not sure what this area was used for originally. Now the staff use it for storage.'

'How do you know about it?'

Harry shrugged. 'I'm observant. More observant than most. I was at the opera one evening when I saw a couple of faces up here. One of the opera girls had smuggled her family in to watch when they couldn't afford tickets. I poked around until I found out how to get up here.'

'So people can see us?' Anna asked, stepping back from the edge quickly.

'If they look up. But they won't be able to see who we are.'

Carefully Anna stepped forward again, leaning on the wooden barrier and looking down on the people below. Many were still in their boxes, talking to their companions, the women fanning themselves in the heat.

'It's not luxurious,' Harry said, pulling up two wooden crates for them to sit on, 'but it is private.'

Gracefully Anna sat down, adjusting her skirts

so the material did not snag on the corners of the box.

'And I brought champagne.'

'You don't like champagne.'

'But you do.'

Their eyes met for an instant before Anna hurriedly looked away. Harry busied himself opening the bottle and pouring out two glasses and handing one to Anna. As she took her first sip the audience down below began filing back into their seats, although there was still a substantial amount of chatter as the second act began.

Harry had seen this opera twice before so he sat back and watched Anna's face as her eyes were fixed to the stage. It was the story of Medea, the priestess in ancient Greece who fell in love with Jason and bore his children, murdering them when he abandoned her. It was captivating and emotional, and as Anna relaxed he saw the first flicker of emotion cross her face. Normally she was so poised, so in control, it was wonderful to see her express what she was truly feeling. As the story unfolded he noticed the gleam of tears on Anna's cheeks, but she was too engrossed in the opera to wipe them away.

Gently Harry leaned in, using his thumb to capture the tiny droplets of salty tears, brushing them away. With his hands still cupping her face she turned towards him.

'It's beautiful,' she whispered.

Using every last bit of his self-control Harry nodded and backed away. He'd never felt such desire as he did right now, never wanted to kiss a woman so much, but he knew it would lead down a path he just couldn't follow.

Quickly he stood, needing to put physical distance between him and Anna, allowing her to watch the last few moments of the opera in peace.

'Thank you, Harry,' Anna said as the applause from the audience began. She stood and crossed the small platform towards him, stopping when they were only inches apart. 'That was one of the best evenings of my life.'

He was unable to stop himself from lifting a hand to place on her upper arm, allowing his fingers to trail over her satiny-soft skin. By the flickering light of the candle she looked beautiful and Harry knew if he didn't step away immediately he wouldn't be able to control what happened next. Her cool grey eyes met his and for a moment the noise from the audience below faded into the background.

It was Anna who stepped away, turning quickly and crossing back to the wooden barrier, pretending to be sorting out her skirts so she wouldn't have to look at him.

Harry hadn't expected the sharp pang of disappointment. No real liaison between them could result in anything good, but it seemed his head and his heart wanted two very different things.

'We will wait for everyone else to leave,' Harry said quietly, 'and then I will escort you downstairs. Your cousin will be waiting for you in your uncle's carriage. I thought it best mine was not seen dropping you home at this hour.'

Chapter Nine

'Great news!' Billy Godden shouted as he ran up the stairs and burst into the office. 'The *Lady Magdalene* has docked in Lisbon. She needs extensive repairs, but the cargo is all in good condition.'

Anna felt a great weight being lifted from her and cautiously enquired, 'And the crew?'

'All safe and accounted for.'

'Thank you, Billy,' Anna said. 'That's wonderful news.'

'Should we arrange for another ship to pick up the cargo, ma'am?'

Before answering Anna took out the small notebook she kept with her at all times that outlined the current position of all the ships the Trevels Shipping Company owned. Quickly she scanned the pages, trying to work out a solution.

'The *Elizabeth Rose* is not due to sail for France

again for another two weeks. We could send her to Lisbon to take the *Lady Magdalene*'s cargo and arrange a replacement for the run to France.'

'Shall I organise it, ma'am?'

'Please do, Billy.'

As he left Billy paused by the door. 'There's a package out here for you,' he said, picking it up and placing it on the desk.

Anna felt a chill creep over her entire body and quickly sat down in her chair before she collapsed. The package was nondescript from the outside, just a brown box tied up with string. There was no note attached, no card to say who it was from, but Anna knew immediately it was another unwanted present from her tormentor.

She hesitated before pulling at the string. It would be easy to throw it away, discard it without looking inside. That would be one way of taking back control, but she knew she couldn't do it. She *needed* to know what was inside, what part of her life they were attacking now.

For a moment she wondered about sending word to Harry, asking him to come and open the package for her, but as soon as the thought occurred she abandoned it. Harry wouldn't be around for ever. In a month, maybe two at the most, they would go their separate ways and Anna would again be alone. She disliked the idea of having to rely on anyone else, so she wouldn't.

'You're a grown woman,' she murmured to herself, quickly tugging at the string before she could change her mind. The knot unravelled and with a rapid movement Anna tore off the lid of the box and peered inside.

Thankfully there was nothing as gruesome as a dead animal inside. The box was almost empty, with just a folded square of paper at the bottom. Trying to ignore her shaking hands, Anna lifted the paper and began to unfold it.

As she read the writing on the paper she felt the bile rise in her throat and a swell of nausea from her stomach. It was a list of her every movement over the past week, details of where she'd gone, at what times and who she had encountered. It was accurate and detailed and could only have been obtained by someone who was watching her closely.

At the very bottom of the page was a warning written in capitals.

STAY AWAY FROM LORD EDGERTON

'I want to go ahead,' Anna said decisively as Harry walked through the door.

He must have seen her expression as he didn't waste time with a greeting, instead moving to examine the box on the table.

'When was it delivered?' he asked.

'Some time this morning. Did you hear what I said? I want to go ahead.'

'With the house party?'

Anna nodded. 'I need to know who is sending these packages.' She shivered before continuing, 'I need to know who is watching me.'

'Was it just the note in the box, nothing else?'

'The note is bad enough. Someone's been spying on me, following me.'

The thought of an unknown tormentor trailing her as she went about her daily life made Anna feel so sick she had to walk to the window and throw it open, gulping in a lungful of fresh air.

'You haven't noticed anyone?'

Silently she shook her head. There hadn't even been the hint of a shadow or the feeling of eyes on her. She'd been completely oblivious.

'Why the warning to stay away from me?' Harry pondered.

'Perhaps they truly think I murdered my other husbands and want to protect you.'

'These packages aren't about protection, they're about persecution. It doesn't make sense.'

'I don't care,' Anna said, her voice sounding almost hysterical even to her own ears, 'I just want to stop them.'

She leaned her forehead on the grimy glass, closing her eyes for a few seconds while focusing on her breathing. Quiet footsteps told her Harry was approaching behind her, but for once she didn't tense, didn't feel the stiffening of her muscles that occurred whenever anyone got near.

Softly he placed his hands on her shoulders, not trying to move her or spin her to face him, content with just letting her know he was there. As the seconds ticked past Anna felt some of the tension seep from her body until she was composed enough to step away from the window.

'I want this house party,' she said firmly. 'I want to invite all three of Lord Fortescue's horrible children and I want to get to the bottom of who is sending these packages.'

'I'll arrange a date,' Harry said simply.

'You don't mind?' Anna asked. She'd reacted badly when Harry had pushed for this very plan just a few days ago, but it looked as though he wasn't about to bring up her behaviour.

'I will not have you terrorised.'

Quickly Anna stepped away, busying herself at her desk. Harry's desire to protect her was seductive and she had to concentrate hard not to fall under his spell.

'We should invite some other guests, too. I don't think I could bear being cooped up in a house with just the Fortescue family for a weekend.'

'Do you have any friends you'd like to invite?'

Avoiding Harry's eye, she shook her head. Once she'd had friends, she'd been popular and well liked as a debutante. Even after the death of her second husband she'd had a select group of friends, women she could laugh with and confide in and share the good and bad moments with. Lord Fortescue had put an end to any companionship, systematically isolating her from her limited family and friends until she'd had no one but her cruel husband.

'How about Beatrice?'

'I'd rather she wasn't involved.'

'It might look a little strange if she isn't present.'

'I don't want her getting hurt. If this *person*, this *villain*, catches on to how much I care for Beatrice she might be targeted.'

'Leave the guest list to me,' Harry said with a reassuring smile.

'How will you get the Fortescue children to attend?'

'I'll ask them,' Harry said with a shrug. 'I'm hoping they'll be intrigued enough to accept.'

'Thank you,' Anna said quietly.

'Do I take it our engagement is back on?'

Grimacing, Anna nodded. Right now she would do anything to find out who was sending her these threatening packages, including resurrecting the sham engagement to Harry.

'You look overjoyed at the prospect, Lady Fortescue,' Harry said.

'I'm not sure if we are saving ourselves from scandal or just postponing it.'

'If we wait until some other unfortunate gets caught in a compromising position, the collective attention of the *ton* will be directed elsewhere and we can quietly go our separate ways.' Harry knew they would still be subjected to gossip and rumour, but perhaps they could lessen the speculation by choosing the right time.

'It may work,' Anna conceded.

'And now I wish to take my fiancée out for an afternoon stroll.'

They took his carriage back to the more salubrious part of London and Harry had the driver stop by the Stanhope Gate while they alighted. Despite the sunny start to the day the sky was now moody and overcast, the clouds like great purple bruises spreading across the sky.

'Afraid of a little rain?' Anna asked as she watched him looking up.

'I wouldn't like for you to catch a chill.'

'Always a gentleman, Lord Edgerton,' Anna murmured.

'Not *always*,' he said, a barely perceptible gleam in his eyes.

Anna had relaxed on the carriage ride through London, the tension slowly seeping from her body and the frown lifting from her face as they got further from the docks. He knew it was the unpleasant packages and her mysterious tormentor preoccupying her mind, but he also wondered if the stress of running the shipping company didn't help.

'I was thinking about your shipping company the other day and I don't think I know a single other woman who is so involved with running a business,' Harry said, keeping his voice light. 'It must be stressful.'

He half-expected a frosty response, but instead got a wry smile. 'Careful, Harry, or you'll start to sound like the meddling matrons I receive so much *friendly* advice from.'

'Society disapproves.'

'That is an understatement. I do not fit the expected stereotype of a gently bred lady. I prefer world maps and shipping charts to watercolours and dinner parties.'

'What made you decide to run the company yourself, rather than hire a man to do it?'

Anna smiled again and Harry realised this was the most animated he'd seen her. There could be no doubt she loved her unusual work.

'Aside from the fact that the company couldn't afford it?' She linked her arm through Harry's and they began to stroll through the park as she spoke. 'The Trevels Shipping Company had a grand total of three ships when I took over the day-to-day management last year. We were heavily in debt and didn't have a reliable reputation among the traders that mattered.'

'But you could afford to employ someone to manage the company now?'

'Yes,' Anna said slowly, 'but that's never going to happen. It's my blood, sweat and tears that have gone into the company, my hard work that is just starting to pay off. I will not hand it over to someone else to ruin it.'

'I can see it has been an important part of your life,' Harry said, aware he was stepping dangerously close to a line he shouldn't cross, 'although one day you might feel differently. I'm sure you will want to marry again, have children—your focus would shift.'

The main problem would be that most husbands wouldn't want their wives traipsing off to the docks every day to do a job that wasn't even suitable for a woman of a lower class.

'That isn't an issue,' Anna said with a smile on her lips, but fire in her eyes. 'I will never marry again.'

It was said so vehemently that Harry missed a step.

'Of course you'll marry again,' he said before he could stop himself.

'Oh, really, Lord Edgerton, you know my mind better than I, I suppose?'

'I just meant you're young, you're beautiful, you're from a good family.'

'You forget half of society thinks I murdered all three of my husbands. Not many men would want to take on the Black Widow as their wife.'

'No one actually believes that...' He paused and corrected himself after receiving an admonishing stare, 'Well, not many people actually believe that.'

'It is of no concern. *I* do not wish to marry

again, so it doesn't matter if anyone would have me or not.'

'Do you not want children?' Harry asked.

Anna's face softened and there was a look of regret in her eyes. 'I always hoped… But it wasn't meant to be. Enough, let's talk of something else. How about you? Have you someone in mind to settle down with?'

Over the past six months he'd attended every ball, accepted every invitation and valiantly tried to find a wife who was respectable and suitable, but also likeable. He wanted a companion, someone he could tolerate sharing breakfast with every day for the next thirty years, someone who would make a good mother to his children. He wouldn't consider anyone he thought there was even a small chance he might fall in love with. Years of witnessing the explosive rows between his parents, seeing the hurt and betrayal in his mother's eyes as his father disappeared with another of his mistresses, was enough to tell him love only set you up for hurt in a marriage. His parents had married for love, his mother had been infatuated with his father throughout their union and she had suffered years of pain and heartache. No amount of passion was worth that.

'No one in particular.'

Smiling, she pulled away slightly and regarded his face for a moment or two. 'Let me guess, you're looking for an accomplished young woman, someone beautiful and poised, someone who was born for the role of countess.'

Harry smiled, too, playing along. This was a new side he was seeing of Anna. He felt as though slowly he was breaking through the façade, knocking down the wall she'd constructed to keep everyone out brick by brick. For the first time she was teasing him and she'd actually opened up a little about her hopes for the future, although he'd clearly got the message that the subject of her past was still strictly out of bounds.

'Only women from the purest aristocratic stock may be considered,' Harry joked.

'So you *do* have someone in mind?'

'No.'

'But you do want to marry?'

'Of course,' he answered before thinking, but then considered the question. He'd always been expected to marry, to carry on the Edgerton family name and ensure the status and wealth built up over the last few centuries didn't dissipate and leave the immediate family. It was his role in life, just as much a responsibility as running the large estate in Kent and looking after his mother and sister now his father had passed away.

'It's strange, isn't it—we're brought up being told we must marry well, make a good match in life, that sometimes we don't consider what we really want.' Anna looked off into the distance as she spoke, her expression inscrutable.

'What is it you want?' Harry asked.

'Peace. But we were talking about you. You don't give much away about yourself, Harry. You're a hard man to get to know.'

'Nonsense. Everyone tells me I'm amiable enough.'

'Oh, you're amiable, more than amiable, but in the weeks that we've known each other you haven't told me much about yourself.'

'That can't be true.'

'You're very good at getting others to talk, Harry, so much so that they forget you haven't said much about your life.'

'What do you want to know?'

'I can ask you anything?'

'You can ask...' He trailed off, grinning. 'I might not answer.'

They strolled arm in arm for a few minutes in silence. Every time Harry tried to speak Anna stopped him, admonishing him for interrupting her train of thought. It was a beautiful day in the park, despite the menacing clouds overhead. The trees that lined the pathways were beginning to fill out with their new leaves and dotted along the grass verge were the earliest blooms of spring flowers. Harry realised he felt content and more at peace than he had in a long time.

'What's your dream, Harry?' Anna asked eventually.

'My dream?'

'What do you want most in the world?'

He considered for a few moments. In most people's eyes he was blessed. He owned a large country estate which provided a decent income, had had a distinguished career in the army before he'd left after his father's death and could afford to spend most of his time as he pleased.

'Happiness for my family. For my sister and mother. A good marriage to a decent man for my sister, for her to settle down and have a family.'

'That is a very selfless dream,' Anna said quietly.

Perhaps it seemed that way to someone else, but Harry knew if his sister were happy he would be able to shed the guilt that followed him everywhere. If she could move on with her life, return to society and find herself a husband, then he might be able to forgive himself for failing her so badly.

'Is she not happy now?' she asked.

Harry shrugged, hoping he could deflect Anna's interest on to a different subject. Apart from Rifield, who'd been his closest friend since their days in the army together, no one knew the full extent of Lydia's despair following the scandal she'd suffered last year.

'She's eighteen,' he said slowly. 'It is difficult to know what an eighteen-year-old girl is thinking at the best of times.'

That much at least was true. This past year Harry had tried to get closer to his sister, tried to break down some of the barriers Lydia had constructed to shield her from the outside world, but in truth he hadn't made much progress. When he was at home in Kent he insisted she dine with the rest of the family, that she go out on rides with him and spent time strolling through the grounds with their mother. Lydia complied, but although she was physically present, it was still obvious her mind was elsewhere.

'So you say your sister won't have her debut this year?' Anna asked.

The Season in London was just winding down,

with most of the *ton* spending the warmer months outside the city on their country estates. The best time to reintroduce Lydia to society would be at the start of the next Season in the autumn, but Harry doubted she would be ready for that.

'No. She had attended a few functions when she was seventeen,' he said, trying to keep his voice light, 'but nothing this past year.'

Out of the corner of his eye he saw Anna frown in confusion. Normally once a young woman had made her debut she attended as many balls and soirées as possible. To find a suitable husband you had to be out there actively looking and being seen.

For a few moments they walked on in silence, skirting round the edge of a small pond, nodding in greeting to the few couples they passed. It was quiet in the park; one of the first fine days of spring had caught people unawares and as yet they had not ventured out from their sitting rooms and gentleman's clubs. If the good weather continued Hyde Park would be crowded in a few days. Harry was grateful they didn't have to stop every few paces to talk to some acquaintance or other, but he did wish there would be a distraction before Anna could ask any more difficult questions about his sister.

'Will she be there at the house party?'

'Yes,' Harry said slowly. She'd be there, but he probably wouldn't be able to cajole her into socialising.

'And your mother?'

'She doesn't mix much since my father's death.'

It wasn't the whole truth, but Anna didn't need to know the intimate details of his mother's anxiety. She'd always been of a nervous disposition, but these past few years her circle of comfort had shrunk and shrunk until she wasn't happy anywhere but home and only then when there were no strangers about. She'd spent her entire life tormented by the love she'd felt for her husband, but now he was dead she was overcome by grief and foreboding.

'It sounds like you have a lot of responsibilities,' Anna said softly as she guided him to a bench situated under a towering oak tree.

They sat side by side, Anna's hand resting in the crook of his elbow, looking out over the park. Despite the almost depressing talk about his family Harry felt a peculiar sense of contentment sitting here with Anna. Once her icy demeanour had cracked she was warm and interesting, and she was sensitive enough to know when not to push him further with her questions.

'Tell me about your time in the army,' Anna said.

He shifted slightly, wondering how to start. The years he'd spent in the army were some of the best of his life. He'd enjoyed the sense of purpose, the camaraderie, the knowledge that the junior officers and soldiers relied on him for guidance and advice. Of course there were bad parts, too—battles where he had lost friends, skirmishes he hadn't seen the point of.

'For most of my service I was posted to the Cape,' Harry said. 'It was hot, it was volatile and it was beautiful.'

'It's unusual for a first son to go into the army,' Anna said quietly.

It had been more than unusual—it had been a subject of much argument and debate with his father. Of course his family hadn't wanted him to join the army, but after the cloistered life of university Harry had felt lost, directionless. His father was still strong and capable of running the family estates so Harry had felt surplus to requirements. His solution had been to join the army.

'My mother sobbed for an entire week when I

informed her of my plans,' Harry said grimly. 'But I was young and I'd already made my decision.'

'So they sent you to Africa.'

'Not immediately. When I joined the army the conflict with Napoleon was just in its infancy. I was deployed to various places, but much of the fighting was done at sea. It wasn't until I went to the Cape that I saw much in the way of action.'

It had never been his role to be at the forefront of a battle. His talents at negotiating, his ear for languages and his ability to blend in with different groups of people meant he was often used for the intelligence-gathering side of things before a conflict or negotiating a resolution afterwards.

Just before he could regale her with any tales of swashbuckling heroism a movement on the other side of the pond caught his eye. It was another couple, the man dressed in a garishly coloured jacket and the young woman giggling coquettishly. Normally he wouldn't be in the slightest bit interested in the romantic liaisons of anyone else, but there was something about the way the man walked that made every muscle in his body tense and gave him the sensation of ice in his veins.

'Harry?' Anna said, turning towards him and placing her free hand on his upper arm.

Everything faded into the background, everything except the man approaching ceased to exist and Harry felt his body move without instruction. As if wading through treacle he stood and walked towards the couple, his hands bunching into fists by his side. The man hadn't seen him yet, he was too engrossed in the words he was whispering to his companion, too enamoured with the sound of his own voice to notice Harry approaching.

'Mountfield,' Harry growled.

At first Captain Mountfield didn't seem to recognise him and this made Harry even more irate. The scoundrel had ruined his sister, nearly been the cause of her death, and he didn't even recognise Harry.

'Lord Edgerton.' The name finally passed Captain Mountfield's lips after a few seconds.

The seconds ticked past as the two men stared at one another, the tension mounting until the lady on Captain Mountfield's arm gave a nervous titter.

'You haven't introduced me, darling,' she said.

Harry didn't even look at her, finding it impossible to tear his eyes away from the only man in the world that he had ever hated.

'Miss Francesca Pont,' Captain Mountfield said quietly, his eyes never leaving Harry's.

'A pleasure to make your acquaintance, Lord Edgerton,' Miss Pont twittered.

All the hurt and distress his sister had suffered over the past year flitted before his eyes and Harry felt his fists tense. After five years in the army he abhorred violence, but right now it wasn't his rational brain in control of his body.

'Hit me and you'll regret it,' Mountfield hissed.

After Lydia and Mountfield had been found in a compromising position and the captain had refused to do the honourable thing and marry Lydia, Harry had challenged him to a duel. Captain Mountfield had refused, laughing in Harry's face. He'd said he would tell the world all the dirty little details of his affair with Lydia if Harry didn't leave him alone. Of course Harry had backed down, but part of him still really wanted to face this scoundrel with a gun or a sword in his hand.

'I'll remind all of society exactly how your sister disgraced herself last year.'

'Be careful of the company you keep, Miss Pont,' Harry said, stepping back and letting the couple past.

His whole body was shaking as he watched them walk away. As they disappeared into the distance he let out a muted growl and turned to look for some inanimate object to take out his pent-up rage on. Instead he found Anna standing behind him. Gently she took his hand in hers and squeezed his fingers.

'I know a little about hatred,' she said softly, 'so I know how hard that must have been to let him walk away. Whatever he did, however you want to punish him, your love for your sister prevailed over that.'

Harry studied Anna's face, letting his eyes roam over her pale skin, the curve of her perfectly pink lips and into her cool, grey eyes. As he focused on her he felt some of the rage start to seep away and his muscles begin to relax.

'I don't believe in fate,' Anna said as she linked her arm through his and began to lead him back the way they had come. 'I don't believe that bad people get punished for their deeds, but perhaps one day whatever it is that he holds over your sister will not matter any longer and then you will be able to expose him for the scoundrel that he is.'

Chapter Ten

The carriage sped down the country lanes, winding this way and that over the rutted road, making it impossible for Anna to stay in one place on the narrow cushion, let alone focus on the book in her hand. Across from her sat her maid Grace, somehow managing to doze despite the jolting of the carriage. She felt a cautious optimism about this weekend. She dared not believe this might be the day they exposed her tormentor, but underneath careful layers of realism she was a little hopeful. It would be wonderful not to be always looking over her shoulder, not worrying about who might be watching her and following her. For months she had felt a sick anticipation every time the butler entered with a letter or a package.

Settling back on to the seat, one hand gripping the small ledge below the window, Anna turned her focus to the scenery outside. If her calculations were correct she should be arriving at Halstead Hall very shortly. Harry had gone on ahead a few days earlier to get everything prepared for the weekend and for propriety's sake she was arriving along with the other invited guests.

All in all they had agreed on a guest list of twelve. It included the three Fortescue children, as well as the wives of the new Lord Fortescue and Mr Ronald Fortescue. Mr Lionel Fortescue, Anna's brother-in-law, had sent his apologies, but was spending a few months in Scotland. They'd ruled him out as a likely suspect as it would be difficult for him to orchestrate the sending of the packages from so far away and by all accounts he'd been in Scotland for over two months already.

Harry had invited a couple of old friends, single young men who were there to keep the peace and also to entice Miss Antonia Fortescue to attend. She was in search of a husband and Anna suspected the only reason she'd agreed to come to the gathering was the prospect of wealthy, titled gentlemen in a confined area.

To finish off the guest list there was also Harry's sister Lydia and the local vicar and his wife from the village of Halstead. All in all a strange party, but Anna knew the purpose of the event wasn't to enjoy herself or make friends, it was purely to find out who was tormenting her.

Nevertheless she felt a surge of excitement as the carriage swerved into a wide driveway and Halstead Hall came into view.

It was a beautiful old house, set in magnificent rolling Kentish countryside. As they rattled up the long drive Anna could see a group of deer in the distance, the tiny fawns frolicking alongside their mothers. The house itself looked old but well maintained, perhaps originally Elizabethan, but with extra wings added over the centuries as was common in many of the country estates.

At each end of the property was a tower, complete with crenellations, and over the heavy front door was a coat of arms. Looking at Halstead Hall, she was in no doubt it was the home of one of the oldest families in England.

The carriage came to a stop and a footman was at the door immediately, offering her his hand to help her down. As her feet hit the floor the footman stepped back and Anna saw Harry emerge from the house, a delicate-looking young woman on his arm.

'Lady Fortescue,' he greeted, taking her hand and brushing a kiss against her knuckles. 'Welcome to our home.' His eyes twinkled in the sunlight and Anna knew he was enjoying himself already. In the short time she'd known Harry it had become clear he was an intelligent man, made for more than the dull life of the wealthy gentleman. She didn't know much about his time in the army, but whenever he mentioned that part of his life he grew animated and his eyes lit up with enthusiasm. She supposed helping her find out who was sending her the unwelcome packages took him back to his army days a little.

'This is my sister, Lady Lydia Pershore. Lydia, this is Lady Fortescue.'

Anna stepped forward and dipped into a curtsy in front of the young woman, as was the correct formal greeting. Lydia looked a little overwhelmed, so as she rose Anna gave her a conspiratorial smile.

'You must call me Anna,' she said.

'I am Lydia.'

'I have been wanting to meet you ever since your brother first spoke of you,' Anna said, gently linking her arm through Lydia's. She'd heard the gossip, pieced together a little of what had happened to Harry's sister a year ago after she'd witnessed the confrontation between Harry and Captain Mountfield in Hyde Park. According to Beatrice, the scandal had been monumental, although her cousin seemed to think many things were worthy of that title. No one had seen or heard from the disgraced Lydia since she was found with very few clothes on in the arms of an army officer. As often seemed to be the case, Beatrice couldn't even remember the army officer's name, it was the daughter of an earl the society gossip had focused on.

Whatever had happened Anna didn't want to know any more. She knew better than most how malicious gossip could hurt. No matter what rules of propriety Lydia had broken, Anna had no doubt she had been punished more than enough in the months since.

'Am I the first to arrive?' Anna asked.

'I was meant to invite other people?' Harry asked, barely able to keep the smile from his lips.

'It would probably make for a more pleasant weekend without the Fortescues,' Anna admitted.

Harry led them inside, and Anna tried not to look around with open-eyed amazement at the beautiful entrance hall. Her family had been wealthy, as had two out of three of her husbands, but never had she been anywhere with such plush furnishings.

'We should have time for a quick tour,' Harry said as they passed through the hall into a sitting room illuminated with the afternoon sunlight.

'Won't the other guests be arriving soon?' Anna asked.

'I might have told them an hour later,' Harry said, not a hint of embarrassment for his deception evident in his voice. 'I wanted to show you Halstead Hall first, without the Fortescues trying to push you down the stairs or poison your teacup.'

'Harry,' Lydia admonished with a gasp.

He shrugged. 'The awful thing, dear sister, is that it could happen.' He turned to Anna. 'Come with me.'

Taking her by the hand, he pulled her quickly into room after room after room, explaining what they all were in a couple of words before moving on. He reminded Anna of an excited young boy, eager to show his new friend his home.

'The music room,' he declared as they entered a large room with a grand piano at one end. 'Perhaps you'll play for me one day.'

Letting go of Harry's arm, Anna walked the length of the room and stood behind the piano, running her fingers across the shiny veneer on the lid before gently caressing the keys. As a young girl she'd spent hours playing the piano, loving the emotion that could be expressed in a single piece of music. No other instrument had the versatility of the piano, allowing soft, gentle notes to be followed by the loud, marching tunes.

'Perhaps,' she said, pressing a couple of the keys, hearing the perfectly tuned notes and wondering if she would ever feel that same love for music as she once had.

After a few moments they moved on, the tour taking her through the dining room and out on to the terrace before returning to the house.

'Let me show you to your room,' Harry said, leading her up the sweeping staircase to the first floor.

He unlocked the door to a large room filled with natural light. In the centre was a four-poster bed, flanked by two comfortable-looking armchairs. A dressing table and a wardrobe made up the rest of the furniture, but it was the view that commanded the most attention. Two large windows, both with window seats, looked out over the parkland. Rolling green hills dotted with oak trees stretched as far as the eye could see.

'This bedroom has one of the finest views in the house,' Harry said softly. He was standing right behind her, so close she could feel his breath on her neck. Ordinarily she would feel unsettled by having anyone so close to her, but not with Harry. She'd realised over the last few weeks that she felt safe with him, a peculiar sensation for someone who was used to living in fear, always wondering where the next unprovoked attack would come from.

'Thank you,' she said, turning to face him. He didn't step away, instead moved a fraction closer, his hand reaching out to find hers. Anna looked up into his eyes, felt her heart pounding in her chest and couldn't deny any longer the physical pull she felt whenever Harry was near.

For a long few seconds he studied her face, his free hand reaching up to brush her hair back from her forehead. Her skin tingled as his fingertips made contact and she shivered with anticipation as he traced a route past her temple and around her ear.

Never before had she wanted to be kissed as much as she did right now and as Harry stepped away she had to choke back a cry of frustration.

'Let me show you my favourite part of the house,' Harry said, taking her hand and pulling her from the bedroom, striding so quickly along the corridor Anna almost had to run to keep up. They passed door after door, room after room, so many that after a minute Anna had lost count. 'This way,' he said, leading her through a tiny, inconspicuous door at the end of the corridor, then up a tight spiral staircase. As they climbed the temperature dropped a few degrees and Anna got a sense of what Halstead Hall would have been like a few hundred years ago soon after it was first built. The walls were smooth stone and at regular intervals there were iron brackets on the walls, no doubt for a lighted torch to guide the way in the dark.

They emerged at the top of one of the towers Anna had noticed when she'd first alighted from her carriage. Although the day was still and calm, up here there was a little breeze, enough to rustle her skirts and whip the loose strands of hair across her face.

Carefully they picked their way over the uneven flagstones to the edge, where Harry leaned easily on the low stone wall. Anna wasn't nearly so confident in the old stone's stability, instead choosing to stand a pace back from the parapet.

'It's beautiful,' Anna said, shielding her eyes from the sun as she looked out over the rolling countryside.

'You can see for miles. I used to come up here when I was a boy and spend hours daydreaming.'

'It's very peaceful.'

'That's why I wanted to show you.' He handed her a heavy iron key. 'I know this weekend might be difficult for you, so many people who dislike you under one roof. If it ever gets too much, then I wanted you to have somewhere private, some-where safe to come.'

Anna felt the weight of the key in her hand, swallowing the lump that was forming in her throat.

'Thank you,' she said softly.

'There are only two keys—you have one and I the other. If you come up here and lock the door behind you, then only I will be able to follow you.' He paused, continuing slowly, 'If you do come up here, could I ask that you lock the door after you come back down. It doesn't do to have the tower easily accessible to everyone.'

'Of course.'

For a few minutes they stood side by side, look-ing out over the countryside. Anna had the sense Harry wanted to say something more, but he couldn't find the words.

'I know this weekend will be hard for you,' he said eventually, 'but do you think I could ask a favour of you?'

'Anything.'

'You shouldn't agree before you know what I'm asking,' Harry said with a mischievous glint in his eyes. 'I could be requesting you join us for dinner in just your undergarments or run naked through the halls at dawn.'

She fixed him with an admonishing stare.

'Of course I wouldn't do that to my lovely fi- ancée...'

'Pretend fiancée,' Anna corrected him.

'Would you help my sister a little?' he asked, his expression turning serious again.

'Help in what way?'

'You're so good at being in society, socialising with people, even when you know they're saying horrible things about you. I don't know if you just don't care what other people think, or if you're very good at putting on a show of not caring, but it's hard not to admire you for it.'

Harry's words came out quickly. He was anx- ious, Anna realised. For the first time since they'd met he was actually nervous.

'Lydia gets very upset by people, by the unkind things people say...' he sighed '...even the unkind things she imagines people might be thinking.'

'That's no bad thing,' Anna said quietly.

'You don't. Do you?'

She shrugged. Of course being called a mur- derer, a black widow and a harlot hurt, but long ago she'd realised they were only words and they could only do her damage if she let them. She supposed in a perverse way she had Lord Fortescue to thank for making her so strong, so resilient. He'd called her names and accused her of all sorts of untrue things every single day of their marriage—after a while she'd learnt to block out most of what he said.

'I've had a lot of practice at ignoring them,' Anna said. 'It's hardened me, made me cynical and untrusting. You don't want that for your sister.'

'She's so unhappy,' Harry said quietly. 'I just want her to be happy.'

Anna reached out and placed her hand over his.

'I will do anything to help you,' she said, stepping closer. 'Whatever you think is for the best.'

Harry was doing so much for her, going above what anyone could ever expect of him to help her find out who was tormenting her, the very least she could do was try to help his sister find her confidence in socialising again.

Chapter Eleven

Standing outside, Harry forced a smile to his face as Miss Fortescue stepped down from her carriage. Despite the almost permanent sneer he could tell she was impressed by Halstead Hall. To him it was just home, but he knew it was one of the grandest residences in the country.

'Miss Fortescue, welcome to Halstead Hall.'

She inclined her head, shot a look of disgust at Anna and allowed the butler to show her inside.

'Please take your time to settle into your room. We shall meet for drinks before dinner, at seven in the drawing room.'

'She looked happy to be here,' Anna said as she watched her stepdaughter and a flustered young maid disappear into the house. 'Remind me how you persuaded me this would be a good idea?'

Harry suppressed a grin. Throughout the arrival of the guests Anna had stood by his side, elegant and poised, but distant. He was reminded of the first time he'd met her at the Prendersons' ball. It had taken a lot of work for him to slowly break down the barriers she'd erected around herself, but slowly he felt like he was getting through. Seeing her formal behaviour crack when there was no one else around warmed him, probably more than it should.

'Just think, three days and hopefully we will know which of the Fortescue children is sending you those packages,' Harry said, giving her arm a quick, reassuring squeeze. He had also noticed that she'd stopped flinching whenever he touched her now. Early on in their acquaintance she'd jumped every time he brushed against her, as if expecting something awful to occur because of the contact. Now she didn't pull away at the slightest touch and seemed comfortable walking arm in arm with him.

'How are we going to work out which of them is guilty?' Anna asked, narrowing her eyes as another carriage appeared on the horizon.

'It's simple. We observe them, provoke them to anger and watch to see how they react, who threatens you, who seems to want to cause you the most harm.'

'It seems a little unsubstantial,' Anna said. 'The

Fortescues aren't dim-witted, they will be on their guard while they are here.'

'Then we confront them,' Harry said with a shrug. 'One by one, ideally in the company of the other guests, and we watch their reaction to that. I've dealt with enough scoundrels in my time to know if one is lying.'

Anna nodded slowly, but Harry could see she wasn't quite convinced.

The next carriage was pulling up to the house and this time Harry didn't have to force a smile on to his face. He recognised the coat of arms painted on its side and sure enough, before the carriage had come to a complete halt, Rifield was jumping down. Anna had initially been concerned at the idea of involving his friend in their attempt to uncover the perpetrator behind her persecution, but Harry had reminded her that Rifield would be perfectly placed to see what people were saying when neither Harry nor Anna was present. He had been glad when Anna had agreed.

Harry watched with curiosity as his old friend turned and took the hand of first an older woman, then a younger one and helped them alight.

'Rifield,' he greeted warmly, clasping his old friend's hand.

'Foxton sends his apologies,' Rifield said as he

gripped Harry's hand firmly. 'Been struck down with a bad chest and couldn't make the journey.'

Sir Thomas Foxton was another of Harry's old friends and meant to be making up the numbers this weekend as well as providing a little moral support. Although roughly the same age as Harry and Rifield, their friend suffered with repeated chest infections no doctor seemed to be able to cure, hence Harry wasn't overly surprised by the cancellation.

'I have brought Mrs Wright and her charming daughter, Miss Caroline Wright, with me,' Rifield said. 'Didn't think you'd mind.'

Harry turned to the two women. He recognised them both, thought he had probably danced with Miss Caroline Wright at a ball the past Season.

'Mrs Wright is a friend of my mother's,' Rifield explained, 'and Miss Caroline Wright made her debut this year.'

'A pleasure to meet you. You are very welcome at Halstead Hall,' Harry said, greeting first the mother and then the daughter. 'May I introduce Lady Fortescue.'

Anna stepped forward and greeted the newcomers formally, smiling at the young Miss Wright who recoiled away before she could stop herself.

'Harrison, please ask the maids to make up two

more rooms and escort Mrs Wright and Miss Caroline upstairs. We will meet for drinks at seven in the drawing room,' Harry addressed his efficient butler.

Once the two women had disappeared inside Rifield turned to Anna.

'Lady Fortescue, I have heard so much about you,' he said.

'Hasn't everyone?' Anna sighed. 'Lord Edgerton tells me I'm quite notorious.'

Rifield threw his head back and let out a hearty chortle.

'I'm intrigued to find out who our villain is this weekend,' Harry's friend said. 'It'd all be rather exciting if it wasn't so ghastly.'

'You wouldn't be so keen on this weekend if you knew our guests of honour well.'

'The Fortescues? They do have a bit of a reputation. I've met the new Lord Fortescue and his younger brother, but never had the pleasure of Miss Fortescue.'

'She's husband hunting,' Anna said, a wicked gleam in her eyes, 'and you're just the sort of man she's looking for.'

'Now I see why Edgerton was so keen to get me here.'

'There's no denying it, you're bait, old friend,' Harry said, clapping Rifield on the back.

'I am completely at your service, madam,' Rifield said with a theatrical bow.

'And now I must go and change for dinner,' Anna said, bidding the two men farewell.

They watched her go, both standing in silence as she glided gracefully up the stairs and out of sight.

'I see why you're infatuated,' Rifield said quietly. 'There's something rather enchanting about the notorious Lady Fortescue.'

'I'm not infatuated,' Harry protested.

'Good. Then you won't be mad I decided to invite Miss Caroline Wright to this little party.'

'You're interested in her?' Harry asked. In all the years he'd known Rifield he hadn't known him to favour any young woman, despite his romantic views on life.

'Good Lord, no. She's pleasant enough, I'm sure—my mother certainly approves of her, and you know how difficult she is to impress. No, I brought Miss Wright here for you to get to know.'

'Why on earth would you do that?' Harry asked.

'She's exactly what you told me you're looking for—respectable, reliable, amiable. Perhaps a little dull, but she's generally well liked. And I can't see you being burdened by falling in love with her.'

Harry exhaled loudly.

'Don't be like that. She's just what you say you want.'

'You're worse than a meddling mother,' Harry said. This wasn't the first time Rifield had introduced him to some young debutante. Normally on paper they looked perfectly pleasant, but in the flesh there was something missing, some quirk that irked Harry more than it should. 'And bringing her here for this weekend, what were you thinking?'

Rifield shrugged. 'If she's the one for you, then why waste time?'

'Has it escaped your memory that I'm currently engaged to Lady Fortescue.'

'Pretending to be engaged,' Rifield corrected him.

'I can hardly court Miss Wright while the world thinks I am promised to Anna.'

'Don't worry, I explained the situation to Miss Wright, she's understanding.'

'You did what?' Harry forced himself to lower his voice. 'What did you tell her?'

'Just that you had proposed to Lady Fortescue to save her from a scandalous situation, not of your own making, of course. And that once the scandal had blown over you would both be going your separate ways.'

'Rifield, I know you have the best of intentions...'

'Always, old chap. Just want to see you happy and settled.'

'But I do wish you hadn't invited Miss Wright. This weekend is going to be difficult enough without having to pretend to be interested in a dull debutante.'

'Not pretend, Edgerton. Miss Wright could be the woman who becomes your wife.'

The idea sent an unwelcome shiver down Harry's spine. He knew he was meant to be looking for someone respectable and amiable, but the idea of actually having to choose a wife made him shudder every time he thought about it.

'Just give her a chance, Pershore,' Rifield said, calling his old friend by his family name just as he had in the army before Harry had inherited the title. 'You might find you like her. I'll keep an eye on Lady Fortescue while you woo Miss Wright, although by all accounts Lady Fortescue doesn't need anyone to defend her.'

'I wouldn't be so sure,' Harry murmured. Anna was fantastic at projecting a strong façade to the world, but underneath she was just as vulnerable

as any other young woman. As she had been widowed three times it was easy to forget she was
still young, still only a few years older than Lydia.

'Just think, in three days' time you could have
found out who is sending Lady Fortescue those
ghastly packages and secured yourself a wife.'

Anna hesitated before knocking, her hand hov-
ering a few inches from the wood. She'd asked
one of the many housemaids which room was
Lydia's and the young girl had directed her to a
quieter wing of the sprawling house. Now she was
here she wasn't sure what she was going to say,
but she'd promised Harry she would try, so she
steeled herself and knocked.

'Come in,' a soft voice said.

The room was beautifully decorated, the walls
covered in wallpaper of an oriental design and
the curtains and bedsheets matched. Lydia was
sitting on the window seat, gazing out over the
countryside, only turning to face Anna after a few
moments. She was still wearing the dress she had
been earlier that day, despite there being less than
an hour until dinner.

'We didn't get a chance to talk earlier,' Anna
said, stepping into the room and closing the door
behind her.

The woman in front of her looked a little like Harry, she had the same dark hair and piercing blue eyes, but her features were much softer, her frame more petite. Although she wasn't as thin as some young debutantes, she looked a little frail and her skin had the translucent quality that hinted at an indoor lifestyle.

'Harry's told me about you,' Lydia said quietly. 'He admires you very much.'

'He is almost alone in that regard.'

Lydia cocked her head to one side, regarding Anna for a moment before motioning to a chair. Anna sat, aware that she felt a little nervous. It was important to her that she didn't fail Harry in this, not because he would blame her, but because he had done so much for her and asked for so little in return.

'I am not a popular woman in society.'

'He didn't tell me that,' Lydia said.

Anna shrugged. 'You'll probably pick up on some of the dislike these next few days.'

Immediately Lydia looked away. 'I'm not sure I'm going to come down tonight. I feel a little unwell.'

'I understand,' Anna said. 'For a long time I wished I could just hide away for ever.'

'I'm not hiding.' Lydia paused. 'Did he tell you

what happened? Did he tell you what everyone thinks of me?'

Anna shook her head. 'I can guess enough, though. Thousands of women go through the same thing. Some scandal, some disgrace, the man gets off lightly, boys will be boys after all. The woman is ripped apart by the gossips.'

'Is that what happened to you?'

Laughing, Anna shook her head. 'No, society thinks I murdered my husbands.'

Lydia's eyes widened and for the first time Anna saw a hint of a smile on the young girl's face.

'Ridiculous, isn't it? But I had three husbands in the space of six years, and my stepchildren from my last marriage really did not like me. A rumour was started and I was the perfect target.'

'You must think me overdramatic,' Lydia said quietly. 'You're dealing with all of this and I—' She broke off, her voice wavering.

'Not at all.' Anna stood and crossed the room, sitting down next to Lydia. 'I spent months hiding away in my uncle's house. For a while I thought I would never attend another ball or accept another invitation ever again.'

'What changed?'

'I was given the right motivation to start social-ising again. My uncle asked me to chaperon my young cousin and it was something that I wanted to do.'

Lydia nodded, her gaze wandering until it focused on a spot somewhere in the distance.

'No matter what your brother says, what anyone says, it is perfectly fine for you never to socialise again, if that is what makes you happy,' Anna said, trying to find the right words to make Lydia see she was in control of her own life. 'But if it doesn't, if you want to go to balls and socialise and dance until the early hours, then a little malicious gossip is not a good enough reason to hide yourself away.' She paused, allowing the young woman time to digest her words. 'It's your life, Lydia. Only you know your hopes and dreams, and only you can change your future.'

'I don't know if I can bear it,' Lydia said quietly. 'Walking into a room and knowing everyone is talking about me.'

'Then walk in next to me. I will guarantee you people will be too busy wondering who I am going to marry and murder next to think about the scandal between you and your young man.'

Slowly Lydia nodded and Anna felt like shouting for joy. There was still a sadness about Harry's sister, something deep-seated and almost melancholy, but she could see her words had penetrated through to Lydia's mind and hopefully the young woman would at least consider them before deciding what to do.

'Shall I help you dress?' Anna asked.

'Would you?'

'Of course. I often help my cousin, Beatrice, get ready before a ball.'

Together they selected a demure white dress with a bright blue sash and carefully Anna helped Lydia into it. Aware of the minutes ticking by, she styled the young woman's hair simply but elegantly, sweeping most of her locks back and securing them at the back of her head, leaving some wisps to frame her face.

'Ready?' she asked as Lydia inspected herself in the mirror.

There was a moment's hesitation before Harry's sister nodded, then arm in arm they left the room.

Chapter Twelve

The conversation was flowing in the drawing room and Harry took a step back to watch the assembled guests. The Fortescues were huddled together in one corner, heads lowered as if discussing something important. Another group, much more friendly in demeanour, stood in the centre of the room as Rifield entertained them with tall tales from his time at university a decade ago.

The only people missing were Anna and his sister. Every few seconds he found himself glancing at the door, wondering who would come through. He barely dared to hope Lydia might decide to join them, but perhaps the safety of a small group in a familiar environment might entice her.

'You seem distracted, Lord Edgerton,' Miss Wright said as she slipped away from the main group and came to his side.

'Not at all.' He flashed a sunny smile, at the same time finding his gaze wandering again to the door. Even if Lydia didn't show, then Anna should be here by now.

'Mr Rifield told me a little of your situation,' she said, touching him lightly on the arm to bring his attention back to her. 'I think it is wonderfully selfless what you are doing for Lady Fortescue.'

Harry blinked, unsure how to answer.

'I know the engagement is not real,' Miss Wright whispered, leaning in so only he could hear her words. 'There aren't many gentlemen who would risk their own reputations for a stranger.'

'It seemed the right thing to do,' Harry murmured.

'You're too generous, I'm sure, Lord Edgerton. Mr Rifield said that Lady Fortescue was about to be embarrassed and you stepped in and proposed to save her from scandal. Is that what happened?'

'More or less,' Harry said vaguely.

'I admire your discretion,' Miss Wright said, in a tone that hinted that she wished she could know more.

'How did you find your first Season, Miss Wright?' Harry asked, trying to move the conversation on to safer ground.

'Tolerable. I enjoy the balls and the socialising,

but now the Season is over I am keen to focus on my charity work.'

'What do you do?'

'My mother and I are patrons of an orphanage in Bath.'

Rifield was right, Miss Wright was just the sort of young woman he should be considering for a wife. She was well liked in society, from a good family and even did charity work. Why then did he find the idea of spending more than a few hours in her company completely unappealing?

Harry opened his mouth to compliment Miss Wright for taking on such a cause, but before the words left his tongue he was distracted by a movement at the door. As he turned his head he saw Anna stepping into the room, dressed in a simple pale green dress made of fine silk, cinched in at the waist with a white ribbon. As always she looked poised and elegant, with no hint of the nervousness Harry knew she must be feeling deep inside. Her expression remained serious as her gaze swept over everyone in the room until her eyes met his. It could have been his imagination, but he was sure he detected just the flicker of a smile, a crinkling of her eyes, as she spotted him, and then as if nothing had happened she moved on. Harry watched as she stepped to one side, glancing behind her. To his amazement Lydia followed her into the room, looking nervously at Anna for reassurance. Anna took his sister by the arm and whispered something in her ear. He couldn't believe his eyes when Lydia actually smiled and for the first time in over a year he felt a little surge of hope.

'May I introduce my sister, Lady Lydia Pershore,' Harry said as Anna and Lydia came to join them.

Miss Wright greeted the two women, smiling kindly at Lydia, although Harry noticed she barely spared a glance for Anna.

'You look lovely, Lydia,' Harry said, taking his sister's hand and kissing her gently on the cheek. He always felt as though she were a delicate porcelain doll, about to crack at any moment, and as such he knew he treated her with too much caution.

'Anna helped me to dress.'

For a moment he felt like picking Anna up and twirling her round, and proclaiming himself as her eternal servant. He wasn't sure how she had convinced his sister to come downstairs, to put on a ballgown and do up her hair, but he would be grateful for ever that she had.

'What a fine gown you are wearing tonight, Miss Wright,' Anna said.

For the first time Harry looked at what Miss Wright was wearing, taking in the pale pink dress, rich with embroidered patterns over the bodice area.

'Thank you, Lady Fortescue. Do you like it, Lord Edgerton?'

Harry murmured an inane compliment, picking up on the tension between Anna and Miss Wright. He supposed in order to entice Miss Wright to the house party Rifield had made Harry out to be completely blameless and chivalrous in the situation he found himself in with Anna. As such, Miss Wright probably didn't have too good an opinion of Anna, even before you took into consideration her reputation among the *ton*.

He was thankful when his butler announced dinner was ready to be served and his guests all started to make their way through to the dining room.

Without thinking he stepped forward to take Anna's arm, but before his fingers touched her skin she gave a subtle shake of her head, glancing towards Lydia as she did so.

'Allow me to escort you to dinner, Miss Wright,' Rifield said, coming up to their little group and taking the young woman's arm and whisking her away before she could protest.

'Lydia, can I escort you in?' Harry asked.

His sister smiled again, placing her hand daintily in the crook of his arm. Together they walked side by side into the dining room. Harry glanced back at Anna, the last one left in the drawing room. She had no one to escort her in to dinner, she would have to walk alone into a hostile environment, and not for the first time Harry wondered how she managed to stay so composed.

Small steps, Anna told herself, *one foot after another*. It was tempting to run away, to flee upstairs to her bedroom, lock the door behind her and shut out the world, but she knew that wasn't the way to solve anything.

Without having to think Anna went through the routine of putting on her invisible armour. Head held high, shoulders rolled back, chin tilted, facial features set into an impenetrable, neutral position. Every day of her marriage to Lord Fortescue she'd done exactly the same thing, from waking up in the morning until she went to bed at night.

Gliding into the dining room, she saw that everyone else had taken their places; there was just one seat empty, between the new Lord Fortescue and his brother Mr Ronald Fortescue, two of her adoring stepchildren.

Anna sat, inclining her head in greeting to the men on either side, before turning to face the woman seated directly opposite. She was relieved it wasn't Miss Fortescue—being completely surrounded by Fortescues would have been too much to bear.

'Antonia tells me you're still running that grubby little shipping company,' Lord Fortescue said part way through the first course.

The eldest of the Fortescue children, the new Lord Fortescue resembled a bull in both looks and temperament. Easy to anger, slow to think, his round face and short neck seemed always to be flushed an unsightly shade of red. He looked much like his father, so much so that Anna had to remind herself it wasn't her late husband sitting next to her when she caught a glimpse of him out of the corner of her eye.

'Indeed,' she said.

'I suppose it's better than whoring.' Lord Fortescue laughed heartily at his own joke, thumping the table with a beefy fist and making the soup jump off Anna's spoon.

'I wouldn't know,' Anna said quietly when he'd finished laughing. 'I have only experience of run-

ning the company, not working in any other oc-
cupation.'

'I don't know,' Mr Ronald Fortescue said from
her other side, leaning in closer so only the three
of them could hear what he was saying. 'Surely
only a woman of experience, *a professional*, could
lure three husbands into marriage in such a short
time.'

Ronald Fortescue was the youngest of the three
children, but also the sharpest. He was cruel, vin-
dictive and Anna suspected he had inherited many
of his father's worst traits.

'Don't forget victim number four,' Lord Fortescue said through a mouthful of soup. He waved
his spoon in Harry's direction.

'How is your wife, Mr Fortescue?' Anna asked,
turning to her left. The new Lady Fortescue, wife
to the eldest Fortescue son, was sitting further
up the table, but Mr Ronald Fortescue's wife was
not present. Anna suspected she had once again
gained an injury she could not easily hide.

'Mrs Fortescue suffers from her nerves,' he said,
adding under his breath, 'Stupid woman.'

'I suffered from my nerves a lot when married
to your father,' Anna said quietly, her voice hard.
'But isn't it peculiar I haven't suffered at all since
his sad passing?'

Lord Fortescue pushed his chair out noisily from the table and stood up, his face turning an even deeper shade of red.

'Ladies and gentlemen,' Harry called from the top of the table, interjecting before Lord Fortescue could say anything he might regret. 'It may be a little unorthodox, but can I propose a little game while we eat.'

Anna felt Lord Fortescue's eyes boring into her as he reluctantly took his seat. She flashed a glance at Harry, who gave her a quick, reassuring smile. He might have put her in this situation, insisted that she be thrown in straight away to sit between the two Fortescue brothers, but he was there keeping an eye on things, ready to step in if things got too heated.

'Some of us know each other very well, but others are not so well acquainted. Seeing as we are a small party, I suggest a little game to allow us to get to know one another better.' He paused as a footman took away his empty bowl of soup. 'In turn we must each tell the table three things about ourselves, things that not many people would know. Two of those things will be true, the other a lie. As a group, we have to work out which is the lie.'

A murmur went along the table as the assembled guests discussed the unorthodox idea with their neighbours.

'Let me start,' Harry said, standing up. 'I was once attacked by a lion in Africa,' he said. 'My favourite drink is champagne. I can speak four languages fluently.'

Anna felt the shift of focus from her to Harry and allowed herself a small sigh of relief. After living with her last husband she could maintain a composed façade for days on end, but she was a little out of practice and she disliked the scrutiny of the Fortescue children.

'No one can speak four languages, that must be a lie,' Mr Ronald Fortescue said.

'Wait,' Mrs Wright called. 'If that was the lie, then it would mean he's been mauled by a lion in Africa.'

'Vicious beasts, no one survives a lion attack,' Lord Fortescue said. 'I witnessed a man get torn to pieces by a lion as if he were no more than a rag doll during my time in Africa.'

'Lord Edgerton did serve in the army, if my memory is correct,' the local vicar said. 'And I think he was posted to Africa.'

Anna glanced at Harry and saw him give her a conspiratorial wink. She'd been dubious about

this whole weekend, worried about gathering together all the people who hated her most in the
world, but Harry had promised he wouldn't let
anything untoward happen and for the first time
in a long time she was realising she could trust
someone to do what they said they would.

'Lord Edgerton did serve champagne in the
drawing room,' Miss Wright said. 'And I'm sure
I saw him take a glass.'

'It's got to be the lion. That's the lie,' Lord Fortescue insisted. 'Rifield, you must know.'

'I am abstaining from comment. I've known
Edgerton for far too long for him to have any secrets from me,' Rifield said.

'And you?' Lord Fortescue asked, not deign-
ing to say Anna's name. 'Do you know anything
about your new fiancé?'

'Lord Fortescue, I *know* which statement is a lie.
I won't ruin the game by giving you the answer.'

'Shall we agree on the lion?' the vicar asked.

A murmur of agreement went around the table.

'That's your final answer?' Harry asked.

'Yes, we're right, aren't we?' Lord Fortescue
said.

'Lady Fortescue, would you like to reveal the
correct answer?' Harry asked.

All heads turned in Anna's direction.

'Lord Edgerton can speak four languages,' Anna said. 'And he must have been attacked by a lion, as he strongly dislikes champagne.'

'Surely not,' the vicar's wife said, her eyes widening in disbelief.

'You must tell us how you survived a lion attack,' Miss Wright said, her face a picture of concern.

Anna wasn't sure exactly why Miss Wright had been invited to the house party. She was a last-minute addition, someone Harry had not even been aware of until she'd arrived with Rifield. At first Anna had assumed she was some romantic conquest of Harry's friend, but the pair didn't seem overly interested in one another. Now she was beginning to wonder if Miss Wright had her sights set on Harry and, if so, how he felt about the matter.

Sitting back in her chair, Anna inspected the young Miss Wright. She was plain but not unattractive, her hair was pulled back sharply from her face and her demeanour was earnest and upstanding. All in all she was the complete opposite of Anna and would make a respectable wife for a man worried about his family's, and more especially his sister's, reputation.

'That is a tale for another time,' Harry said. 'Who's next? Miss Fortescue?'

As Antonia stood Anna realised she was still looking at Miss Wright. She was surprised to find it was jealousy she felt at the idea of Harry turning his attention to another young woman. Not that she saw a future between her and Harry, she knew she could never give up her independence again, couldn't bear to take her chances in another marriage, but she did care for him.

Don't be selfish, she told herself silently. She couldn't ever marry Harry, so she should be happy for him to find someone to settle down with. Although she doubted Miss Wright was the right woman for him. Harry needed someone who challenged him, someone who made him laugh and shared his interests, not someone who stood meekly by his side, agreeing to everything he said, no matter how respectable she was.

'I'm not entirely sure…' Miss Fortescue said.

'Just any three facts,' Harry said, flashing Anna's stepdaughter his most charming smile. 'I'm sure whatever you choose will be fascinating.'

'My brothers will have to keep quiet,' Miss Fortescue said. 'I can play three instruments, I once broke my ankle when thrown from a horse and I correspond with friends on three different continents.'

On either side of Anna the two Fortescue brothers looked completely bemused.

'What fascinating facts,' Rifield said in encouragement. 'And you are adept at lying for such a respectable young lady.'

Harry had instructed Rifield to charm Miss Fortescue, in the hope of getting her to open up about her hatred of Anna.

'Three instruments seems rather a lot,' Mrs Wright mused. 'My daughter is talented on the piano and has a beautiful voice, but I wonder if anyone could play *three* instruments.'

'I believe Miss Fortescue could well correspond with friends on three continents. People travel at the drop of a hat nowadays and it is common to have friends in Africa as well as India,' the vicar said.

'Lady Fortescue?' Harry asked. 'Do you have any idea?'

Anna inclined her head gracefully at her stepdaughter. 'I do not wish to spoil the game. I'm afraid I am certain of the answer.'

'What do you know?' Miss Fortescue hissed, causing the whole table to fall silent.

'I was married to your father for a year, part of the family in every way.'

When she had first arrived in the Fortescue household Anna had tried her very best to fit in. Both Lord Fortescue's sons lived elsewhere, but Miss Fortescue was unmarried and as such still resided in the family home. Anna had tried to befriend her, tried to forge an alliance with the unhappy young woman. As the weeks passed she'd realised Antonia was almost as spiteful as her father, so the attempts to assimilate had stopped, but she'd still lived under the same roof as the young woman for a year.

'You play the piano, the violin and the cello to a very high standard,' Anna said, no hint of emotion in her voice. 'You have a friend in India—Miss Fiona Dotwell, if I'm not mistaken—and a friend in Egypt, as well as many correspondents in this country.' Miss Fortescue opened her mouth to speak, but Anna carried on. 'And you were thrown from a horse when you were ten years old, but you broke your wrist and not your ankle.'

The silence stretched out as Anna finished speaking, none of the assembled guests wanting to come between the two women.

'Is Lady Fortescue correct?' Harry asked quietly after thirty seconds had passed.

'She is correct,' Miss Fortescue confirmed.

'I did try to be your friend,' Anna said quietly, angling her head to Antonia so the other guests wouldn't be able to hear.

'You seduced my father, betrayed him and may well have killed him. You were never a friend of mine.' Miss Fortescue's voice was not so quiet, projecting the accusations down the table. As the silence stretched out two spots of colour appeared on her cheeks and with a jerky, rushed movement she stood, dropping her napkin and pushing her chair back with a loud scrape. 'Please excuse me, I have a terrible headache all of a sudden.'

Miss Fortescue left the room, throwing Anna a look of hate on her way out. As the other guests tried to fill the ensuing silence with embarrassed chatter, the Fortescue brothers both turned to Anna.

'You're a disgrace,' Lord Fortescue muttered in her direction.

Mr Ronald Fortescue was looking at her with more curiosity than contempt. 'Why are we here, Lady Fortescue?' he asked quietly.

'Would you believe me if I said to mend the family rift?'

Mr Ronald Fortescue laughed, a spiteful, ugly

chortle. 'I don't believe a word that comes out of your mouth, dear Mother.'

'Then perhaps it would be better if I said no more.'

Chapter Thirteen

It was another unseasonably warm evening for so early in the spring so Harry had instructed the servants to throw open the doors to the terrace from the drawing room. After dinner the women had filed through, leaving the men in the dining room, discussing whatever it was they discussed when the women left.

Anna surveyed the room. Mrs Wright and Miss Wright were perched on two straight-backed chairs, talking to the vicar's wife. Lydia stood awkwardly to one side, as if unsure if she should join in the conversation. She'd remained quiet throughout dinner, barely saying a word, but she had eaten a little, sipped on some wine and answered any questions directed only at her.

'Tell me,' Anna said, approaching Lydia and taking her arm, 'what do you think of our guests?'

A small smile flickered across Lydia's lips, only

present for a second, but welcome all the same. 'They're a little odd,' Lydia whispered. 'Individually I'm sure they're all perfectly pleasant.'

Anna grimaced—she wouldn't call Miss Fortescue or her brothers perfectly pleasant in any situation.

'But it is a strange group to be gathered together.'

'Did your brother tell you why he arranged this house party?' Anna asked.

Lydia shook her head. 'A little, but not much.'

Harry probably thought he was protecting his sister, shielding her from the unpleasantness in the world, whereas in truth he was likely just isolating her more from the real world.

'The three guests, Lord Fortescue, Mr Ronald Fortescue and Miss Antonia Fortescue, are my stepchildren,' Anna explained, drawing Lydia to one side. 'They all completely despise me—they have done since the moment I married their father and it has only got worse since his death.'

Lydia looked at her with wide eyes and Anna wondered if she was doing the right thing. Part of her thought it would be good for Lydia to be involved with the wider world again, to have something to think about other than her own unhappiness, but she also realised she was probably telling Lydia this against Harry's wishes.

Quietly she explained about the packages and the letters, about her suspicions that it was one of the Fortescue children behind the campaign of hatred. As they talked she saw Lydia slowly become more animated, more interested.

'Do you think they'll do something while you're here?' Lydia asked after Anna had finished her story.

'That is what we hope. Then we can catch them at it and put a stop to the packages once and for all. Will you keep your eyes open for anything suspicious?'

'Of course.'

'Lady Fortescue.' A voice behind Anna made both her and Lydia jump. 'Please forgive me for the interruption.' It was Miss Wright, smiling sweetly. 'I was hoping you might like to join me for a stroll along the terrace. It is such a lovely evening.'

Anna allowed the other woman to take her arm and lead her out to the terrace, checking over her shoulder that Lydia was not too uncomfortable at being left alone.

'What a beautiful evening,' Miss Wright said as they walked away from the dining room.

'Indeed.' Something about this young woman made Anna raise her guard, but she smiled politely and waited for her to say whatever it was she wanted to say.

'I understand the nature of your agreement with Lord Edgerton,' Miss Wright said quietly.

'Oh?'

'No one could say he is not chivalrous, coming to your aid to save you from scandal, but I fear such a kind and generous man might be taken advantage of in that sort of situation,' Miss Wright said smoothly.

'Taken advantage of?' Anna asked mildly, feigning confusion.

'We all know this engagement between you is nothing more than a ruse, something that Lord Edgerton plans to break when the time is right,' Miss Wright said. 'But I fear an unscrupulous woman might pressure such a kind-hearted man into a more lasting agreement.'

'For a woman who only met Lord Edgerton and myself today you seem to have a lot of insight into our situation,' Anna said, keeping her voice impassive.

'You have a reputation, Lady Fortescue, and not a good one. Any connection with you is not good for Lord Edgerton, or his sister. And everyone knows *she* can't afford to have any more scandal attached to her name.'

'I was under the impression Lord Edgerton was a grown man and not a child,' Anna said, 'and as such is perfectly capable of making his own decisions.'

'Even the noblest of men can be led astray by a pretty face and a devious mind.'

'Tell me, Miss Wright, do you have intentions on my fiancé?' Anna couldn't help herself. 'Stealing another woman's betrothed is hardly decent behaviour for a respectable woman.'

'Mr Rifield has made it clear that Lord Edgerton wants a respectable wife who is well liked and well thought of by the rest of society. You are neither respectable, well liked or well thought of. I suggest you gracefully step out of the way and let Lord Edgerton get on with his life without the burden of you.'

'Thank you for your advice,' Anna said, inclining her head politely to Miss Wright. 'You certainly have given me much to think about.'

It would be so easy to go on the attack, but Anna had realised long ago that nothing was ever gained by making a dispute public. Quickly, before her anger could get the better of her, she spun on her heel and glided away, ensuring all traces of anger and passion had been cleared from her face before she stepped back into the drawing room.

Holding a flickering candle, Harry climbed up the winding staircase, feeling his head clear as he breathed in the fresh air. Quietly he stepped on to the parapet, smiling to himself as he saw Anna looking out into the darkness. He'd thought she might be up here. After a challenging dinner no doubt she needed time to process everything that had happened before retiring to bed.

As he stood watching her it became clear she hadn't heard him approaching. She didn't turn round or speak to him, instead lifting her face to the moonlight.

'Anna,' he said, coming up behind her and touching her lightly on the shoulders.

She stiffened and let out a gasp of surprise, but quickly recovered, turning to him with a half-smile.

'You did very well tonight,' he said softly.

'Did I? I couldn't tell.'

'Lord Fortescue's children are absolutely awful. You were wonderfully detached from their spitefulness,' Harry said. He'd watched her throughout dinner, admired the way she hadn't risen to any of the cruel comments the new Lord Fortescue or his brother had made. He'd known she was skilled in hiding her emotions, but until tonight he had never seen anyone deal with such outright disdain with so much dignity.

'Remind me why this is a good idea,' Anna said, turning away and resuming her perusal of the night sky.

'One weekend of discomfort will be worth it if we can put an end to the persecution you've been suffering.'

'Perhaps you're right,' she said, a hint of sadness in her voice.

Carefully Harry reached up and adjusted the shawl around her shoulders, covering the exposed skin against the chill of the night. His fingers lingered, feeling the heat of her body even through the thick wool of the shawl.

'Why are you doing this for me, Harry?' Anna asked, turning to face him.

'I told you before, no one should have to suffer what you're going through.'

'That's too noble,' she said with a little laugh.

'We might not really be engaged,' Harry said, stepping closer so their bodies were almost touching, 'but over the last few weeks I've come to care for you, Anna.'

Her eyes met his and he felt as though she were

searching his entire soul, the deepest recesses of his being.

'I do not like to think of you alone, suffering,' he said.

He wanted to kiss her then, even though he knew it would only complicate things. Before his rational mind could make him step away Anna had swayed towards him, one hand reaching up to touch his face. With her fingers on his cheek, her eyes looking into his, Harry knew a kiss was inevitable and with a low groan he gave in and covered her mouth with his own.

She tasted sweet and her lips were warm, just as Harry had imagined them to be. As he kissed her a torrent of desire crashed through him and he looped an arm around her waist, pulling her closer to him. Even in the midst of passion Harry knew this was wrong, but nothing in the world could have stopped him.

Anna's fingers trailed down his cheek, tracing their way along his neck and coming to rest on his chest. The skin where she'd touched him felt as though it were on fire and his entire body was on edge, as if each and every nerve was waiting to discharge.

With a soft sigh she pulled away.

'I'm sorry, Harry,' she said. 'I shouldn't have done that.'

He half-expected her to flee, that was what most women of his acquaintance would have done after a situation such as this, but instead she embraced him, wrapping her arms around him and burying her head in his shoulder.

'You're a kind man, Harry Edgerton,' she said, her voice muffled by his clothes. 'And I am a foolish woman.'

Gently he lifted her head so she was once more looking into his eyes. For a moment he forgot all the reasons why they couldn't be together, forgot his resolve to find a wife he could never fall in love with and Anna's vehement objection to the idea of ever marrying again.

'Can we forget this ever happened?' she asked. 'I value what we have too much for this to ruin things.'

'Of course,' Harry said, knowing he was lying. He wouldn't ever be able to forget how her lips felt on his, the taste of her mouth in his own, the way her body fitted against his as if they were made for one another.

She smiled at him then, a smile that could melt the heart of any man, then turned and slipped down the staircase back to the main house. Harry stayed where he was for a few minutes, looking out at the stars and wondering when his life became so complicated.

Chapter Fourteen

As the first light of dawn filtered through the thick curtains Anna rose from her bed, slipped into a dress she could fasten without the help of a maid and quietly left her room. She'd always risen early, always enjoyed the peace of a new day before the household started to wake, but today she felt heavy and tired.

She'd barely slept, too many conflicting thoughts racing through her mind, whipping her up into a state of confusion and anxiety and chasing away even the possibility of sleep. Every time she tried to settle Harry's face would flash before her eyes and the memory of his lips on hers, his fingers on her skin, pushed out anything else clamouring for attention in her mind.

Of course the kiss had been a mistake. Anna wasn't sure what had come over her. There had been something almost magical about the moment up at the top of the tower, something irresistible about Harry.

He was unlike any man she had ever known, although she supposed a list of five wasn't very many to compare to. Apart from her three husbands and her father—a man who had frowned upon displays of affection or sentimentality—the only man she'd ever been relatively close to was her beloved uncle. Despite living for a few years as a widow in between her marriages she'd kept herself quite private, never been in a position to start an illicit affair, never indulged in an inappropriate friendship with a gentleman, until now of course. Nevertheless, she knew Harry was different to other men. He was kind and generous, perhaps too generous. He took the problems of others and made them his own, often shouldering the burden when he shouldn't have to. There was no arguing he was a good man.

After Lord Fortescue's death Anna had vowed never to marry again, never to give a man that ultimate power over her. While married she'd suffered daily at her late husband's hands. He was a cruel man and a crueller husband, and she had the scars to prove it. Even after knowing Harry for just a few short weeks she knew he would never beat her, never raise his hand in anger, but all the same she needed to keep her distance.

It would be all too easy to fall for Harry, to find herself seduced by his charm and his kindness, and once again to lose her autonomy, to become a wife rather than a woman of independence.

'Keep your distance,' she murmured to herself as she glided down the stairs, turning back on herself in the grand hallway to slip through the door to the kitchens below where she thought she might find a door a little easier to open than the heavy oak that guarded the grand entrance.

Outside the air was damp and in the distance Anna could see wispy tendrils of mist floating low over the hills. With the sun just starting to peek over the horizon it looked more like a fairy-tale land than England and Anna found it difficult not to smile. Despite the reason she was here, despite all she'd suffered over the years, she couldn't help but appreciate this moment. Right here, right now she felt happy and it was a long-forgotten emotion.

As she stepped on to the immaculately kept lawn that swept the entire length of the back of the house she could feel the dampness seeping through her shoes and knew it wouldn't be long until the hem of her dress was sodden with water, but even this was not enough to make her turn back.

In the distance she could see two deer, a mother and her baby, trotting through the parkland, and closer, just twenty feet away, a group of rabbits were hopping about in the early morning air.

Anna walked for a few minutes with no certain destination in mind, just content to be out in the fresh air. As she headed away from the house the outline of a summer house became visible, the white boards reflecting the sun. Without too much thought she headed for the small structure, but as she drew near she heard a faint sobbing.

Pausing, Anna wondered whether to push on or retrace her steps before anyone saw her. She didn't like to leave whoever it was inside the summer house in distress, but she also knew all too well how sometimes a witness to sorrow was the last thing that person might need.

Quietly she stepped up to the open door and looked inside. For a moment she thought it was Lydia sitting on the bench—the woman had the same dark hair, the same delicate, almost fragile physique. As she looked up Anna realised this woman was older, but most certainly related.

'I'm sorry to intrude,' Anna said. 'I heard you

crying, but I understand if you wish to be left alone.'

'Come sit,' the woman said, brushing the tears away from her eyes. 'You must think me very foolish sitting here crying all by myself.'

'Not at all.' Anna meant what she said. She didn't know what troubles this woman faced and sometimes a few quietly shed tears in private were all the outlet a woman was allowed.

'You must be Lady Fortescue,' she said with a soft smile. 'Lydia told me all about you last night.'

'Lady Edgerton?' Anna ventured, guessing this must be the countess, Harry's mother.

Anna had thought it a little strange the countess had not been present to greet the guests as they'd arrived, or been part of the gathering the evening before, but Harry had hinted that his mother suffered deeply from her nerves.

The older woman frowned, looking past Anna and her eyes glazing over slightly.

'You must be careful, my dear—an ill wind follows you here.'

Anna glanced over her shoulder, shivering slightly, knowing it was from the damp morning air but wondering what Harry's mother was looking at.

'Would you like me to take you back to the house, Lady Edgerton?' Anna asked.

Harry's mother sighed and Anna saw her hands were trembling in her lap. Cautiously, moving slowly so as not to alarm the older woman, she reached out and placed one of her hands over the top of Lady Edgerton's fingers. Momentarily Lady Edgerton stiffened, but then seemed to relax a little.

'There has been much heartbreak here.'

'I know, Lady Edgerton,' Anna said placatingly.

'My poor Lydia. She's so sensitive, so delicate.'

Looking at the countess, Anna knew Lydia had inherited more than just her looks from her mother. Harry had hinted that his mother was prone to fits of melancholy and was plagued by her nerves, and now Anna could see just what a toll this had taken on her.

Suddenly the older countess's eyes swung back to Anna's, focusing intently on her.

'He's very taken with you.'

'I'm not sure…'

Lady Edgerton shook her head vehemently. 'He is very taken with you. Nothing good can come out of it.' She wrung her hands together, squeezing and pinching at the skin until Anna felt like reaching out and pulling them apart. 'First Lydia and now him, how am I to bear it?'

'Bear what, Lady Edgerton?'

'Losing them. My lovely children. First my husband and now them.'

Anna wanted to point out that she hadn't lost either of her children, Harry and Lydia were still resident at Halstead Hall, still very much alive, but didn't want to add to the older woman's distress.

'It nearly killed me when poor Lydia—' She broke off, letting out a sob. 'My poor heart, it won't stand any more pain.'

'Please don't suffer on my account, Lady Edgerton.'

'They say you're engaged to my son,' Lady Edgerton said, turning and fixing Anna with a hard look.

'Your son is helping me through a difficult time.'

'He must marry a nice girl. A respectable girl. He needs to settle down and produce an heir with someone from a good family.' Lady Edgerton's voice was becoming higher in pitch and more hysterical with every syllable. Anna wished she knew how to calm Harry's mother, but was aware a few poorly chosen words could have the opposite effect.

'I'm sure he will, Lady Edgerton.'

'How can he, when…?'

'Mother.' Harry's voice was quiet but firm and both women turned in surprise to look at him.

The silence stretched out, Anna feeling as though she couldn't be the one to break it, but feeling decidedly uncomfortable being in the middle of the tension between mother and son.

'Let me escort you back to the house,' Harry said kindly after a long minute of silence. 'You'll catch a chill in this damp air if you stay out any longer.'

'Yes, dear,' Lady Edgerton said.

Gently Harry took his mother's arm, flashed an apologetic smile over his shoulder at Anna and led the older woman back over the damp grass towards the house.

'You must think my entire family mad,' Harry said, ten minutes later as he met Anna on the lawn in front of the summer house.

'Not at all.'

'Sometimes I do,' he murmured, running his free hand through his hair, resting it at the nape of his neck before letting it fall to his side.

'All families have their challenges,' Anna said.

'What a wonderfully uncontroversial way to put it.'

Harry offered Anna his arm and they walked side by side away from the house across the wet lawn. He was a naturally early riser, normally one of the first awake in the household, but this morning he'd opened his curtains to see Anna strolling through the gardens just as the sun was rising above the horizon. When he'd gone out to meet her he hadn't expected to find his mother sat in the summer house in just her flimsy nightclothes.

'My mother hasn't been the same since my father passed away,' Harry said quietly, feeling as if he needed to tell Anna his family weren't completely crazy.

'There's no need to explain anything, Harry.'

'She was always nervous, but nothing like this. Now it seems she's governed by worry and superstition.'

'Were she and your father close?'

He grimaced, remembering the blazing arguments, the screaming matches that he would watch from the top of the stairs, his parents oblivious to his presence.

'They loved each other,' he said slowly. 'Completely adored each other, especially at the beginning.'

There had been good times, Harry remembered, the walks they would all take together though the fields, his parents arm in arm and smiling up at each other. But as the years went on the good times had diminished and instead their lives had been full of arguments and rows.

'They loved each other *too* much. It wasn't healthy to have so much passion in a marriage. They were always destined to hurt one another.'

'Surely love in a marriage is a good thing,' Anna said softly.

Harry shook his head vehemently. 'Mutual respect and companionship, that's what a good marriage is built on, not love. My parents loved each other so much it was destructive, especially for my mother. As time went on, after an argument my father would goad her, flaunt his latest mistress in front of her. He knew it would destroy her, but he still did it. And this was to the woman he loved.'

'That doesn't sound like love…' Anna murmured.

'But they did love each other, madly at first. It turned bad and ruined them both.'

'And your mother's still mourning him?'

'Ever since he passed away she's shut herself off from the rest of the world, and it was worse after Lydia…' He trailed off.

'It sounds like you've had a lot to deal with these last few years.'

'No more than any other head of the family,' he said. 'They don't tell you what a difficult job having responsibility for the ones you love actually is.'

'Does your mother have a companion?' Anna asked.

He shook his head. 'She and Lydia used to be inseparable, but I think Mother became a little too overbearing even for my sister.'

'Are you happy, Harry?' Anna asked quietly, the question causing him to pause and look at her.

'Happy?'

'Yes, happy.'

'I suppose so. At least I will be when Lydia finds a husband and is settled.'

'You're a very kind man,' Anna said, looking up at him, her cool grey eyes piercing into his core, 'but you must remember to please yourself as well as others.'

'What do you mean?'

'Correct me if I'm wrong, but society tells me you are looking for a wife.'

He shrugged—it wasn't a great secret.

'But instead of looking to find someone you actually care about, someone who you can see would make you happy, you're looking for a woman who is respectable and dull.'

'As I said, I don't believe in love matches. For centuries people have been marrying for much more sensible reasons than love.'

'Are you looking to save the Edgerton family name, to marry a woman so respectable she could champion Lydia back into society?'

Harry sighed—the thought had crossed his mind on more than one occasion. 'A respectable wife certainly wouldn't hurt the reputation of this family, but that is not the main criteria I am basing my search on.'

'What is?'

'I'm looking for an amiable young woman who would make a good mother to my children, a respectable countess, someone I like, but don't feel anything more for.'

'What about love, Harry? What about happiness?'

'I think my marriage will be much happier if love doesn't complicate it.'

'What happened to your parents doesn't have to happen to you,' Anna said.

'Were you happy?' he asked, slightly more abruptly than he meant to. 'In your second marriage, the man you married for love?'

'No,' Anna said without hesitation. 'But I see now it was an infatuation with a dashing young man, not true love.' He watched as Anna hesitated and he realised she was wondering whether to give up a little more about her own past.

'I've had three marriages, Harry, none of them particularly happy, but one was the worst year of my life. I wouldn't want anyone to suffer through a marriage like that.'

Harry watched her intently. From the little things she'd said, from the reactions she had whenever anyone touched her, he'd worked out her last marriage had been difficult, but now he was wondering if it had been more than that.

'Marriage is for life,' Anna said, stopping and turning to him, 'and I wouldn't like to think of you being stuck with someone who didn't make you as happy as you could be for the rest of your life.'

Rifield had said the same thing many times, had cautioned Harry about choosing his wife based on purely her reputation and her amiability, but they didn't understand, neither of them did.

'I thank you for your concern,' Harry said quietly, 'but our situations are very different.'

Anna sighed, turning to smile at him brightly after a few seconds. 'It is none of my concern, I know that,' she said, patting him on the arm like an elderly aunt. 'You have been so kind to me, I do not like to think of you as unhappy, but I will keep my views to myself.'

There was an awkwardness between them for a few minutes and Harry was reminded of the evening they had first met in Lord Prenderson's study. Anna had been stiff and formal then, but as the weeks had passed by she had revealed more of her true self, little by little.

'Let us return to the house,' Anna said, her expression inscrutable. 'Your guests will be rising for breakfast shortly and it is probably wise we are not seen out in the gardens together with no chaperon.'

The walk back to the house only took a couple of minutes and as Harry left Anna in the entrance hall he found himself mulling over her words. His views on marriage weren't that unusual. Most of the unions between titled ladies and gentlemen were arranged for far less sensible reasons than he was proposing. Most people of his acquaintance married for money, a title or links to an influential family. He was merely looking for a wife he could rub along well with for thirty years, someone who could never hurt him because he wouldn't be head over heels in love with them.

He'd seen the destruction a marriage built on love could cause—he wasn't about to impose that on his own life or his future children.

Chapter Fifteen

'Pall-mall,' Harry had announced to the guests who had made it down for breakfast. 'It's the perfect day for it.'

Now about half of the party had traipsed out to the gardens where Harry was enthusiastically hammering the hoop into the grass and setting out the course. To one side, just off the patio, Harry had set the heavy wooden mallets and the hefty ball, and as she watched the rest of the guests emerge from the house Anna walked over and picked up one of the mallets, testing its weight in her hand.

'I hope you're not planning to use that as a deadly weapon,' Rifield said quietly in her ear, smiling as he did so.

From most people it would have been an unkind reference to the rumours of how her husbands had died, but Anna could detect no malice in Harry's friend.

'Who wants to go first?' Harry asked.

There were six of them in total: Harry and Anna, Rifield, Mrs and Miss Wright, and Lydia. The Fortescues had all taken breakfast in their rooms and were yet to emerge to join the other guests. The vicar and his wife had returned home the evening before, but would be joining them for dinner again tonight.

'I'm not sure it is entirely appropriate for a young lady…' Mrs Wright said, eyeing up the ball and mallets.

'Perhaps you gentlemen could show us how the game is played,' Miss Wright suggested.

Anna took a seat on the patio alongside the three other women and watched as Harry and Rifield hefted the mallets and took some preparatory swings.

'The aim of the game is to hit the ball along the course and through the hoop at the end in the least number of hits,' he explained.

'I've never seen pall-mall being played in a garden before,' Miss Wright remarked.

Harry went first, hitting the ball a good distance with his first swing before lining up and aiming for the hoop further down the garden. The ladies all let out a cheer as the ball shot through the hoop on the fourth hit.

'Your turn, Rifield,' Harry said.

Rifield stepped up to the starting point and tapped the ball, sending it hurtling across the grass. It took him five hits to get the ball to pass through the hoop and by the time it sailed under the metal bar the spectators were all laughing at his antics.

'Who is next?' Harry asked.

'If you would be so kind as to show me how to hit the ball,' Miss Wright said, standing up and ignoring the warning glance from her mother.

Miss Wright took the mallet from Harry and positioned herself as he directed. Reaching around her waist, Harry showed her how to hold the heavy wooden mallet, how to line up the hit with the hoop at the other end of the garden and the desired force to hit the ball with. Although their bodies did not touch at any point Anna felt a sharp stab of jealousy and had to remind herself that Harry was not really her fiancé to covet.

Miss Wright hit the ball along the garden with delicate little taps, succeeding in pushing it through the hoop after eight hits.

'Lady Fortescue?' Harry asked as he and Miss Wright headed back to the patio.

Anna stood, allowing Harry to lead her to the start point.

'Have you played before?' he asked.

'No.'

'Would you permit me to assist you?'

She nodded, allowing Harry to adjust her grip on the mallet, show her how to position her body and finally loop his arms around her waist much as he had done with Miss Wright. Their bodies didn't once touch, but every second she was aware of his presence just inches away. As she hit the ball for the first time, sending it spinning across the garden, she felt his breath on her neck and had to force herself to concentrate on the game before her.

'Good hit,' Harry called, a trace of admiration in his voice.

Anna squared her stance, looked backwards and forward between the hoop and the ball a few times and then swung the mallet again. The ball bounced, flying along the course and Anna felt a swell of pleasure. She liked to do things well.

'Four hits,' Harry called from further up the garden. 'If I'd have known you were this good I'd have tried harder.'

Anna handed the mallet over to Lydia and watched as the young woman tapped the ball gently down the garden. Harry was with her every step, every hit.

'He's so good with his sister,' she heard Miss Wright murmur to Mrs Wright.

'Many men wouldn't have the patience to mollycoddle a young woman of such tepid character,' Mrs Wright whispered.

'It is certainly a point in his favour.'

As if Harry needed any more points in his favour. He was an earl, from one of the oldest families in England. He owned a large estate and beautiful property, and probably many more houses dotted around the country. He'd served his country while in the army and now was devoted to serving his family.

'You'd have to get the sister married off quickly, though,' Mrs Wright murmured. 'No sense in having to share Lord Edgerton's attention.'

'I'm sure there would be no shortage of candidates once a suitably large dowry was suggested,' Miss Wright said, looking thoughtfully at Lydia. 'And it would do the poor girl good to make a life of her own.'

'Ah, Miss Fortescue,' Harry called as Lydia hit the ball through the hoop at the end of the course. 'You're just in time to play pall-mall.'

Anna turned to see her stepdaughter walking

stiffly on to the terrace. There was still no sign of her brothers and Anna wondered if they had decided to pack for London.

'I do not play games,' Miss Fortescue said.

'Nonsense, everyone plays games.' Harry motioned towards Rifield, who summoned his most charming smile. 'Rifield will show you how it's done.'

Stepping back off the course, Harry wandered back to Anna's side, picking up a glass of water from the table on his way.

Quietly they watched Miss Fortescue stiffly allow Rifield to demonstrate how to play pall-mall, wondering whether she would hit him with the mallet if he got too close.

'I think she's developing a soft spot for Rifield,' Harry murmured, quietly enough so only Anna could hear him.

'I don't wish to be uncharitable, but I don't think Miss Fortescue is capable of affection.'

'Under that unwelcoming demeanour there might be a romantic side struggling to get out.'

Anna had lived under the same roof as Miss Fortescue for a year. She very much doubted there was a hidden romantic under the spitefulness, but she had been wrong about people before.

The sun peeked out from behind a cloud as the

rest of the guests got into the spirit of the game and for a few minutes at least it felt like they were at a normal, amiable house party with friends rather than people who detested her.

To everyone's surprise Mrs Wright, who had to be coaxed from her seat on the patio, won the game of pall-mall, managing to knock the ball through the hoop in just three hits. She reddened at the congratulations and hurriedly returned to her seat before she could be pressed into repeating the performance.

'Time for archery,' Harry declared.

'Are you mad?' Anna hissed at him as he took her arm and led her to a different part of the garden. Up ahead three well-worn targets had been set up and closer to the house a selection of bows and arrows lay on the ground.

'Can't have my guests getting bored,' Harry said.

'Someone is threatening me and you provide the deadly weapons to help them make good on their threats.'

'No one will harm a hair on your head while you are under my protection,' Harry said so confidently it left Anna speechless.

As the footmen carried the seats from the patio, arranging them a little distance away from the targets, the guests chattered and eyed up the assorted bows on the ground.

By the time the ladies were seated Lord Fortescue and Mr Ronald Fortescue had joined the group and each were eagerly inspecting the bows, picking them up to feel the weight and testing the tautness of the string.

'Brings back memories of the good times, eh, Lady Fortescue?' Mr Ronald Fortescue said.

Anna fixed him with an icy stare, but decided not to answer.

'Perhaps we should play Fortescue rules,' Lord Fortescue murmured to his brother. 'Might get rid of our little problem with the settlements.'

'Fortescue rules?' Harry asked Anna, quietly so he wouldn't embarrass her.

The two Fortescue men laughed at their private joke and Anna felt an unfamiliar rage building inside her. Of course she could control it—during the terrible months of her last marriage she'd felt everything from terror to rage to sorrow, but she'd become expert at hiding every emotion, of constructing a wall to hold back her feelings. Now there was no need, no reason to remain calm and detached. No one to hurt her, no one to make her regret her actions.

'Lord Fortescue has suggested we play Fortescue rules,' Anna said, her voice ringing clear and loud, silencing the rest of the guests.

The look of surprise on her two stepsons' faces was enough to encourage her to go on.

'My husband, the late Lord Fortescue, always had an archery target set up on the lawn, with a bow and arrows handy.'

'That's quite enough, Lady Fortescue,' Mr Ronald Fortescue hissed.

'No, no, Mr Fortescue, you suggested Fortescue rules, I'm just explaining them to our companions.'

'I really don't think...' Lord Fortescue bumbled, his face turning an even deeper shade of red than normal.

'My dear husband, the late Lord Fortescue, was very particular in how he liked the members of his household to behave,' Anna said, seeing the horrified fascination in the faces of the assembled guests. It wasn't the done thing to discuss the intimate details of a marriage, especially when a peer of the realm was involved, but everyone was hanging on Anna's every word. 'If I had committed a transgression he felt was very severe, he liked to punish me in novel and *amusing* ways.' Amusing to him, certainly not to her.

'That is quite enough, Lady Fortescue,' the new

Lord Fortescue said, grabbing Anna by the arm roughly.

Immediately Harry had intervened, taking Lord Fortescue's wrist and squeezing until he let go, muttering in pain.

'He would make me stand in front of a target, just like this,' Anna said, walking slowly up to the middle target. She stood with her back to the board and spread out her arms. Everyone was watching her, no one able to tear their eyes away. 'And then he would ask me if I was afraid.'

The first time he'd done it Anna had thought it a joke. She'd laughed merrily at her new husband until he fired an arrow that thunked into the target so close to her shoulder it tore the fabric of her dress.

'I think he wanted me to be afraid,' Anna said, looking directly at the three Fortescue children, each in turn. Not one of them would meet her eye.

'You deserved everything you got,' Miss Fortescue said after a few seconds, her voice no more than a low whisper, but Anna heard every word all the same.

'For what? For laughing too merrily at the dining table? For playing the piano too loudly in the middle of the day? For receiving a letter from a schoolfriend?' All transgressions she had been punished for.

'You were an unfaithful harlot...' Miss Fortescue said, echoing her father's words, even her father's tone.

'It's just not true. You know it and he knew it.'

'Shut up,' Miss Fortescue whispered. 'Stop slandering a dead man's name when he can't defend himself.'

'We both know what your father did to me...'

'Shut up, shut up, shut up.' Miss Fortescue's voice raised from a whisper to a croaky shout.

Anna should have seen the flash of desperation in Miss Fortescue's eyes, should have stopped there, but she felt liberated, finally free of the hold her late husband held over her even after his death. If she wanted to she could tell the whole world what a cruel violent man Lord Fortescue had been.

'He—' She didn't get to say any more. Time seemed to move slowly as she saw Miss Fortescue lift the bow that was in her grip, pull back the string and loose the arrow. Anna was frozen, unable to move, the arrow heading straight for her when Harry's solid body careened into hers, knocking her to the ground.

Silence stretched out, no one moved for what felt like an eternity. Finally Harry shifted, moving the weight of his body on to his arms and pushing himself up.

'Are you hurt?' he asked, cupping her face with his hands.

She considered for a moment. She felt a little winded from where he'd landed on top of her, but she wasn't hurt. Slowly she shook her head.

With everyone's eyes on her, Anna stood, turning to inspect the arrow in the target, still quivering from the impact, embedded right where her head would have been if Harry hadn't pushed her to the ground.

Miss Fortescue let out a sob, covered her mouth with her hand and fled swiftly in the direction of the house.

'I shall see to my sister,' Mr Ronald Fortescue said quickly, beating a hasty retreat, closely followed by his brother.

Anna felt her pulse begin to slow as she looked away from the target and up into Harry's reassuring eyes.

'What an action-packed morning,' Rifield said, his eyes still wide with shock.

'I will escort Lady Fortescue to her room,' Harry said, taking Anna's arm.

'Good idea.' Rifield leaned in. 'Don't worry, I'll look after your guests. Take all the time you need.'

As Harry led her gently across the lawn they heard Rifield gathering up the rest of the bewildered guests and suggesting a nice sedate stroll about the gardens.

Chapter Sixteen

'I'll kill him,' Harry growled, pacing backwards and forward across Anna's bedroom floor. He shouldn't be in here, certainly not alone with the woman he was pretending to be engaged to, and most certainly not with the door firmly closed and locked.

'If you mean my late husband, he's dead already,' Anna said, calmly, with that little shrug of the shoulders he was coming to like so much.

'He used to stand you in front of the target and shoot arrows at you? That's disgusting, it's barbaric.'

'Only in the first few months of our marriage,' Anna said quietly.

Somehow he didn't think Lord Fortescue had stopped due to a reformation of character.

'Did he harm you? Is that why he stopped?'

Harry stopped pacing in front of Anna and held

her gently by both upper arms, looking her over head to toe as if for arrow wounds.

'No, whatever else Lord Fortescue was, he was a good shot, could hit where he wanted to on a target with an arrow from thirty feet.'

'So why did he stop?' Harry asked quietly, wondering if he really wanted to know.

'He liked to see the fear in my eyes, to know he had absolute control not just over my body but also my mind, my emotions.'

'You can't mean to say you stopped being afraid.'

Anna looked down at the ground for a few seconds before answering, 'I stopped caring. I stopped caring whether the arrow hit me or not.'

He couldn't find the words to respond for a few seconds. It was unconceivable, a husband putting his wife in such danger, all for a little amusement, to see the fear in her eyes. What kind of man... what kind of *monster*...could do such a thing?

'Did he do other things to you?' Harry asked, his voice no more than a whisper. He had to know, but at the same time dreaded her answer.

'Harry,' Anna said, raising a hand and trailing her fingers down his face, 'you don't need to know.'

No wonder she'd been so adamant she would never marry again.

'Tell me,' he said, raising a hand so it covered hers, looking deep into her unwavering grey eyes.

'We should…' Anna started to say.

'There's no rush. Rifield will keep the rest of the guests busy. Tell me.'

With a sigh Anna turned away. He thought she would refuse again, tell him to get out of her rooms, perhaps even start packing to return to London, but instead he saw her fiddling with the fastenings of her dress.

'Help me,' she said, looking over her shoulder.

'What…?'

'You wanted to know, so help me.'

Motioning to the fastenings at the back of her dress, those normally a maid would help her with, Anna began to pull at the pale green cotton. In a daze Harry stepped forward, his fingers fumbling as he reached out for the first of the fastenings. He couldn't deny he'd thought about undressing Anna, couldn't deny he'd imagined this moment a thousand different ways. He'd desired her from the moment their bodies had careened into one another in Lord Prenderson's study, but never had he thought he would be undressing her in the middle of the morning in his family home.

After a few seconds he'd loosened the dress just enough for Anna to slip it down. The rustling of material revealed a thin white cotton chemise, which went from the top of her back to well below the knee, covering her body and preserving her dignity, but Harry felt as though he were looking at her naked. As he watched she tugged at the ties at the front of the chemise.

'Anna?' he asked, trying to be a gentleman, trying to give her the opportunity to stop.

'You wanted to know, you wanted to see.'

'Stop,' he said, hearing the lack of emotion in her voice. The last thing he wanted was for her to do anything against her will. 'Stop, Anna.'

She shook her head, pushed the chemise from her shoulders and pulled down. Harry heard himself take a sharp intake of breath as the skin of her back was exposed. Her skin was milky white, just the colour of the cream off the top of the finest milk. He'd touched her hand, her arm, her cheek enough times to know the skin would be soft and velvety to the touch.

Latticed across her back were a half-dozen pale scars. Long and thin and straight, there could be no mistake they'd been made by a rod. Without thinking Harry raised his fingers and gently touched one of the scars. It was well healed and one day far into the future probably would disappear, but to make such a scar would have required a deep wound and a cane wielded with a monstrous force.

'He beat you,' Harry said quietly.

'Among other things.'

He had so many questions, so many things he wanted to ask, but hearing the emptiness in her voice Harry gripped the edge of her chemise and tugged it back up over her shoulders.

He gently tightened the fastenings of her gown and once she was dressed again Anna turned to face him.

'Why?' he asked.

'I don't think you'd understand, Harry,' Anna said with a small, brave smile.

'Try me.'

'He was cruel. He was evil. He revelled in holding power over me, by seeing the naked fear in my eyes, by finding new ways to torment me.'

'He did this to you for a whole year?'

Harry felt sick to his stomach, roll after roll of nausea working its way through his body. Who could do such a thing to such a woman? Who could do such a thing to anyone?

'It was worse at the beginning. I learnt to submit.'

'Submit?' He echoed the word with horror.

Anna shrugged. 'I conducted myself in the manner he wished me to, after a few months of beatings. I sat straight, didn't fidget. I didn't look at anyone else when we socialised, didn't speak to anyone else except on his express command. I did everything he told me to. Everything.' There was disgust in her voice, as if she thought she should have been stronger, should have stood up to her late husband more.

'That made him stop?'

Anna laughed, but it was humourless. 'No. Of course not. He always found an excuse, always found a reason.'

'How did you survive?' Harry's words were hushed, awed, and he saw Anna close her eyes for a moment before answering.

'I don't know,' she said, as the tears started to glisten in her eyes.

In two steps she was in his arms, her head buried deep in his shoulder, her body racked with sobs. Harry wrapped both arms around her, pulled her close and stroked her hair. Murmuring soothing sounds, he held her minute after minute, wondering if this was the first time Anna had allowed herself to crack a little, to cry about the terrible things she'd suffered during her year of marriage.

As Anna cried Harry felt a rage like no other building inside him. Here was a kind and gentle woman who had been terrorised throughout her marriage, persecuted by the man who was meant to protect her.

'Did they know?' Harry asked, as Anna pulled away for a second, wiping the tears from her cheeks.

'Who?'

'His children. Those cretins I have invited into my home.'

When Anna didn't meet his eye Harry had his answer.

'Promise me you won't do anything, Harry,' Anna said, regaining some of her usual poise.

'I can't do that. They knew what their father was doing to you, yet they did nothing?'

'What could they have done? I was his wife, his property.'

'Not his property,' Harry protested. 'You're a person, a woman, not a piece of furniture he can smash up on a whim.'

'The law is very clear, Harry. Once a woman marries everything she has, including her person, belongs to her husband.'

'Not to abuse and injure.'

'He can do whatever he likes. Lord Fortescue used to discuss with his cronies the best size and thickness of rod to keep a woman in line. Apparently it is frowned upon to use a rod thicker than a man's thumb.'

Unable to resist a quick peek at his own thumb, Harry felt the blood surge to his head.

'He beat you with a rod as thick as a thumb?'

'I'm not sure he stuck to that rule exactly. I think the rods he used were often thicker.'

'Did he…?' Harry closed his eyes, knowing he had no right to ask the question, but somehow needing to know the answer. 'Did he rape you?'

'It would have been well within the law,' Anna said, 'but no, he didn't. He was unable to…' She trailed off, staring at a point on the wall. 'Sometimes I wondered if it would have been better if he wasn't unmanned, if his rage for me would have been less.' She shook her head as if trying to get rid of an unpleasant thought.

'How did you bear it?' Harry asked, knowing that many women would have been completely destroyed.

'I didn't have a choice. He was my husband, until one of us died.'

'I don't know how you survived,' he said quietly, 'but I'm glad you did.'

Anna rested her head on Harry's shoulder. For a whole year, ever since Lord Fortescue's death, she'd clung on to the secret of the abuse she'd suffered, not wanting to taint anyone else with it, not trusting anyone with her secrets. Today, as she'd stood in Harry's garden, listening to her stepsons chuckling at the memory of just one of the many terrible ways their father had sought to demean and terrorise her, she'd felt something snap inside her. She didn't have to be afraid any more. Her husband was dead and his children couldn't touch her. Whoever was sending her the packages and threatening letters didn't know who they were up against. She'd survived a year of physical and psychological torture, she could survive a few nasty surprises in the post.

When Harry had escorted her back to her room she hadn't meant to tell him quite so much and certainly had never planned on dropping her dress and chemise to expose her back and the scars that told a little of the beatings she'd received. There was something about him that made her want to open up, to share her secrets and share her past, to let him into all the dark corners of her soul that she didn't even dare to peep into.

'I suppose the Fortescues will leave now,' Anna said quietly, 'before we can work out which of them is sending the packages.'

Immediately Harry sprang to his feet and strode to the door.

'Please don't do anything,' Anna said, her voice calm but authoritative.

'I won't stand by while those brutes walk away, thinking there is no shame in laughing at how their father abused you.'

'Please, Harry. I ask you not to do anything.'

He hesitated and she felt a weight lift from her as he crossed the room and cupped her face in his hands.

'Stay here,' he instructed.

Of course she followed him, having to run through the corridors to keep up with his long, purposeful strides.

He flung open the door to Mr Ronald Fortescue's room, catching him shouting at his valet who wasn't packing quickly enough for his master's liking.

'What is the meaning—?' Mr Ronald Fortescue asked, his question cut off as Harry barrelled into him.

There was a short tussle, but it was obvious from the outset Anna's stepson hadn't a chance against Harry's superior size and strength, and especially not when he was bursting with fury.

'Did you know?' Harry asked, his voice low but dangerous.

'Know what?' Mr Fortescue tried to sound defiant, but there was a tremor in his voice.

'Did you know what your father was doing to her?'

'I... I...'

Harry flung him away, disgusted, and Mr Fortescue staggered back.

'Why are you sending Lady Fortescue the letters and packages?' Harry asked.

A look of genuine confusion passed across Mr Fortescue's face.

'What?' he asked.

'Not him,' Harry growled and walked from the room, catching Anna's hand and pulling her behind him.

Next on his list was the new Lord Fortescue, Anna's oldest stepson.

'What the devil—?' Lord Fortescue started to bluster as Harry burst into his room.

'I'll be quick,' Harry said. 'I want you out of my house as much as you want to leave. Why are you sending Lady Fortescue packages?'

'Packages?'

Even Anna could see Lord Fortescue was not lying. He had no idea what Harry was talking about. That was two off the list, leaving only Miss Fortescue.

'Come on,' Harry said, pulling Anna behind him again, marching her along to her stepdaughter's room.

This time Harry knocked and waited for the door to open a crack instead of bursting in. Even in his anger he couldn't bring himself to act ungentlemanly towards a female guest in his house.

Miss Fortescue's face was pale and drawn and Anna realised with a jolt of surprise that she had been crying. Red-rimmed eyes and the red tip of her nose gave it away, as did the three handkerchiefs discarded on the bed.

'What will you do to me?' Miss Fortescue asked, managing to stand up straight and look Harry in the eye as she spoke.

'Do to you? Nothing.'

'I thought you might summon the magistrate.'

'Antonia,' Anna said, stepping forward, 'I'm sure what happened in the garden was an accident.'

Shifty eyes hinted that it perhaps wasn't entirely accidental, but Anna chose to ignore it.

'At least I'm sure you never meant to hurt me. Sometimes when we hear something we don't like we react in a way we can't control.'

Miss Fortescue nodded as if in agreement, still unable to meet Anna's eye.

'I won't summon the magistrate—in fact, I will let you leave here with no further consequences to your actions, if you answer a couple of questions truthfully,' Harry said, his voice stern. 'If you refuse to answer or lie to me then I will need to reconsider what I do about the incident in the garden.'

Smoothing down her skirts, Miss Fortescue motioned for him to continue.

'I understand you dislike Lady Fortescue and have done since she first married your father.'

'Yes,' Miss Fortescue answered, her voice quiet but clear.

'Why?' Anna asked the question before Harry could continue, realising she had many theories on the reasons her stepchildren hated her so much, but no definite answers.

For a few seconds she didn't think Miss Fortescue would answer, but then a petulant mumble came from her mouth, a cascade of reasons why she'd disliked her father's new wife from the moment they'd met.

'My mother had been dead less than six months when you seduced my father. You're six months younger than me, it's disgusting, and we all know you only married my father for his title and his money.'

Most of what Miss Fortescue said was true. Anna had married Lord Fortescue when he should still have been in mourning for his first wife, but it hadn't been her choice. What Miss Fortescue didn't know, and Anna was certainly not going to tell her stepdaughter now, was that her father and Anna's father had met to discuss a possible marriage before the first Lady Fortescue had passed away, when she was lying sick in her deathbed.

'We women are not often lucky enough to choose our own fates,' Anna said quietly. 'I did not ask to marry your father, did not even know who he was before the arrangement was made.'

Miss Fortescue looked away rather than acknowledge the truth in Anna's words.

'What do you think you will gain by sending me those horrible packages?' Anna asked softly.

'What packages?'

Just like her brothers there was no hint of guilt on Miss Fortescue's face, just a look of mild confusion.

'Never mind,' Anna said. 'I wish you a safe journey, Antonia.'

Chapter Seventeen

Anna pulled her shawl tighter around her shoulders and shivered. It was a beautiful sunny day, but still early in spring and the sunshine couldn't make up for the crisp bite of the April air.

After ensuring the Fortescues had all been escorted from his property Harry had gone to check on the rest of his guests, promising Anna he would slip away as soon as possible and come meet her here in the formal gardens. His voice had brokered no argument when he'd insisted they needed to talk further, and Anna found she couldn't be angry with his authoritarian tone as she agreed they should discuss the events of the morning.

Watching two blackbirds tapping at the grass with their beaks, Anna sank back on to the stone bench, allowing her body to relax. When she had been married to Lord Fortescue she had got into the practice of always sitting straight, never slouching, even when she was alone, just in case her husband surprised her and found her in a position he did not approve of. It was a hard habit to break, but slowly Anna was finding she could will her body to relax if she reminded herself no one would ever again reprimand her for sitting comfortably.

With her eyes closed she turned her face up to the sun, enjoying the warm rays as it peeked out from behind a cloud. It had been a strange morning, one of high tensions and dramatic revelations, and she felt physically tired from all the excitement. When she'd stepped in front of the target, meaning to shame her two stepsons into realising how their father had treated her was not acceptable, and most certainly not a topic to find merriment from, she could never have envisaged how the morning would turn out. She hadn't planned on sharing a little of the abuse she'd been subjected to with Harry, certainly hadn't ever imagined she would have dropped her dress quite shamelessly to let him see the scars on her back. It had been an impulsive action and at the time had seemed the best way to show him the physical damage her late husband had inflicted. And physical scars were a lot easier to explain than mental ones.

'Sorry,' Harry said, striding along the gravel path towards her, 'that took longer than anticipated.'

'Are the rest of your guests mollified?'

'Thankfully we're only a small group, otherwise someone would be bound to talk.'

It was true, seeing as the local vicar and his wife were only joining them at dinner and the Fortescues had now all left, the remaining guests at this little house party included only Mrs Wright and her daughter, Rifield and, of course, Lydia.

'Will they stay?' Anna asked.

'I think so. Unless you'd prefer me to cut our house party short.'

There were pros and cons to staying and leaving. The main point of the party had been to find out which of the Fortescues had been sending Anna the packages. Now it looked as if they were going to have to look elsewhere for the culprit. However, Anna didn't feel overly inclined to head back to London just yet. Harry's estate was peaceful, even more so now the Fortescues had all left, and she secretly relished the idea of spending another couple of days here enjoying his company.

'Did you believe them?' Harry asked as he offered Anna his arm and they began to walk through the formal gardens. 'You know them better than I do.'

She considered for a few moments. It would have been easy for any of them to lie, easy for them to anticipate the question and feign confusion, but she hadn't seen any deception in any of her stepchildren's expressions. None of them had known about the packages or the threatening letters.

'I believed them,' Anna said. It was horrible to say it out loud for it meant admitting she had another enemy, one she knew nothing about.

'I believed them, too,' Harry said thoughtfully. 'Complete waste of time, this house party. I'm sorry, Anna.'

'There's no need to be sorry.'

'It was unnecessary. We could have just confronted the three of them in London without having to put you through the torment of staying under the same roof as them.'

They fell silent as Harry led her around the freshly dug-over borders, which no doubt in summer would hold a dazzling array of brightly coloured flowers.

'We will have to regroup,' Harry said, sounding every inch the military officer. 'Make a list of everyone who might hold a grudge against you.

Any servants you have dismissed, business rivals, clients who feel your shipping company has done them wrong. We will go through the list systematically, questioning everyone until we find the culprit. Never fear, we will get to the bottom of this matter.'

Anna had to suppress a smile. 'I just want to forget about it for a couple of days,' she said. 'Forget about the packages and the letters and the unknown person who hates me so much they feel moved to be so cruel.'

'There's no time like the present. Why don't you draw up a list and we can discuss it after dinner tonight?'

'Harry, did you listen to a word I just said?'

'I just think we should keep up the momentum on this.'

'And I said no,' she said firmly.

'But we could use this time…'

'I said no, Harry,' Anna repeated. 'I want to have a couple of days where I feel normal, where I'm not always thinking about what the next package might contain, what the next letter might threaten.'

'If you're sure.'

'I'm sure. When we return to London we can go back to searching for whoever is tormenting me. For the next couple of days I wish to at least pretend I'm a carefree young woman.'

They fell silent, continuing their stroll through the gardens, each lost in thought.

'Anna, what you told me earlier,' Harry said eventually as they made their way on to a tree-lined boulevard, 'I can't stop thinking about it.'

At least he was honest. Most people would skirt around the subject, dropping hints that they wanted to know more, but never asking directly.

'What would you like to know?' she asked.

'Did your other husbands…?'

She shook her head. 'My first husband was much older than me, benignly uninterested in our marriage, but never unkind. Captain Trevels I barely saw after our marriage vows until he returned home when he was so unwell he couldn't sit up in bed without my help.'

'Just the thought of Fortescue hurting you…' Harry trailed off, shaking his head as if the image was too much.

'I think violence and abuse in marriage is much more common than we all care to admit,' Anna said quietly. 'I survived, Harry, that's all that matters now.'

'But the awful things people say about you and after all you've endured.'

Anna shrugged. 'I told you once before a little gossip isn't the worst thing in the world,' she said. 'I don't care what people say about me. They cannot hurt me like my late husband hurt me. He is dead and I am free, and no amount of horrible gossip will ever change that.'

'I can see why you never want to marry again,' Harry said softly.

She doubted he truly understood. Of course she never wanted to put herself in a position where a husband could physically hurt her again, where it became legal for a man to beat her, as long as the rod wasn't *too* thick. What she doubted he realised, what she doubted anyone could realise unless they had been in a similar situation, was her complete reluctance to ever give anyone power over her life again. Now she lived by her terms, did as she wished, talked to whom she wished, ran her business and accepted or declined invitations as she desired. No, nothing was worth giving up that control.

Chapter Eighteen

Harry was glad to see Anna at breakfast the next morning. She'd understandably been reluctant to rejoin the other guests for the afternoon stroll into the village and for dinner yesterday, and had sent her apologies. This morning she looked bright and fresh, her head held high as she took her place at the breakfast table. No one mentioned the events of the day before and, if they had, no doubt Anna would shut down any enquiries politely but firmly.

'What shall we do with the morning?' Harry asked, smiling at his assembled guests as they finished breakfast. In truth, he wanted nothing more than to whisk Anna off to a remote corner of his estate and show her not all men were cruel, but he knew that was never going to happen. With great effort he focused on Miss Wright, who was looking at him with her encouraging dark eyes. Rifield was right, he should be thinking of finding himself a nice, amiable bride and here was one served up without any effort, but he just couldn't find any enthusiasm at the idea of getting to know her.

'How about a scavenger hunt?' Rifield suggested. Harry could always rely on his friend to fill a long silence with a suggestion.

'How would that work, Mr Rifield?' Miss Wright asked.

'We draw names out of a hat for our partners and then in pairs we set off around the estate and have to find three items of interest. The couple with what is judged to be the most interesting item by everyone else wins.'

'What a lovely suggestion,' Mrs Wright said, her eyes already gleaming. No doubt she was hoping her daughter would be paired with either of the eligible young gentlemen.

Harry went to fetch some paper from his study and wrote the six names down on pieces of paper, folding them in half before placing them in Miss Wright's proffered bonnet.

'Miss Wright, would you like to pick the first two names?'

She dipped her slender hand into the bonnet and took out two pieces of paper.

'Mother and Mr Rifield,' she said, her tongue darting out over her lips as she spoke.

Rifield moved soundlessly over to Mrs Wright, as always uncomplaining in doing his bit to help Harry out.

'Lydia, would you like to pick the next two names?' Harry asked.

His sister had barely said a word all day, but he supposed it was something to be celebrated that she was still socialising rather than retreating off to her room.

With her cheeks flushing Lydia stepped up, dipped her hand into the bonnet and took two names.

'Miss Wright and myself,' she said, glancing nervously at her chosen partner.

Harry felt like shooting his fist up into the air. That left him and Anna, just the person he wanted to spend the morning with, and now good fortune or fate had thrown them together.

'I am quite happy to swap with one of you young ladies,' Mrs Wright said. 'It wouldn't feel right me enjoying the company of such a lovely young gentleman when he could be with someone closer to his own age.'

It was an obvious attempt to pair her daughter

off with Rifield, but Miss Wright shook her head and took Lydia's arm.

'Not at all, Mother, I'm very much looking forward to spending the morning with Lydia.'

'What are the rules?' Harry asked, eager to be off.

'Two hours to find three interesting items from around the estate. Nothing from inside the house.'

'Shall we start?' Harry asked, offering Anna his arm.

She looked up at him with warmth in her eyes and Harry knew immediately where he wanted to take her for the morning. They might not find many interesting items, but right now winning the game was the last thing on his mind.

'This way,' Harry murmured quietly in Anna's ear, guiding her away from the other couples.

'Where are we going?' Anna asked.

'Somewhere private. Somewhere I guarantee you will love.'

'That is a bold statement, Lord Edgerton,' Anna said, a small smile lighting up her face.

After finding out what she had endured through the year of her marriage Harry wanted nothing more than to put a smile on her face. That was what this morning was about. Tomorrow he would think about his future, tomorrow he would work on getting to know the respectable and slightly bland Miss Wright, but today he would dedicate to making Anna smile.

They walked briskly, fast enough to stop the chill in the air from bothering them, Anna peeking out from underneath her bonnet every few seconds to glance up at his face. Out here in the countryside, without anyone else watching them, it was hard to believe she was the same Lady Fortescue the gossips whispered about, the same Lady Fortescue who had a reputation for being icy and unapproachable. Here she was just a vulnerable young woman, a young woman who made his pulse race every time he looked at her.

'Where did you grow up?' Harry asked, as they came to the top of the hill and began their descent into a shallow valley.

'My family home was in Hampshire,' Anna said, 'but we spent most of our time in London. My father didn't much care for country life.'

'And you?'

She looked up at him, tilting her head back so he could see the soft line of her jaw and the delicate skin of her neck.

'I love the countryside,' she said. 'I think I'd be happy if I never had to set foot into London again.'

'Then I think you'll like where I'm taking you.'

Harry had been treading this very path for nearly thirty years, often escaping on his own during his childhood to come and explore the dense forest in the valley. It only covered a small area, but the trees were close together, their leaves tangled and dense overhead, and the paths covered in moss. It felt like a little enchanted forest in the middle of Kent.

They left the long grass on the hillside and stepped into the wooded area, and immediately next to him Anna gasped. Harry suppressed a smile.

'It's beautiful,' she said.

Along the edges of the overgrown path were hundreds upon hundreds of bluebells, their violet flowers hanging low, a carpet of colour against the green. The flowers stretched out into the distance, crowded between trees, huddled into clearings and growing even where the light barely penetrated.

Anna rested her hand lightly on his arm, allowing him to guide her through the dense forest along the barely visible path. Once, when he was young, Harry's father had ordered the forest to be tidied, the trees chopped back, the paths cleared, but Harry and his sister had begged him not to spoil the magical place. Their father had relented and now Harry loved to stroll in the dappled sunshine whenever he came home.

'How is your mother?' Anna asked as they walked.

'Let's not talk of our families for once.'

'What do you wish to talk about?'

He knew this was the wrong time to start a flirtation. Anna had made it very clear she wasn't looking for a romantic relationship and who could blame her after all she had suffered in her last marriage, yet sometimes he thought he saw a flicker of attraction in her eyes.

'How about us?' he said, gripping her firmly as she stumbled on the uneven path and taking the opportunity to pull her a little closer to him.

'Us?' She turned to him with amusement in her eyes. 'Which *us* would you like to talk about? The *us* who are pretending to be engaged? Or the *us* who are foolishly trying to play at tracking down this mysterious person who's sending me horrible packages?'

'How about the *us* who's walking arm in arm through a beautiful wood on a sunny spring afternoon.' She was exactly the sort of woman he *couldn't* marry, someone he knew he might very well fall in love with if he spent too much time with her, but still he couldn't stop himself from imagining a future they couldn't have.

'That *us* is nothing more than a fantasy,' Anna murmured.

So he had been right, she did feel the spark between them.

'Sometimes it is fun to indulge in fantasy,' Harry said, bending down to whisper in Anna's ear.

'As long as everyone is clear that is all this is,' Anna said, turning her grey eyes to look at him, searching his face for reassurance.

'I know nothing can happen between us, Anna,' Harry said, his lips almost tickling her ears. 'You're hardly the mild wife I'm looking for and you have plenty of reasons never to want to marry again, but don't you want to forget that for one afternoon?'

When she didn't say anything, Harry felt his heart soar. For just one afternoon they could be irresponsible, they could pretend they were unencumbered young lovers.

'If we were courting,' Anna said, 'what would you say to me?' Her voice was light, her manner so different to how she'd been just hours earlier. He wondered how many people got to see this side of Anna and doubted it numbered more than one or two in the past few years.

'Most men would tell you how the sunlight glints off your coppery hair and your lips curve into the most wonderful smile. They would sing odes to your grace and compare you to a rose on the most magnificent summer's day. They would profess to be blinded by your beauty and over-come by your sweet nature.'

'But not you?'

'Not me. The things I admire about you are a little less superficial, although I do have to admit every time I look in your eyes I forget every thought in my head...' He paused, seeing Anna unsuccessfully try to suppress a smile under her bonnet. He loved how her lips quivered ever so slightly as she fought her urge to grin. 'I love the determined look you get on your face whenever you talk about your company. I love how to the world you can seem dignified and aloof, but then I see a tiny smile, a tiny flicker of amusement in your eyes and I know what you're really think-ing. I love your courage and determination to hold your head up high no matter what and I even love how you think you have to deal with everything alone.'

'That's quite a list of things you love,' Anna said quietly, her face completely unreadable.

For a moment Harry felt a panic seize him as if someone had him by the throat and was slowly squeezing. Of course he didn't *love* Anna. He loved lots of things about her, but that wasn't the same as love. He admired her, it was hard not to. And he *liked* her, there wasn't a single other person in the entire world he enjoyed being with as much as Anna, no one else even came close. But love was another matter. Love was... Well, love was...

He took a deep breath. This was why he could never let this relationship go any further. It would be so easy to fall in love with Anna, so easy to share an intense and passionate relationship, and that was exactly what Harry didn't want for himself. A nice, bland wife, someone he could share a calm and placid marriage with.

'If I was courting you, I'd need to declare myself early,' Harry said glibly. 'You would have a number of suitors, of course.'

Anna smiled at this. 'All lining up to become the fourth victim of the Black Widow?'

Harry bent down, plucking a handful of wild bluebells and arranging them into a messy bouquet.

'For my lady,' he said with a theatrical bow,

pulling back the flowers as Anna reached out to take them. 'In exchange for a kiss.'

'That is quite a steep price for a bouquet of flowers.'

'That depends...' Harry said.

'On what?'

'On how much you want to kiss me.'

For a long few seconds Anna just looked at him, that inscrutable expression on her face.

'No consequences?' she asked. 'After we return to the house we go back to how we were?'

He couldn't believe she was asking the question. It meant she was actually considering kissing him.

'No consequences,' he said. 'We never even mention it again.'

'They are particularly beautiful bluebells.'

'Surely worth a single kiss.'

'Perhaps.'

Gripping her hand, Harry pulled her gently from the path and into the woods, stepping a path that he'd known since he was a boy, yet was all but invisible to the naked eye. Carefully he picked his way across gnarled tree roots and through ferns as tall as his shoulder until they came to a clearing. It had been years since he'd last set foot here, but barely anything had changed. There was still the huge trunk of an oak tree lying on the ground where it had fallen many years ago in a storm, still the dense silence of the forest, interrupted only by small creatures rustling through the undergrowth, still the same earthy scent and the same dappled sunshine.

'No one will stumble across us here,' Harry said, watching as Anna perched on the edge of the felled tree and then taking his place beside her.

'This is rather a convenient spot,' Anna said, looking at him with a small frown. 'Did you plan on bringing me here all along?'

Not consciously, although he did wonder if somewhere deep down he'd known what he wanted to happen and had engineered everything to make it as he'd pictured.

'No plans,' he said, 'but perhaps some unacknowledged desire pushing me subconsciously towards this place.'

Slowly he reached up and gripped one end of the ribbon that secured Anna's bonnet under her chin. A gentle tug was all it took to untie it and carefully he lifted the bonnet off her head.

'Do you think anyone would notice if I pulled down your hair?' Harry asked. For weeks he'd been wanting to see Anna shake her coppery locks loose, to see her hair cascade over her shoulders and down her back, but even he knew that was too much to ask. Only a husband or a lover ever got to see their woman's hair unfastened and loose. No respectable young lady would ever take down her hair in public.

He felt his pulse quicken as Anna raised her hands to her hair, slowly pulling out the pins. One after another, each allowing another few strands to uncurl and tumble over her shoulders.

'Maybe I *should* write an ode to your hair,' Harry murmured, lifting his fingers and running them through her loose curls.

His fingers lingered as they brushed against her neck, picking out all the spots he wished he could kiss. There was a hollow just behind her earlobe that begged for his lips, but Harry knew he had to tread carefully. If he didn't control himself he might find himself ravishing Anna in the middle of the clearing and that would ruin all their plans.

Tentatively Anna reached up and touched Harry's shoulders, gripping them gently and pulling him closer to her.

'What was the price for my flowers?' she asked.

'Two kisses.'

'Two kisses? That seems rather steep. Surely I did not agree to that.'

'I'm sure you did, my lady.'

Their bodies were close now, thighs side by side,

separated only by the thick layers of her skirts, swaying closer together with every passing second.

Slowly, taking his time, Harry leaned in, the desire in him building to an excruciating high as he watched her close her eyes and tilt her chin, inviting him to kiss her. His lips met hers, gently at first, revelling in the sweet taste of her mouth, the softness of her lips, the warmth of her skin. He stiffened as her tongue flicked out to meet his and felt his entire body clench and tighten as she clutched at his shoulders and pulled him closer.

His hands were moving now, caressing her neck, her shoulders, her back. He wanted to touch her everywhere, run his fingers over every exposed bit of skin. He felt her breasts brush against his chest and wanted more than anything to push down her dress to expose the milky skin beneath and to trail kisses over the most private parts of her body.

'Harry,' Anna whispered, inflaming his desire even more as he heard his name on her lips.

He wouldn't have ever pulled away. If it were up to him they would still be locked together as the sun set on the horizon and the day turned to night, but Anna must have had more self-control as she eventually sat back, her eyes a little glazed and her mouth beautifully pink.

'That was unfair, Harry,' she said after a minute.

'Unfair?'

She nodded. He understood. They might have laughed and joked about never mentioning their little intimacy again, but it would be impossible to forget that kiss. It *was* unfair. Right now he couldn't remember a single reason why he and Anna couldn't be together. He liked her. He desired her. He wanted to get lost in her kisses all day long. There was a small voice in the back of his mind shouting about duty, but Harry found it very easy to silence as he glanced again at his fake fiancée.

He never thought Anna would kiss him again, despite upping the price of the flowers to two kisses, but as he turned back to her he wondered if he was in heaven as her fingers snaked around his neck, tickling the skin before she leaned in closer.

There was nothing gentle or delicate about this kiss. Harry found it impossible to hold back. All the pent-up desire that had been building over the past couple of weeks erupted and he found himself gripping Anna hard, kissing her as if they would never get the chance again. She returned his passion, running her hands over his body and kissing him deeply.

He couldn't help himself, he needed more. With dextrous fingers he traced the edge of her dress, where fabric met the skin of her chest. Anna stiffened for a second and then melted into him, pressing his hand deeper under the fabric. Inch by inch he exposed the silky-smooth skin of her breasts, pushing at her dress and chemise, knowing he had to see her, had to taste her.

'Harry,' Anna whispered, a plea for more that inflamed him like nothing else could.

With an almost imperceptible ripping of fabric Harry managed to push her dress down, taking a moment to watch how the soft cotton pooled at her waist, wishing it would just fall over her hips and leave her completely naked.

'I need to kiss you,' he said, his voice gruff with pent-up desire.

She nodded, her eyes wide, and before she could say anything his lips were on her skin again. He trailed kisses from her collarbone to the groove between her breasts, finally pausing before capturing one dusky-pink nipple in his mouth. Anna sighed, a sound that went straight to his very core, and out of the corner of his eye he saw her head drop back, her eyes glazed with desire.

After a few seconds of teasing and kissing he moved his lips to her other breast, eliciting the same deep sigh, and he wondered if it was the most perfect sound in the world.

It would have been so easy to lay her down, to strip her entirely naked right here deep in the forest and worship her body until the sun went down, but reluctantly Harry pulled back. He wanted her badly, but this wasn't the right way. Despite being a widow and not a shy virgin Anna was still vulnerable and he wouldn't be the man to take advantage of her, not like this. Even if he had to suppress a groan as he looked at her wonderfully dishevelled appearance.

Wordlessly Anna moved away a few inches, as if she didn't trust herself to remain quite so close. He felt bereft without her body pressing against his, but contented himself with watching her straighten her dress and pin her hair up. In the dappled sunlight she looked like some Greek goddess, some deity sent to bewitch and bedazzle him.

'I'm sorry. I couldn't help myself,' Harry said eventually.

'Don't apologise,' Anna said softly. 'It was wonderful.'

Harry knew then how close he was becoming,

how close he was to falling in love. He needed to distance himself, to step away from Anna and her sweet, strong nature and her beguiling looks, but right now that seemed impossible to do.

'We need to find something to take back from our scavenger hunt,' Anna said, standing and brushing small pieces of moss from her skirts.

'A bluebell,' Harry said, plucking one of the hundreds that surrounded the small clearing and tucking it carefully in the pocket of his jacket so the head of the flower poked out the top.

'Weren't we meant to bring back three things?'

'Let's pretend we forgot that part.'

He'd promised her they wouldn't discuss the kiss, the intimacy, promised her things would go back to normal, but he wondered if her heart was still hammering in her chest. He couldn't imagine never thinking about those few minutes in the clearing again—right now it seemed like it would be at the forefront of his mind for eternity.

'We should return,' Anna said, placing her hand in the crook of Harry's elbow. 'Otherwise we will be late and the others might get suspicious.'

'Perhaps we could linger just a few minutes more,' Harry suggested hopefully. It really was beautiful under the trees and out here he didn't have to share Anna with anyone else.

'The whole purpose of this pretend engagement is to save us both from further scandal and gossip,' Anna said, trying to look haughty, but instead just looking delightfully dishevelled. 'And all we've done these past few weeks is jump from one scandalous situation to the next.'

She was right: first their little trip into the darkness of the Carmichaels' garden, then the unchaperoned private platform to watch the opera from, then the kiss at the top of the tower and now this wonderful interlude in the forest. They hadn't really been behaving as they should, but Harry found he couldn't regret it.

'We're among friends here,' he said. 'Who is going to care if we return a little late?'

'Perhaps the upstanding Miss Wright and her mother,' Anna said, casting a sideways look at Harry.

He shook his head, but couldn't find the words to refute Anna's statement. He didn't really know Miss Wright or her mother well. They might be the sort of people who loved to be witness to a scandal so they could tell all their friends.

'She's pursuing you,' Anna said, just the tiniest hint of emotion in her voice.

Now wasn't the time to talk about this. Not five minutes ago he'd been kissing Anna, completely lost in her, willing to give away his fortune for just a few more minutes alone with her. He couldn't think of any other woman right now, even if there was no way of him and Anna having a future.

'Do you mind?' he asked.

Anna sighed, not answering for a few seconds, before shaking her head. 'I don't mind you having admirers, Harry. As much as I like you I know we aren't really engaged and one day soon we will go our separate ways. But I do want you to be happy and I'm afraid you'd be marrying Miss Wright for all the wrong reasons if you did court her.'

She'd said the same to him before, only a couple of days ago.

'People get married for all sorts of reasons,' Harry said. 'Money, titles, allegiances. Love doesn't often come into it. Why would my reasons be any different?'

'You deserve happiness, Harry,' she said, stopping abruptly and turning to face him. 'And an unhappy marriage is not a good start to a happy life.'

'That's exactly why I want to marry some respectable young woman that I can see myself tolerating for the rest of our married lives. Much better to have contentment than passion.'

'Toleration is no substitute for love,' he heard

her murmur, but she shook her head and dropped the subject.

They continued walking in silence, emerging from the woods and back into the long grass before finding the path that led back up the hill to the house. As they began the descent to the house they saw Miss Wright and Lydia walking arm in arm back from wherever their scavenger hunt had taken them.

Next to him he saw Anna surreptitiously smooth down her creased skirts and pat at her hair so no one would suspect anything untoward had happened between them. The tear in the fabric of her dress she'd cleverly concealed by holding it together with a hairpin and arranging a few loose strands of hair over the new seam.

'Lord Edgerton,' Miss Wright called as the two pairs neared each other. 'Lydia has been telling me of her love for music.'

He glanced at his sister and was surprised to see a hint of excitement in her eyes.

'My mother is hosting a small piano recital next week at our London house and I have invited Lydia along. Of course you'd be welcome to accompany her.'

No invitation was forthcoming for Anna, but he pushed this to the back of his mind.

'Would you like to go, Lydia?' he asked, hardly daring to hope.

With a small nod his sister indicated she would and Harry felt like falling to his knees and praising every saint that had ever lived. A piano recital was hardly a bustling ball, but it was a start. It was a social event that his sister had agreed to go to and without him having to cajole her a single bit.

This morning was turning out to be a great success. With a spring in his step he turned towards Halstead Hall, trying to stop the triumph from showing on his face.

Chapter Nineteen

'Play for me,' Harry murmured in Anna's ear, sending shivers down her spine. They were in the drawing room, awaiting the other guests to gather before dinner, and Anna had gravitated towards the piano without realising it.

'I haven't played for anyone in years,' she said, trailing her fingers along the keys.

'I heard you, a few weeks ago when I came to visit you for the first time at your uncle's house. You were good.'

'I play for myself, when no one else is around, but I don't think I've had an audience in the last five years.'

'Indulge me,' Harry said.

'I think I've indulged you enough today,' Anna muttered, flushing as she remembered their intimacy in the clearing. She hadn't been able to look at Harry for the rest of the day without feeling the heat rise in her cheeks and the blood pound in her ears. Never had she felt the kind of attraction she did for Harry. Of course she'd found men attractive before, but with Harry it went deeper. Her body craved him, but it wasn't just a primal desire, there was so much more.

'Please.'

With that one word she melted. Before her marriages she hadn't realised how attractive good manners were.

Carefully she sat on the piano stool, arranging her skirts around her.

'Do you need any music?'

She shook her head. Dozens of pieces were seared into her brain from years of practice. It might have been a few years since she last played them, but once learnt a piano piece wasn't something easily forgotten.

Stretching out her fingers, she began to play, choosing something which started slowly, building in tempo and difficulty as she gained confidence. After a few minutes she felt all her worries lifting from her shoulders, all the uncertainties, all the dilemmas just fading away. Right now the only thing that mattered was the music.

As she finished the piece and drifted back to earth she became aware of Harry again, standing far too close for propriety, especially as the other guests were expected in the drawing room at any moment. He laid a hand on her shoulder, his fingers trailing against the bare skin of her neck, the contact sending tiny jolts through her body.

She dared not turn to face him, knowing he would have *that* look in his eyes, the one she found impossible to resist. He would suggest a kiss and before she knew what was happening they would be in each other's arms when the rest of the guests arrived for pre-dinner drinks.

'Tell me why you don't play much any more,' Harry said, his voice quiet.

'Lord Fortescue didn't like it,' Anna replied simply.

'I like it.'

She turned to face him then, wondering when this strong, kind man had crept into her heart where he certainly did not belong. No man did.

'I like it, too,' she said.

Perhaps, a little voice in her head said. *Perhaps he is your chance at happiness.*

She did feel happy when she was with him, more happy than she had been in years.

The door to the room opened and Miss Wright entered with Lydia, the two women arm in arm.

'What marvellous music,' Miss Wright said,

smiling sweetly at Anna. 'We couldn't wait to see who was playing.'

'Lady Fortescue is very talented,' Harry murmured, stepping away slowly as if trying not to draw attention to how close he'd been standing.

'Perhaps you could play for us after dinner,' Miss Wright suggested.

Anna inclined her head, knowing it would seem petty if she said no. Hopefully she could just play one piece and then someone else would take over. Both Miss Wright and Lydia would be proficient at playing the piano—all young women of good birth were, although not many enjoyed it as much as she did.

Within a few minutes their party was complete with Rifield escorting Mrs Wright into the room. They were just about to move into the dining room when the door opened again and Lady Edgerton entered the room, her hair hastily pulled back and her dress crumpled, but nevertheless dressed for dinner.

'Mother,' Harry said, frowning. 'I didn't expect you to join us.'

He moved quickly to his mother's side, bending his head and talking quietly, trying to stop everyone from overhearing.

'I should be here,' Lady Edgerton said, wringing her hands.

'There really is no need. If you would be more comfortable in your rooms…'

'No. I can't hide away on such an important night. I must be here. I can't fail you.'

Harry flashed his sister a concerned glance, but Lydia just shrugged and he had no choice but to escort their mother in to dinner.

'Thank you for a lively weekend,' Rifield said, lifting his glass once everyone was seated. 'It has been most memorable.'

Anna's eyes darted to Harry's. She certainly would never forget the moment they'd shared in the clearing and the rest of the weekend wasn't easily forgotten either.

'I wanted to say something,' Miss Wright said, ignoring the plate of food in front of her and fixing Anna with a steady stare. 'Many things have happened this weekend that I am sure the rest of society does not need to know about and I wanted to assure you, Lady Fortescue, that they will not hear any details from me or my mother.'

Mrs Wright nodded her head in agreement.

'Thank you,' Anna said quietly.

'Well said,' Rifield agreed. 'There is no need

for any details from this weekend to be discussed by anyone who wasn't here.'

All eyes were on her as Anna took a sip of wine to wet her throat. 'Thank you all for your kindness. I feel I must apologise for the drama that unfolded over the weekend and embroiling you all in that. It was never my wish for things to happen as they did.'

Harry gave her a reassuring smile and Anna felt the corners of her mouth quiver as she tried to maintain her serious façade.

'Please, don't apologise,' Miss Wright said. 'I don't know anything about the difficulties you faced in your last marriage, Lady Fortescue, or the disputes you have with your stepchildren now, but I do understand they must be substantial if Lord Edgerton is willing to put his own reputation on the line to try to resolve some of these issues. Especially as your engagement is not a true one.'

Stony silence followed for a few seconds. Most people around the table knew Anna and Harry had agreed to pretend to be engaged while the gossip died down, but no one was meant to say it out loud.

Harry cleared his throat, but before he could speak there was a clatter of cutlery as his mother dropped her fork.

'Not true?' Harry's mother asked. 'What does she mean, Harry?'

'I'm sorry,' Miss Wright said quickly. 'I just assumed everyone knew.'

Anna scrutinised the young woman. She looked mortified by letting slip something she shouldn't, but there was no way to be sure if the mistake was genuine or not.

'Mother,' Harry said, his voice steady with no hint of the trepidation he must be feeling at trying to explain the situation to his mother.

'None of your clever words, Harry, tell me truthfully—are you engaged to this woman or not?'

'It's not that simple.'

'I don't see what about the question is difficult to answer. Are you engaged?'

Anna felt her heart hammering in her chest. She knew the answer, she'd always been the one going around reminding everyone that their engagement was only for convenience, a ruse only to be maintained until society had found someone else to gossip about. Nevertheless she found herself holding her breath.

'No, Mother.'

Deflating, Anna bowed her head so no one would see the disappointment in her eyes. His answer was never going to be anything but *no*. All the same, some part of her had wanted him to proclaim his affection for her, confess that although their arrangement had started off as a way to avoid a little bit of scandal it had ended with him falling in love. After this morning in the clearing she knew he desired her, just as she did him, but part of her was hoping for something more than that, something deeper.

'No?'

'I found myself in an embarrassing situation,' Anna said. 'Lord Edgerton was chivalrous enough to step in and offered to pretend to be engaged until the scandal was forgotten about.'

'Harry, is this true?' Lady Edgerton asked, a tremor in her voice.

He inclined his head.

'What on earth were you thinking? What about your reputation? This family's reputation?'

'You raised me to think of others,' Harry said quietly. 'Lady Fortescue was in need and I was in a position to help.'

'But this will ruin you. No decent woman will associate with you now.' Her voice was becoming shriller and shriller and Anna could see Harry glancing uncomfortably at the rest of the guests. 'This was your idea, wasn't it? A way to trap my son into marriage.'

Anna shook her head. She didn't want to tell everyone that Harry had insisted on their fake engagement, that he wouldn't take no for an answer.

'It was my idea, Mother,' Harry said abruptly. 'Lady Fortescue is a friend, she needed my help and I was more than happy to give it to her.'

'You're ruined, we're all ruined. There will be just as much scandal when you break off the engagement.'

The countess was probably right, Anna reflected. They wouldn't avoid all gossip by pretending to be engaged and then ending their relationship, but at least it gave them some power over when and how they made the announcement.

'You're ruined,' Harry's mother repeated.

'No, I'm not. I am an earl and a wealthy one at that. I come from one of the oldest families in England and I will have absolutely no problem in securing a respectable wife.' Harry spoke firmly but quietly, his tone brooking no argument, and Anna was glad to see his mother looked a little mollified, although her hands were still shaking as she picked up her fork again.

'It's not good,' she mumbled to herself as she began eating. 'It's not good.'

Harry flashed Anna an apologetic glance, but she shook her head, a minute movement that she hoped portrayed that she wasn't upset by the revelation.

Of course it was a lie. Inside Anna was crying, although she wasn't quite sure why. She'd been the one pushing Harry away on every occasion, the one who had insisted over and over again that she did not ever want to marry. And she didn't. It was just…

She couldn't finish the thought, there were too many things that made her like Harry. Time and time again he'd swooped to her rescue, calmly dealing with whatever new problems arose. He was kind, but more than that he truly wanted to help people in meaningful ways. And then there were his kisses. Anna knew she would never be kissed like that again. Every time she looked at him she felt her pulse quicken and her skin flush. Just the memory of their kiss earlier in the day made her feel giddy with excitement.

'I am so sorry,' Miss Wright was murmuring to Harry. 'I just assumed everyone knew. We're such an intimate group after all.'

'Please don't apologise. Everyone but my mother was aware of the situation, and it was my fault for not enlightening her sooner.'

Anna saw the fingers that brushed against Harry's arm and forced her gaze down to her plate. It didn't matter, she told herself. She found Harry attractive, she enjoyed his company, but they were never going to end up together. That meant she had no right feeling jealous when Harry didn't brush away Miss Wright's hand or when he leaned his head in closer to hear what she was saying.

Anna tried to excuse herself after dinner, but was pressed into playing a couple of pieces on the piano before she could persuade Miss Wright to take over. Despite her objections the young debutante looked thrilled to be able to show off her own musical talents, Anna thought, acknowledging her thoughts as uncharitable.

Rather than returning to her bedroom, she slipped out on to the patio, meaning to take a stroll around the gardens to clear her head before bed.

'It's a beautiful night,' a voice came out of the darkness, making Anna jump and let out a small cry. 'Sorry to startle you.'

It was Lydia, who must have also slipped away between the dining room and the drawing room, sitting on a low stone bench and looking up at the stars.

Anna walked the length of the patio and perched on the bench beside Lydia, feeling the cold of the stone even through the layers of undergarments and skirts.

'I'm sorry about Mother,' Lydia said quietly.

'There's nothing to apologise for.'

'You must think us an odd family.'

'Every family is a little odd in their own special way,' Anna said, reflecting on the peculiar foibles of her own family.

Lydia gave a short, sharp laugh. 'I suppose that's true.'

'I understand you are going to be accompanying Harry to London next week,' Anna said, trying to keep her tone light. If she understood correctly this was the first time Lydia had agreed to go out into society since the scandal with Captain Mountfield last year, so quite a monumental event.

Lydia shrugged, looking down at her shoes that were peeking out from under her dress. 'Miss Wright invited me to a piano recital. I thought it might be a pleasant way to spend an evening.'

Cautiously Anna searched for the right words. Just one ill-timed comment could be enough to push this nervous young woman back into her self-protective shell. 'It'll be a small, select group, I'm sure.'

Sighing, Lydia looked up at Anna. 'I suppose you think me very foolish,' the younger woman said.

'Why do you say that?'

'Hiding away here when you've been so brave to face the people who call you names and whisper about you.'

'I think everyone deals with it in a different way,' Anna said. 'Neither is right or wrong.'

They were silent for a few minutes, both looking out into the dark garden and the starry sky beyond. The night was clear, probably the reason there was a noticeable chill in the air, but Anna felt no compulsion to get up and go inside, not yet. She had an instinct Lydia hadn't quite finished with what she was trying to say, despite her silence.

'The first night you were here, when you came and helped me dress for dinner, you said something to me,' Lydia said after a few minutes. 'You told me it was my life, that my decisions were my own and that if it made me happy I could stay away from society for ever.'

Anna remembered saying the words and nodded.

'I've thought a lot about what you've said over the last few days and I realised you were right. I'm not happy shut away here, of course I'm not, but the only person keeping me here is *me*.' Lydia bit her lip and Anna was reminded how young

Harry's sister was. At just eighteen she'd coped with so much already; no one this young should be having to make such monumental decisions. 'It's just that I've locked myself away for so long, I don't know...' She trailed off, shaking her head as if she couldn't find the words.

'You feel like by trying to return to a normal life you're acknowledging how you've been living these past months was the wrong course and that doesn't feel right?' Anna ventured. She'd felt the same thing.

Lydia nodded, her eyes wide. 'I don't think I could have even thought about going to a piano recital or even socialising with Harry's guests here a few months ago, maybe not even a few weeks ago.'

'That's perfectly natural,' Anna said, giving Lydia a quick squeeze on the arm. 'Time heals most wounds, even to our most fragile characteristics like our self-confidence. In a year's time you'll feel completely different to how you do now. In five years' time this part of your life will be a distant memory and when you're fifty and surrounded by children and grandchildren it will just be a short episode of a rich and varied life.'

Lydia gently placed her hand in Anna's and

looked up at her. 'Thank you,' she said quietly. 'I can see why Harry cares for you so much.'

Anna felt a lump beginning to form in her throat. She knew Harry cared for her, it was obvious in everything he did, every way he tried to help her—the problem was she was starting to care for him rather deeply, too.

'Your brother is very kind,' Anna said carefully, trying to keep any hint of emotion from her voice.

'He tries to help everyone,' Lydia said. 'He's been like it ever since we were young. But he really does care for you.'

'I value his friendship.'

'There's nothing more between you?' she asked, her tone hopeful.

'Your brother is looking for a quiet, scandal-free society wife,' Anna said, 'and I am certainly not that.'

'But if he weren't? If he were able to follow his heart and choose the wife he wanted?'

'He doesn't believe in following his heart,' Anna said quietly. 'He thinks love has no place in a marriage.'

'Foolish man,' Lydia said with a shake of her head. 'Our parents…' She trailed off. 'Has Harry told you about our parents?'

'A little.'

'They were very much in love and they made one another miserable. I think it was worse for Harry, they'd mellowed a little by the time I was aware of what was going on, but they still sometimes had huge rows.'

'That's why Harry would never marry anyone he cared for. It seems so obtuse, thinking history would repeat itself.'

'And he is nothing like our father. Father might have loved Mother fiercely at the beginning of their marriage, but he was selfish and thought only of himself. A man who truly loves a woman wouldn't parade a string of mistresses in front of her eyes, he wouldn't say things purely to cause hurt.'

'Harry would never do that,' Anna agreed.

'Foolish man,' Lydia said again. 'I suppose he thinks he needs to protect me as well, marry someone with a good reputation, someone who might ease my passage back into society.' She shook her head. 'I just want him to be happy.'

They sat in silence for a few moments, both contemplating the reasons Harry was set on orchestrating his own unhappiness.

'What if he realised he was wrong?' Lydia asked. 'What if he realised he wanted to marry you, someone he *did* care for?'

Anna couldn't meet Lydia's hopeful eyes. Of course she'd considered this very scenario, imagined Harry being free of responsibility, free of the fear that he might care too much for his wife, and asking her to marry him. Part of her would say yes without any hesitation, the part that acknowledged she was well on her way to falling in love with him. Then the sensible part of her stepped forward and made her remember her vow never to marry again, not because she was against breaking a vow, but because of the reasons behind the vow. She would never give a man that power over her again, not even a man as kind and generous as Harry.

'I don't think I'll ever marry again,' Anna said eventually.

'He'll end up with someone like Miss Wright. I know that's the kind of wife he thinks best for him, someone pleasant and dull and respectable. And although my brother can make the best of most situations, a wife who does not challenge and stimulate him, who he does not care for, would make even him miserable,' Lydia said.

'I thought you liked Miss Wright.'

Lydia pulled a face that reminded her so much of her cousin Beatrice, Anna wanted to wrap her arms around the young woman.

'She's perfectly *nice* to my face, but I'm not convinced she doesn't talk about me behind my back.'

So Lydia was much more astute than Anna had given her credit for.

'Even if she doesn't, she wouldn't make Harry happy and that's what is important. He doesn't look at her like he looks at you.'

Smoothing down the satin material of her dress to keep her hands busy, Anna inclined her head, not trusting herself to speak.

'Of course I appreciate what he's trying to do for me, but sometimes I wish he'd be a little less selfless.'

'Perhaps you should tell him that,' Anna suggested.

Lydia sighed, but nodded all the same. 'He still looks at me as if I'm going to shatter at any moment.'

'It must be hard seeing someone that you love suffer,' Anna said.

'I know. And I know every time he looks at me he sees me up on the rooftop, thinking about doing something very stupid, but I just want him to get past that, to see I'm not the same person any more.'

Anna tried to keep her eyes from widening at the revelation Lydia had just made. She'd known

Harry's sister had been brought very low indeed by the scandal following her liaison with Captain Mountfield, but she'd never imagined the young woman had tried to take her own life. But Lydia hadn't revealed the depths of her desperation in a bid for attention, so Anna wouldn't make a fuss of it.

Keeping the shock from her face, Anna said kindly, 'He will. Give him time. Let him see you socialising a little, let him see you enjoying yourself and smiling and slowly he'll realise how you've grown and moved on.'

'But it might be too late by then. He might have already married someone who will make him miserable.'

Anna didn't have an answer for that. Knowing Harry, he probably would have. It was going to take a long time for Lydia to find her confidence, to start socialising and for Harry to see that she was slowly getting better.

'Talk to him then,' Anna urged. 'Tell him all this. Explain how you're feeling, how you've grown. Perhaps that will be enough.' Perhaps it would be enough to show him he didn't need to marry a respectable woman for his sister's sake, but it wouldn't do much to shift his deep-seated belief that marrying someone he actually cared about would only end in disaster.

They sat in silence for a few more minutes, both lost in thought as they gazed up at the clear night sky.

Chapter Twenty

The rain was hammering on the stairs as Anna dashed out of the carriage and up to the Shipping Company office. Even though she was only out in the open for at most twenty seconds she was dripping wet by the time she swung the door shut behind her. Rainwater dripped from her hair, down the front of her dress and even off the tip of her nose. The hem of her dress was discoloured and muddy and already she could feel the wet material beginning to stick to her skin. The weather was a far cry from the beautiful days of Harry's house party, but Anna couldn't find it in herself to be miserable.

In the three days that had passed since she had returned home she'd felt light and high-spirited, so much so that both her cousin and uncle had commented on numerous occasions. Beatrice had pushed her again and again to talk about what had occurred during her trip to Kent, but Anna had wanted to keep the memories to herself, as if in sharing them they might escape and diminish.

Now, even shivering in her damp clothes, she found she couldn't keep the smile from her face. Nothing had been resolved, they still didn't know who was sending her the horrible packages, but the memory of the time she'd spent with Harry was in the forefront of her mind.

'Dreadful weather,' Mr Maltravers bellowed as he came bursting through the door without knocking. Normally Anna would stiffen at his presence, but today she even managed to smile at her business rival.

'Good morning, Mr Maltravers,' Anna said, wiping the wet tendrils of hair from her face.

'What are these rumours I hear about you being engaged to some blue blood?' he asked abruptly, without any of the normal pleasantries.

'Lord Edgerton. He's a good friend.'

'But are you engaged? I saw the chap a couple of weeks ago and he didn't deny your connection, but I'd hoped you'd have seen sense by now.'

Mr Maltravers had proposed to her formally three times, but managed to bring up informal proposals in almost every conversation they had. Anna wasn't sure if he wanted her or her Shipping

Company more, but he was determined to pursue her despite the multiple rejections.

'Yes, we are engaged,' Anna said. Perhaps this would finally discourage him from proposing yet again.

'Man like him won't have any business sense,' he said, shaking his head. 'The company will be run into the ground within six months.'

'What makes you think he will take over?' Anna asked.

Mr Maltravers barked a harsh laugh. 'Of course he will. No man would let his wife run a shipping company. It's unheard of.'

'We live in modern times, Mr Maltravers.'

'If you care about the company you should marry me. I'd whip it into shape in no time and you have to admit we rub along pretty well.'

Anna couldn't stand the man and had made it quite clear that they didn't *rub along* well at all, but he was just so persistent.

'I thank you for your proposal, Mr Maltravers, but you see I am engaged to Lord Edgerton,' Anna said, wondering what she would do once they broke their sham engagement and Mr Maltravers proposed again.

He moved towards her, dripping rainwater all

over the wooden floorboards, and took her fingers in his large hand.

'I've admired you for a long time, Lady Fortescue. Your beauty and grace do not belong in this office, and I will make it my goal to be the one to free you from this work. I will not give up hope that one day you will be my wife. I hate to see a woman alone and vulnerable. There are too many terrible people in this world ready to take advantage, ready to hurt a woman who doesn't have a strong man to protect her.'

Anna was saved from answering as the door flew open and Harry came bounding in, grimacing as he wiped the water from his face.

'Am I interrupting?' he asked, his eyes flickering from Maltravers to Anna, resting on their linked hands, but his smile never slipping.

'Ah, the fiancé,' Mr Maltravers said, summoning a small bow of his head and a polite smile for Harry. 'You are a very lucky man, Lord Edgerton.'

'I am thankful every minute of every day.'

'I shall leave you,' Mr Maltravers said. 'Consider what I said, Lady Fortescue. You know where I am.'

They waited until Mr Maltravers's footsteps had

faded into the distance, covered by the hammering sound of the rain on the roof before moving.

'Should I be concerned?' Harry asked, shrugging his soaking overcoat from his shoulders and draping it over the coat stand.

'Mr Maltravers has been suggesting marriage almost every week for the last six months. I haven't been tempted so far.'

'He's a man of good taste.'

Anna shrugged. 'I'm not sure if it's me or the company he wants more.'

'Trust me,' Harry said, moving closer and lifting her hand to his lips, 'it's you.'

Anna's heart was pounding in her chest as he lingered with his lips on her skin and she imagined those very same lips tracing a path up her arm and across her body.

'What are we doing, Harry?' she whispered. 'We both know this can't lead anywhere.'

Slowly he dropped her hand and stepped away, his eyes never leaving hers.

'You are a very difficult woman to resist,' he murmured.

Anna couldn't hold his gaze, moving away and shuffling papers on her desk, not even noticing when the water droplets from her hair smudged some of the ink on her important documents.

'I was hoping to steal you away from your work for a couple of hours.'

Ever since she'd met Harry she had been spending a little less time at the Shipping Company office and a little more time socialising. In truth, she didn't mind. The company was beginning to do well so didn't need such close supervision and Anna knew it was healthy to have a more balanced lifestyle. All the same she hesitated.

'Just two hours,' Harry said, 'and then I'll deliver you back here myself and offer my services as your personal scribe, accountant and odd-jobs boy for the afternoon.'

It was hard to resist him.

'Two hours?'

'Two hours, no longer on my honour.'

Harry ran first, dashing to his waiting carriage and flinging the door open, waiting for Anna to make her way down the stairs before helping her up. Once she was seated he bounded inside, giving a shout for the coachman to set off, sparing a thought for the poor man sitting in the pouring rain.

He swept his hair back from his face, brushing the droplets of water from the tips and realising he was fighting a losing battle; his entire body was wet, a few more drips weren't going to make much difference.

Across from him Anna was tentatively touching her own hair as if wondering if any kind of style could be salvaged from the sodden tendrils.

'Where are we going?' Anna asked, settling against the backrest while rearranging her skirts.

'I have a surprise for you. Did you know we've been *engaged* for an entire month now?'

'You're proposing that we celebrate the one-month anniversary of our fake engagement?'

'We may not get to two months,' Harry reminded her softly.

She turned her head to look out the window then, studying the empty streets with an air of nonchalance and not for the first time Harry wished he could tell what she was thinking. Every day they spent together she warmed to him more, so much so that Harry was certain that she *liked* him, even cared for him, but he just couldn't tell if there was anything more to it than that.

On his part he knew he was falling for her. Ever since their kiss in the clearing at Halstead Hall he'd fallen asleep dreaming of her body pressed beside his and woken up tight with desire. And more than the physical attraction was his need to see her every day, to just be with her. He found himself making up excuse after excuse to call on Anna at home or at her company's office. It would only take one little slip and he would be professing his undying love for a woman he could never marry.

'Will you be attending the piano recital this evening?' Harry asked, steering the conversation to neutral ground.

Anna sighed. 'I'm not sure I'd be very welcome. I think Miss Wright only invited me because your sister insisted.'

'What does it matter why you were invited?'

'I think Miss Wright would prefer to have your attention to herself,' Anna said quietly.

'And I would prefer it if you were there.'

This earned him a little smile before she turned back to the window and continued her perusal of the empty streets.

'Harry, where on earth are we going?' Anna asked after a few minutes.

Instead of heading towards the more illustrious part of town their coach was weaving its way through the back alleys of Southwark, an area no sensible aristocratic lady would ever venture and gentlemen only went to have their vices satisfied.

'Nearly there,' he said cheerfully, poking his head out of the window for a second.

Two minutes later the carriage stopped and Harry instructed Anna to wait while he jumped down and rushed towards a nondescript door. After a hurried conversation with the occupant he ran back to the carriage and motioned for Anna to get down.

'If you're trying to sell me into service in a brothel, I won't be pleased,' Anna grumbled, but underneath it he could tell she was intrigued.

They ran inside where a young woman waited to show them into a tiny kitchen with a welcome fire.

'Anna, meet Miss Polly Proctor, daughter of the very talented cook in my London house.'

'Pleased to meet you, your ladyship.' Polly bobbed a curtsy, looking completely overwhelmed to have two titled visitors in her home.

'Lovely to meet you, Polly,' Anna said kindly.

'Would you like a cup of something warm, your ladyship? And please take a seat by the fire.'

Anna took the proffered seat, thanking Polly for the warm cup she pressed into her hands a few minutes later.

'What beautiful girls,' Anna said, motioning to the two toddlers who were gripping on to Polly's skirt and following their mother around the kitchen closely.

'My twins. Gilly and Kate.'

'They're lovely. A credit to you.'

As the two women talked about children Harry sat back and listened contentedly. If there was any topic of conversation that could unite women from all different backgrounds it was the subject of children. Soon Polly had relaxed enough to giggle and chat freely and one of the two girls was sitting happily on Anna's lap.

'Shall I bring them in now, sir?' Polly asked as Anna finished her drink.

'Yes, please.'

'What are we doing here?' Anna whispered as Polly left the room.

'Just wait.'

A minute later Polly came back in, carrying a large wicker basket which she set down in front of the fire. Harry watched as Anna craned her neck to see what was inside.

'I saw how much your cat meant to you,' he said quietly, 'and thought now might be the right time to consider another little companion.'

Anna sank to her knees in front of the basket and peeked inside. Harry saw her face light up at the sight of the kittens, all sleepy and curled up next to their mother, and wanted to capture how she looked right at that moment, the radiance and happiness that emanated from her.

'I need to find homes for them,' Polly said. 'My sister will take two and my next-door neighbour will have one, but the other two don't have anyone to take them. Sir said you might be interested...' She paused, looking hopefully down at Anna.

'I'd love them,' Anna said, stroking the soft fur and murmuring at the tiny kittens.

'You'll take both?' Polly's face lit up. 'Truly?'

'Truly. I wouldn't want to leave one homeless. Which two?'

'Your pick, your ladyship.'

Harry wasn't surprised when she picked out the two smallest, handling them with as much care as if they were her own babies. Both had a distinctive tortoiseshell pattern on their backs, but one had white feet and the other a white tip of tail.

After bidding Polly farewell they ran back to the carriage and climbed up, Anna sheltering her two new kittens from the rain as best she could with her cloak.

'That was a very sweet thing to do, Harry,' Anna said as she settled back into her seat, stroking the two sleeping animals in her lap. 'I don't think anyone has ever been as thoughtful.'

She reached across the gap between them and grasped his fingers in her own, her eyes filled with happiness.

Chapter Twenty-One

'They've been engaged a month and there's still no sign of a wedding date.'

'He's probably realised who he's tied himself to and can't bring himself to go through with the marriage.'

'The Edgertons are a good family, and he's an earl. Of course there was that unfortunate *business* with his sister last year, but it's hardly his fault. He could do so much better than Lady Fortescue.'

'It's a disgrace, such an eligible bachelor being snapped up by a woman who's already got through three husbands.'

Anna suppressed a smile as she listened to the two middle-aged women seated in front of her gossip with no idea she was sitting behind them. She knew both the women vaguely, had been introduced on a couple of occasions, but she had

no qualms about embarrassing them for their unkind words.

'I heard she's already lining up husband number five for after she's got rid of Lord Edgerton,'
Anna said, leaning forward and inserting herself
into the conversation.

Both women spun in their seats, realised it was
Anna who had spoken to them and turned varying
shades of crimson. They gave her disgust-filled
looks and moved away quickly, muttering behind
their fans as they found new seats.

'Making friends?' Harry observed as he slipped
into the seat next to her.

'Just fuelling the gossip about us.'

He raised an eyebrow. 'Trying to prolong the
scandal and therefore our engagement, Lady Fortescue? If I didn't know better I'd say you were
falling for me.'

'Well, according to the gossips you could do *so*
much better than me.'

Harry pretended to preen, then bent down to
whisper in her ear, 'Ah, but they don't know what
a good kisser you are.'

Anna considered this for a moment. 'I think
that's probably a good thing.'

'Perhaps.' Harry's eyes flickered to her lips and
Anna felt an all-too-familiar shiver run down the

length of her spine. All he had to do was look at her in a particular way and she was ready to disgrace herself in front of a room full of witnesses.

'Where's your sister?' Anna asked, trying to distract herself.

'She went to talk to Miss Wright.'

'I'm glad she came.'

'Me, too.'

'Lord Edgerton,' Beatrice, Anna's cousin, said as she flopped down into a seat beside Anna. 'It's lovely to see you, although I'm still miffed I didn't get an invitation to your little party.'

'Blame your cousin,' Harry said, settling back in his seat.

'I do. Anna said your sister was coming tonight.'

At that moment Lydia joined them, greeting Anna and slipping into her seat as Harry introduced Beatrice.

'Come sit with me,' Beatrice said. 'I'd love to hear all the juicy details of what occurred at your brother's house party and Anna is not very forthcoming.'

Anna watched for any sign of discomfort from Lydia, but she seemed happy enough to link arms with Beatrice and allow Anna's cousin to start gossiping.

She caught the flash of hope in Harry's eyes as

he realised Lydia was slotting right in during a social situation and gave him a reassuring pat on the forearm.

'Beatrice will be kind,' Anna whispered. Her cousin might be confident and outspoken, but she was sweet underneath it all. Just the sort of friend Lydia needed.

At the front of the room Mrs Wright clapped her hands, smiling at her assembled guests. All in all there were about twenty-five people in the room, mainly women, but with a smattering of men.

A tall man with a neat little moustache took his place at the piano and began to play. He was talented, hugely so, and within minutes he had the entire room enthralled. As Anna listened she felt the music washing over her and taking her back to simpler times.

Her fingers sought out Harry's and they sat side by side with their fingertips just touching, hidden from the view of everyone else by their position between the chairs. She dared not turn her head sideways, knowing one glimpse of Harry's smile, one twinkle of his eye, and she would do something they would both come to regret.

Too soon the first piece was over and Harry stood, breaking the contact before anyone could see them. Quickly he moved away, ducking out on to the terrace. Anna was just about to follow him when Mrs Wright came and sat down beside her and launched into a long history of how she'd come to discover the talented musician playing for them today. As she spoke Anna kept glancing at the door to the terrace, expecting Harry to reappear. She was completely trapped, unable to go to him, and it felt like torture.

Harry took a long, deep breath of the cold evening air and steadied himself. They'd only been holding hands, not even that, just the gentlest touching of the fingertips, yet here he was about to burst with desire like some green boy.

The door opened and he spun, smiling, expecting to see Anna, knowing that he wouldn't be able to keep his hands from her, but not caring.

'Miss Wright,' he said, trying to keep the disappointment from his voice.

'Thank you for coming this evening, Lord Edgerton,' Miss Wright said, crossing the terrace to him.

'My sister was most eager,' he said.

'I found myself missing your company after we spent the weekend together.'

He wanted to move away, but knew he had to tread carefully.

'I am glad you enjoyed yourself, even with the unpleasantness of the second day.'

'I think you handled that unpleasantness very well, Lord Edgerton. I admire you very much.'

'And I you, Miss Wright.' It was perhaps the wrong thing to say and he realised it as he noticed the flare of triumph in her eyes, but he was just trying to be polite.

'I have been talking to my select group of friends,' Miss Wright said, changing the direction of the conversation so abruptly Harry wasn't sure what was going on. 'I thought it might be prudent if we welcome your sister into our group. We are regarded in society as respectable debutantes, we all involve ourselves heavily in charity work and ensure no hint of scandal touches our names.'

Harry wasn't sure if she were proposing a friendship for his sister or that Lydia would be the charity work Miss Wright's friends engaged in.

'That is very generous,' he said, trying to dampen the feeling of discomfort building.

'I am sure with our support she could re-enter society and find herself a respectable husband. Perhaps not a duke or an earl or a marquess, but most certainly a baron or a second son.'

It was exactly what he'd wanted for his sister, so why did it feel so underhand, so sneaky?

'Of course she would have to engage in charity work and behave in an exemplary fashion, but with a little time I think her little indiscretion could be glossed over.'

'Mmm,' was all Harry could bring himself to say. He wanted Lydia to be accepted back into society, even wanted her to find a good husband and settle down with a family of her own, but this just didn't feel like the right way to go about it.

'It would be my pleasure to help her in this way,' Miss Wright said, stepping closer, but still maintaining an appropriate gap between them. She certainly was a stickler for the rules of propriety.

'That is very kind, Miss Wright,' Harry murmured.

'There was one other little matter I thought I might mention,' she said quietly. 'Your engagement to Lady Fortescue.'

The fake engagement that Harry just couldn't seem to bring himself to end.

'Although I can see Lady Fortescue has some wonderful qualities, she does have a certain reputation. I wondered if you appreciated how much your association with her damages your reputation and, by extension, your sister's.'

'Lady Fortescue is a friend,' Harry said softly

but firmly. 'I would not abandon a friend in their hour of need.'

'But surely you have done enough, Lord Edgerton. And if Lady Fortescue considers you a friend, then she will not hesitate to distance herself from you at such an important time. A respectable marriage for you could make all the difference to your sister's chances.'

It was exactly what Harry had been telling himself for the past few months, but as he looked at Miss Wright and imagined a future with her in it he found himself shuddering and not in a good way.

'Thank you for your concern, Miss Wright,' he said, trying to keep his voice light. 'I shall certainly consider what you have said.'

As a well-brought-up young woman she didn't press the matter any further. There was no way for a respectable debutante to declare her desire for a man to start courting her, especially not outright. Many indicated interest with a flutter of the eyelashes or fleeting glances, but Miss Wright could do no more than curtsy and take her leave.

Harry was still outside five minutes later when most of the guests had trickled back into the large drawing room for the second part of the recital.

He was gazing out over the darkened gardens, his eyes wandering over the immaculately kept grass and the neatly dug borders as a fine drizzle began to fall. He knew he should be grateful to Miss Wright—her offer to take Lydia under her wing was exactly what he had hoped for. With Miss Wright's influence and reputation Lydia's past indiscretion would eventually be forgotten, at least enough for her to find a husband.

If he were truly being selfless and working towards helping his sister recover from the scandal, he'd marry Miss Wright without a second's thought and bring some respectability back to the Edgerton family, but he just couldn't do it. It was ridiculous, Miss Wright was exactly the sort of woman he'd always been determined he'd marry one day: amiable, level-headed and someone he absolutely would never fall in love with. He should be dropping to his knees and begging the young woman to marry him, but he couldn't, not now he'd met Anna.

Running a hand through his hair, he inhaled deeply. He was falling in love and no matter how hard he tried there was no way of stopping it. A sensible man would distance himself, would take himself away from the woman he couldn't stop thinking about, but Harry was in too deep already. The situation was everything he'd always vowed to avoid—a woman he loved, someone he could actually hurt and who could hurt him. Not that he could imagine Anna doing anything to harm him deliberately...

'The performance will be starting again in a minute,' his sister said as she stepped outside. Despite her words she seemed in no rush to return to the audience and gently closed the door behind her.

'Are you enjoying it?' Harry asked, taking her arm as she approached and leading her for a slow stroll along the terrace.

'The pianist is very talented,' Lydia said, 'but it feels a little strange to be out in society after so long.'

'You don't regret coming?'

He found himself holding his breath as he waited for her to answer.

'No. Anna and her cousin, Beatrice, have been very kind and Miss Wright has introduced me to quite a few people. No one has said anything unkind.'

'Good. I wouldn't want you to be unhappy.'

Lydia smiled at him, the impish smile he re-

membered so well from her childhood, one he
hadn't seen much this past year.

'No one would dare with you scowling at them.'

'I don't scowl.'

'You're scowling now.'

Harry didn't have an answer for that, instead
deepening his scowl to make his sister giggle.

'I don't want you to be unhappy either, Harry,'
Lydia said once she'd regained her composure.

'I'm not unhappy.'

'Not now, but you could be. I know what you're
planning and I think it would make you miserable.'

'What do you think I'm planning?'

'Marrying someone you don't love, someone
like Miss Wright.'

'I thought you liked Miss Wright?'

'She's pleasant enough, at least to my face. And
she's probably pleasant enough behind my back.
But pleasant doesn't make a good choice for a
wife.'

'I think I'd like a pleasant wife.'

'Not if that was all there was, Harry,' Lydia said,
her large blue eyes staring up at him with more
wisdom than an eighteen-year-old should have.
'You deserve someone who adores you, who chal-

lenges you, who you think about every moment of every day.'

Anna, his mind screamed, that was who he thought about every moment of every day.

'We've seen what happens when people marry for love,' Harry said softly.

'That wasn't love, Harry,' Lydia said in a voice much older than her years. 'Two people who love each other don't go out of their way to hurt one another. Father was cruel and Mother provoked him again and again. I don't know what their relationship was built on, but that wasn't love.'

Harry frowned, but before he could speak Lydia continued.

'Love is caring for another person more than yourself. It's doing anything and everything to protect them and never knowingly causing them harm. Love is beautiful, Harry, and what our parents had wasn't beautiful.'

'You're eighteen, Lydia…' Harry began.

'I don't pretend ever to have been in love, but I watch people. I can see when two people truly care for one another—they're the happy ones. Not those who marry for money or titles or some other silly reason.' She reached out and squeezed his hand. 'Don't let our parents' disastrous marriage ruin your life. You're not like Father, Harry, you're a better man. I know you would never hurt someone you loved, you wouldn't intentionally hurt anyone.'

'Who would you have me marry?'

She levelled a completely grown-up stare at him that made him wonder where the little girl who loved pony rides had disappeared to.

'Someone who makes you smile when you see her, someone who makes you whistle as you come down for breakfast, someone that has you acting like a carefree young man and not someone with the weight of the world on his shoulders.' She patted his arm as if he were a little boy.

'But if I take a well-respected wife, someone who could help you back into society...'

Lydia grimaced. 'Then you will be unhappy and I will be unhappy because you are unhappy.'

Standing on tiptoes, she reached up and gave him a kiss on the cheek before turning and slipping back into the drawing room. Harry knew he should follow her, but lingered for a few minutes longer, too deep in thought to hear the piano music start again.

Chapter Twenty-Two

'Rebecca Tointon has had four proposals this month,' Beatrice said as she flopped on to Anna's bed, creasing up the delicate silk of her gown in one swift movement.

'Rebecca Tointon is the richest debutante London's ever seen,' Anna said, smiling at her cousin in the mirror. 'And it's not like you haven't had any.'

'Two, that's barely anything. And both were entirely unacceptable. Sir Witlow is barely out of the schoolroom and Mr Gainsborough has a daughter older than me.'

'You've only been out in society a few months,' Anna said soothingly. 'I'm sure an earl or a marquess will fall head over heels in love with you soon.'

'You can joke, but you're engaged to the most eligible bachelor in London. And he's an earl.'

'Pretending to be engaged,' Anna corrected.

Beatrice levelled her with a hard stare. 'No one believes that any more. You two are besotted with each other.'

'I am not besotted,' Anna said, feeling the heat rise in her cheeks as she came out with the lie. 'And Lord Edgerton is just being chivalrous and trying to save me from a little gossip.'

'If that was true he'd have broken the engagement this week when Lady Arrington got caught in a rather compromising position with Lord Wilbraham. Apparently her husband is thinking of *divorcing* her.'

Anna had half-expected Harry to suggest they quietly end their engagement once society was preoccupied with the rather scandalous discovery of Lady Arrington half-naked in the arms of a man who was most certainly not her husband, but he hadn't. He hadn't even hinted that it might be a good opportunity.

'Lord Edgerton has made it very clear he wants to marry a well-respected young woman, not an old widow who everyone gossips about.'

'That's what he thinks he should want, but not what he really wants,' Beatrice said with all the self-assurance of a confident eighteen-year-old. 'He wants you.'

Anna remembered their kisses, the stolen caresses, the looks that turned his eyes dark with desire.

'And you want him,' Beatrice said, holding her hand up to stop Anna from interrupting. 'I know you've vowed never to marry again, you've told me a thousand times, but that doesn't stop you from being besotted with Lord Edgerton. It's rather sweet and tragic, of course.'

A knock on the door halted the rebuke Anna had been forming as Beatrice skipped across the room to answer.

'Lord Edgerton, we were just talking about you,' Beatrice said with a dazzling smile.

In the mirror Anna watched as he raised a questioning eyebrow, but Beatrice just shook her head.

'I suppose I must have something to busy myself with before the rest of the guests arrive.'

Anna saw her cousin give Lord Edgerton a rather salacious wink that she suspected Beatrice had picked up from somewhere and someone entirely inappropriate and felt a prickle of guilt. It was truly scandalous that Harry be in her bedroom with her and Anna felt once again that she wasn't the most conscientious chaperon for the young girl.

As she tried to secure a dainty gold chain with

a teardrop ruby on the end around her neck she saw Harry check over his shoulder and then close the door completely, turning the key until the lock clicked. She felt a shiver of anticipation as he slowly turned back to face her.

'Allow me,' he said, coming up behind her and taking the two ends of the gold chain in his hands. His fingers brushed against her neck as he secured the clasp and then lingered for just a second longer than was necessary. 'I thought we should discuss how to move forward with finding who has been sending you those horrible packages.'

'I haven't received any more,' Anna said, feeling a little disappointed he didn't want privacy for any other purpose. 'Perhaps it was one of the Fortescues and now they've been scared off.'

'Perhaps, but it is unlikely. We both saw their reactions when we mentioned the packages—they didn't have any idea what we were talking about.'

'I don't know who else would want to harm me.'

'No spurned lovers? No spiteful wives who have a reason to hate you? No business rivals who would prefer you cowed and afraid?'

Anna shook her head. She truly couldn't think of anyone.

'No gossips you've publicly humiliated? No men you've turned down?'

'I really can't think of anyone,' Anna said. 'I have not ever had a lover to be spurned and the only man to propose to me in the last year is Mr Maltravers, and he's harmless.'

'Ah, yes, the man who's proposed to you nearly every week for the past six months.'

'But he wouldn't be sending me the packages, it wouldn't make sense.'

Harry looked thoughtful for a moment, then shrugged. 'Let's add him to our list. I'm told unrequited love is a large burden to bear. Anyone else?'

'I will think the matter over tonight,' Anna said with a small shake of her head, 'but I can't think of anyone else at present.'

'We should go downstairs,' Harry said, but didn't move from his position standing behind her.

'The other guests will be arriving soon.'

Anna's uncle, Mr Tenby, was hosting a small dinner party for a select group of friends as he did most months. He'd insisted Anna invite Harry, but most of the other guests would be middle-aged men and their wives, all friendly enough but not overly interesting.

'Perhaps they wouldn't notice if we were a couple of minutes late,' Harry murmured, dropping a hand lightly on Anna's shoulder. Her dress was low-cut with a wide neck, exposing her collarbones and the tips of her shoulders, and now Harry's fingers were tracing a path along the bare skin.

'Harry, we shouldn't,' Anna said, regretting the words as soon as they left her mouth.

'I know.'

He didn't stop, but in the mirror Anna saw he closed his eyes for a moment as if trying to reason with himself.

'What are we doing here, Harry?' she asked quietly.

'We're just two people, pretending to be engaged and finding it damn difficult to keep our hands to ourselves,' Harry said bluntly.

'We should break off our engagement.'

'We will. Just not yet. Give me a few more days.'

'What for, Harry?'

'To enjoy you.'

She turned and stood, facing him so they were chest to chest, body to body. Anna was not small in stature for a woman, but she had to tilt her head back to see Harry's face she was so close.

'Lydia thinks I should marry you,' Harry said, trailing his fingers from her temple down to the tip of her chin. 'She thinks you make me happy.'

'Doesn't she know I wouldn't have you?'

Harry shrugged, leaning in closer. 'She thinks I'd be able to persuade you.'

Right now Anna was feeling as if she would be very easy to persuade.

'It got me thinking, my conversation with Lydia, about what life is all about.'

Anna was finding it hard to concentrate with Harry standing so close. She could feel the heat from his body, the tickle of his breath on her neck and the completely distracting fingers on her skin.

'I started wondering if maybe I'd been approaching things all wrong.'

Managing a non-committal squeak, Anna looked up, knowing it was the wrong thing to do even as she did it.

'I've been too preoccupied with worrying about not repeating my parents' mistakes that I have nearly made an even graver one myself. I thought marrying a woman I cared deeply for would make me unhappy, but really *not* marrying for love would be a much greater source of misery.' He dropped his fingers to her neck, his touch feather-light and oh, so seductive. 'And here you are, a woman I care deeply for, and we're already engaged...'

'Pretending to be engaged,' Anna corrected,

half in a trance-like state. The correction made Harry smile.

'Do you know what would make me extremely happy right now, Lady Fortescue?'

Anna shook her head, hoping with every fibre in her body that it would involve a meeting of their lips.

'Kissing you right here.' He dipped his head and brushed his lips against the patch of skin that sat in the hollow just above her collarbone. 'And here…' His lips moved across her neck, pausing at the angle of her jaw before he groaned softly and covered her mouth with his.

Anna felt time stop. She wasn't aware of anything but Harry's lips on hers, his tongue, his hands, his body. Already her head was spinning and her heart pounding.

Never had she been kissed like this before. None of her husbands had ever made her feel even a fraction of what Harry did whenever his lips met hers.

'What would make you happy, Anna?' Harry asked, pulling away just enough to whisper the question.

She couldn't form any words, couldn't think of anything but Harry's firm body and their slow movements towards her large, inviting bed.

'Tell me,' he murmured, 'what would make you happy?'

She couldn't bring herself to utter the words, couldn't bring herself to admit out loud that she wanted him to lay her down on the bed and make love to her. Despite all the rumours and all the gossip she *was* a respectable widow. She'd only ever shared a bed with her husbands, never even entertained the idea of a lover.

'How about if I kissed you here?' he suggested, moving his lips down to the base of her neck.

Anna heard the sigh leave her mouth before she was even aware of it. Harry grinned and edged her a step closer to the bed.

'Or how about if I kissed you here.' His lips trailed ever lower, dancing across the skin of her chest, pushing against the material of her dress.

Feeling the edge of the bed behind her Anna sank down, looking up at Harry towering over her. Despite his physical advantage in size and strength she felt completely safe with him. Even after thinking she would never trust a man again, it was impossible not to trust Harry.

Holding out her hand, she waited until he'd taken it and pulled him to sit beside her. As soon as he was back on her level his lips found hers again, kissing her so deeply, so passionately, that

Anna felt her head begin to spin. Her hands were on his body, her palms caressing his torso through the layers of his eveningwear, and suddenly Anna realised that she had to feel more of him, to touch his bare skin, to run her fingers over the firm muscles of his back.

Pulling away slightly, she took his cravat and untied it in one swift movement, then moved on to his jacket, pulling it from his shoulders.

'My turn,' Harry said, lifting Anna to her feet and quickly spinning her so he could unfasten her dress. His fingers worked quickly and, before she could compose herself, Anna's dress was pooling around her ankles.

Harry whispered, 'What are you doing to me?' He motioned to the white stockings she wore under her dress. Anna glanced down. She'd put them on to keep out the chill of the cool evening, not as a seduction technique.

While he was distracted Anna quickly untucked his shirt, pulling it off and pausing to lay her hands on his chest. His skin was soft, but the muscles underneath firm and solid, and Anna knew that before the evening was over she would feel her own body pressed against those very muscles.

'Lie down,' Harry said and as Anna fell back on to the bed he gripped the top of one stocking and slowly started to pull the material down her leg. His fingers grazed her skin, sending wonderful sensations all through her body, and soon Anna was offering up the other leg quite shamelessly for him to divest of her stocking.

Soon she was clad only in her chemise, the thin white cotton barely any protection from Harry's burning gaze.

'Do you want me to stop?' Harry asked as he gripped the hem of her chemise. The strained expression on his face hinted at how hard he would find it if she said yes, but Anna knew he wouldn't continue without her agreeing completely. There was no way of hiding from the fact that she wanted this as much as him.

'Don't stop,' she whispered.

It was enough. Within seconds he'd whipped her last piece of clothing off over her head and was regarding her naked body. Anna didn't feel ashamed or self-conscious—this was Harry, he could put even the most timid mouse at ease.

While Harry began to caress her body, Anna reached up and unfastened his trousers, gripping the waistband and pushing them down as far as she could reach.

'I've been dreaming of this for a long time,' he said as he dipped his head and caught one of her nipples between his teeth. 'You've bewitched me, enchanted me, and now I can't stop thinking about you.'

Anna was too overwhelmed by the wonderful sensations coming from where his mouth met her skin to answer coherently.

'I fall asleep every night wondering how you would taste, how you would feel. Imagining touching you here...' he grazed his fingers across her abdomen '...and here...' he moved lower with his feather-light touch '...and here.'

Anna gasped as his fingers sent little jolts of pleasure through her body as he caressed her. Never had she been touched like this, never had she been made to moan in pleasure involuntarily.

'I've even imagined kissing you,' he said, causing Anna to pause. Surely he was kissing her already? As he pushed himself down the bed Anna's eyes widened and she struggled up on to her elbows, only to fall back with a soft whimper as his lips brushed against her most sensitive spot.

'Harry,' she moaned as he kissed and caressed her, her hand bunching the sheets beneath her, holding on tight to try to anchor herself to the bed. Every second that passed made her feel like she would float away on a cloud of pleasure, until something burst deep inside her, consuming every inch of her body.

As she opened her eyes and looked up she saw Harry moving up towards her, looking like some Greek god with bronzed skin and hardened muscles. She gripped his arms, pulling him towards her, and gently he slipped inside her.

He kissed her as their bodies came together and they moved as if one, rising and falling on the soft bed until Anna felt the pleasure building and building before the wonderful release. As she clung tight to Harry's back he stiffened and then collapsed on top of her.

Anna felt herself come drifting back down to earth as Harry raised himself on his arms and looked down at her. She couldn't help but smile, a dreamy, faraway smile. In a few minutes they would have to return to reality and discuss the future, but right now she just wanted to revel in the warm sensation of feeling completely and utterly cherished.

Harry stretched out beside Anna, pulling her body closer in to his and resting his hand on her hip. He knew they should move, knew a rather respectable dinner party was just about to start directly below them, but he couldn't find it in himself to spoil this moment.

He'd known what would happen the moment he'd locked the door behind him on entering Anna's room. If he was honest with himself, he'd known what would happen long before that. Ever since his realisation that he could not marry Miss Wright, or anyone like her, and Lydia's frank words trying to make him see he wasn't anything like their father, that he *could* marry for love and be happy, he'd known it was only a matter of time before he and Anna fell into each other's arms.

'Marry me,' Harry murmured, saying the words into the soft skin of Anna's neck.

'We're already...' she started to say.

'I mean for real. Marry me. Be my wife.'

Anna turned to face him, her eyes searching his. For once the cool greyness that normally hid all her emotions was alive with hope and worry and disbelief.

'I...' Before she could answer there was a quick rap on the door, followed by a low hiss that sounded like muffled words through the thick wood.

Anna sprung up from the bed and began to struggle back into her dress. There was another knock, this one louder and more insistent.

'Anna, open up. Now.'

With a quick glance at Harry, Anna rushed over to the door and opened it a crack. Beatrice hurriedly pushed inside, closing the door behind her. Anna's cousin's eyes widened as she took in the scene. Harry had just had time to pull the bedcovers over himself, but there was no hiding what had just occurred in this bedroom.

'Father sent me to fetch you. All the guests have arrived.'

Harry looked at Anna's completely dishevelled hair, her delightfully pink cheeks and her crumpled dress she'd only managed to get halfway on.

'Tell your father Anna has a headache, a bad one. She won't be able to attend the dinner party.'

Beatrice nodded, glancing at Harry out of the corner of her eye, but not able to bring herself to look at him directly.

'And you?'

'Does your father know I arrived?'

Beatrice shrugged.

'Only one of the footmen saw me come up. I don't think anyone else knows I'm here.'

Harry wrapped the sheet around his lower body, not wanting to embarrass Anna's cousin any further. Quickly he crossed to Anna's small writing desk and took a sheet of paper, penning a quick note of apology.

'Give this to the tall footman, the one with white-blond hair. Ask him to deliver it to your father as if it were just dropped off.' Harry handed her the note of apology along with a couple of shiny coins to ensure the footman's silence.

'And what will you do?' Beatrice asked, then shook her head, holding up her hands. 'Forget I asked, I don't want to know.'

With a backwards glance at her cousin, Beatrice left the room and Anna hurriedly locked the door behind her.

'We'll never get away with it,' she whispered.

Harry shrugged. It didn't much matter either way. If they were found together in Anna's bedroom they would just have to marry sooner and that would suit him just fine. Now he'd made up his mind to follow his heart and not his head he was rather eager to make everything legal.

'Everyone will know and then they'll really have something to gossip about.'

'Hush,' Harry said, crossing the room and taking her in his arms. 'What does it matter?'

Anna looked up at him as though he'd grown a second head.

'Of course it matters. Your reputation will be

ruined completely and by association your sister will be subject to further rumour and scandal.'

'What is it you always say?' Harry asked. 'There are worse things than a little gossip.'

This at least got a smile from her. A little up-turning of the corners of her mouth, but a smile all the same.

'Marry me, Anna,' Harry said again, 'and it won't matter.'

'You don't want to marry me.'

He kissed her, a slow, gentle kiss full of passion and promise, then pulled away and cupped her face in his hands.

'I've been trying to tell myself I don't want to marry you for six weeks,' he said, dropping a kiss on the end of her nose. 'I can't pretend any more.'

He waited, watching the emotions flit across her normally inscrutable face. It was unsurprising that she was hesitating, after her last disastrous marriage she had every right to be cautious, but Harry knew she cared for him and surely that was more important than her worries.

'It's not that I don't care for you, Harry,' Anna said, biting her lip. 'I care for you rather a lot.'

'I love you,' Harry blurted out, unsure where the words had come from, but realising they were true all the same. He did love Anna and he would make damn sure they spent their lives together.

Anna glided towards him, her eyes locked on his. 'I think I might love you, too, Harry,' she said, but there was a hint of sadness in her voice. Harry chose to ignore it and pushed forward.

'Then that's settled. We'll marry as soon as possible.'

Anna shook her head. 'I'm not sure…'

'I love you, you love me. What else is there to consider?'

'I need to think about this. I need some time.'

Harry sank to his knees in front of her and took both hands in his own. 'I promise to cherish you, to protect you, to allow you to flourish.'

'I need time, Harry.'

It wasn't an outright 'no' and with a little work Harry was sure he could turn it into a 'yes'. She was just cautious and rightly so after the abuse she'd had to endure from her last husband. All he had to do was show her he was different, show her how their lives could be together.

With a gentle squeeze of her hand he backed away.

'I can give you time, Anna. I don't want to rush you. Just know that I love you and I want us to be together.'

'You said you wanted to marry someone you would never fall in love with.'

'I was a fool, too preoccupied trying to avoid the harm my parents caused each other, too blind to see what they shared couldn't have been love. I could never hurt you like my father hurt my mother, could never set out to make you cry or make you want to hide in shame. I want to cherish you, protect you, show you how much I love you every single day,' Harry said.

'And your mother? She will not approve.'

'My mother is consumed by her nerves, I'm not sure she'd approve of anything. But I will break the news to her gently and she will come around.'

Anna fell silent, all her protestations answered for a little while.

'Just consider my proposal, Anna. That's all I ask. Think of the life we could have together. Think of the happiness.'

'I might not be able to have children,' Anna said quietly, glancing up at Harry for a second as she spoke. 'Three husbands and not one pregnancy does not bode well.'

He took her hand in his own and kissed her knuckles. 'Then we don't have children.'

'You'd make a wonderful father.'

'And you would make a wonderful mother, but sometimes these things are just not meant to be.'

'I will consider it,' Anna said, a little frown on her face. Harry knew the war that was waging inside her, knew enough about her character and her past to piece together the internal argument that was raging in her head. Part of her wanted to throw caution to the wind and say yes to becoming his wife. She loved him, he loved her, and the carefree romantic was telling her that things would be different this time. The other part of her was much more cautious. She'd been hurt, irreparably so, and didn't want to ever put herself in a position where anyone had power over her again. He just hoped the positive side won.

'I shall call on you tomorrow,' he said.

'I might need more time than that.'

'Then I shall call on you the next day as well.'

'Harry...'

He held his hands up. 'I'm not pressuring you, take all the time you need. We can be engaged for another six months if we so desire. I just don't want to go too long without seeing you.'

'I've got the accounts to go over tomorrow. Perhaps you could call on me at the Shipping Company Office and we could go for a stroll in the late afternoon.'

'I'm looking forward to it already,' Harry said, pulling her in closer and kissing her deeply.

Humming to himself as he slipped out the back door, Harry skirted around the side of the house, quietly opened and shut the gate behind him, and was back on the street without anyone seeing him. All in all it had been a successful evening. He had never planned to seduce Anna, although he had been fantasising about tumbling into bed with her for weeks. And he had never planned on proposing, at least not right then.

Ever since his talk with his sister when he'd realised she was right, he knew he could never hurt Anna the way his father had hurt his mother. He'd been consumed with the idea that he and Anna could have a future. A future where they strolled through his country estate arm in arm, spent long, lazy mornings in bed together, and sat side by side while she worked on her shipping company accounts and he those for running the estate.

For so long he'd been focusing on the wrong things, thinking a dull, amiable wife would stop him from spending the rest of his life miserable, when the exact opposite was the truth.

So here he was, just a man in love with a woman, trying to persuade her to marry him. Harry knew he had a huge grin on his face, he probably looked like a lunatic escaped from an asylum, but he couldn't stop smiling. Anna would come round, if he didn't press her too much, and she'd realise by herself how they were meant to be together.

He was just crossing the street when a movement in a carriage fifty feet away caught his eye. Pausing for just a second, Harry glanced at it, trying not to let on he'd noticed. Sure enough there was a shadow inside, someone shifting behind the curtain, trying not to be seen.

Nonchalantly he continued walking, his natural path taking him past the carriage. As he drew closer he could see the curtains were drawn tightly together and there were no identifying markings on the exterior, no family crests or coats of arms, just plain black paintwork.

He debated whether to fling open the door and expose whoever was sitting inside, but his impeccable manners and good upbringing prevailed. This coach might have nothing to do with Anna or the mysterious packages she'd been receiving. It might simply be two lovers out for a secret assignation who'd chosen this street to stop in at random. Harry rounded the corner, ducked behind the wrought-iron fence so he was hidden by the thick bushes and looked back. The carriage hadn't moved. The coachman was sitting holding on to the reins with a drooped head and Harry wondered if he was dozing. Perhaps he would be able to sneak back and…

Before he could finish the thought he saw the coachman jerk awake and gather the reins tighter. Whoever was inside the carriage was evidently ready to leave. Looking about him, he searched for another carriage, something he could follow in at a discreet distance. There was nothing. Anna's uncle lived in a respectable residential street where many people would have carriages of their own. No need for a hired conveyance to be touting for business.

Cursing, Harry sprang into action. They knew whoever was tormenting Anna was watching her closely. The last package had just contained a list of dates and times and locations where she'd been. This could be his best chance at finding out once and for all who was behind the packages.

He ran at a full sprint down the pavement, throwing himself at the carriage door just as the coachman urged the horses forward. Clinging on to the handle, Harry pulled, opening the door as the carriage started moving. He was balancing on the footplate of a rapidly accelerating carriage and he knew a fall could cause him to have at least a few broken bones. Gritting his teeth, he pushed the door open a little further and threw himself inside.

As he landed on his face inside the carriage he felt the driver pull on the reins to slow the horses, shouting in surprise at his new passenger.

'Mr Maltravers,' Harry said, greeting Anna's business rival. 'What a surprise to see you here.'

'What is the meaning of this…this…intrusion?' Mr Maltravers spluttered, his face rapidly turning crimson.

'I could ask you the same thing.'

'Stop talking in riddles, man, and tell me why you've thrown yourself into my carriage.'

Harry picked himself up from the floor and took a seat across from Mr Maltravers.

'Tell me, why were you outside Lady Fortescue's house, watching?'

'I don't know what you're talking about.'

'Your carriage was stopped outside Lady Fortescue's house.'

'Indeed it was. There's no crime in it.'

'No…' Harry shook his head '…but it is a crime to send threatening messages, to kill a cat and send it to their owner.'

'What are you going on about?' Mr Maltravers bellowed. 'You're making no sense.'

Harry watched carefully and saw a flicker of fear in the portly man's eyes. He knew exactly what Harry was talking about.

'Why were you here, then?'

'Not that it's any of your concern, but I had in mind to pay Lady Fortescue a little visit this evening, then I remembered her uncle was hosting a dinner party so thought it better not to intrude.'

'So why did you not instruct your coachman to leave straight away? You were watching the house.'

'I was doing nothing of the sort. Get out. Take your vile accusations and leave my carriage.'

Harry had seen enough. Mr Maltravers wasn't going to admit he had been the one terrorising Anna, much less explain why he'd done so. Nothing more would be gleaned tonight.

'I must insist you have no further contact with my fiancée,' Harry said. 'Do not visit her on business, do not run into her on the street by accident, do not ever come by her house. Is that clear?'

Mr Maltravers bristled, but did not protest.

'I shall inform Lady Fortescue of this in the morning,' Harry said.

'No, you won't.'

Harry had just turned to get down from the carriage when Mr Maltravers grabbed him by the jacket.

'I saw you go into her room, saw the shadows behind the curtains,' he hissed. 'I don't think you or Lady Fortescue would like the world to know what happened between you tonight.'

Harry shrugged, pulling himself free of Mr Maltravers's grip. 'I don't much care what you tell the world. Soon Lady Fortescue and I will be married and if the gossips want to talk about us, then so be it. There are worse things in the world than a little gossip.'

Quickly he jumped down from the coach, turning to address the coachman.

'Get this scoundrel out of my sight.'

As the coach raced off around the corner Harry glanced back at Anna's window. Now she could go about her life in peace, not always wondering where the next threat was coming from. Tomorrow he'd tell her about Mr Maltravers and, once he'd informed her, he would talk to a magistrate he knew well and see what could be done to keep Mr Maltravers from ever bothering Anna again.

Chapter Twenty-Three

'I'm not sure I believe it,' Anna said. 'I've never liked the man, but I didn't think he was capable of this.'

She sank back into her chair behind the desk and absentmindedly stroked the small kitten in her lap. She'd brought both kittens into the office today as they were already causing chaos around the house, scratching furniture and ripping fabrics. They were sweet little things, just wanting to frolic and play all the time, but they didn't realise yet that the whole world wasn't theirs to paw and scratch.

'I found him sitting in a carriage outside your uncle's house.'

Anna nodded. 'Why would he do it?' she asked. 'I thought he liked me—the man proposed to me often enough.'

'I suspect he wanted to make you feel vulnerable, so you would think you needed a husband to look after you and run to him for comfort.'

Anna shuddered. It was a cruel thing to do.

'I never even suspected him.' Mr Maltravers had suggested she needed protection on a number of occasions, but she'd never thought he was terrorising her to scare her into marriage.

Harry shrugged. 'Sometimes we need to be more wary of the people who act in secret than the people who are unpleasant to our faces.'

'He actually thought it would make me marry him?' Anna asked, incredulous. Mr Maltravers was the last man she would ever consider marrying.

'He didn't admit as much, but I suspect that was the reason. He had no other motive I can see. And he did propose to you rather a lot.'

Anna nodded. 'And I suppose the packages started when I came out of mourning, the point when I *could* start considering marriage again.'

'It's not just me that finds you irresistible,' Harry said, moving closer and taking Anna's hand.

'He killed my cat, he watched me and recorded all my movements.'

'Men can do terrible things when they're thwarted.'

'I was never sure if he wanted to marry me for *me* or for the business.'

'I think we can assume it was you he was obsessed with. I've never known a man to go to such lengths for anything other than an infatuation.'

Anna shuddered, thinking of all the times she'd been alone with the man, all the carriage rides home, the conversations in her office.

'I don't think he would have ever harmed you,' Harry said.

'You warned him to stay away?'

'Of course.'

'I'm glad the matter's resolved,' Anna said with a sigh, taking Harry's hand. 'Thank you. I don't think I truly believed this would ever be over.'

'It's over,' Harry said, pulling her closer to him and kissing her lightly on the forehead. 'I won't let anyone harm you, I won't let anyone threaten you.'

'I just want to forget this all ever happened.'

'And you can, my love. I'll sort things out with the magistrate.'

Anna stiffened and pulled away. She didn't want to involve a magistrate, she just wanted to forget Mr Maltravers even existed, forget about the horrible packages and the feelings of unrest and fear at the thought of being watched.

'No magistrate,' Anna said. 'I don't want to report this.'

'We must, Anna. He's tormented you for months, he can't be allowed to get away with it.'

'No, Harry, no magistrate. I don't want anyone else knowing about this. I don't want to have to relive everything that's happened.'

'You won't have to. I'll talk to the magistrate, make sure everything is kept discreet.'

'I said no, Harry,' Anna stood back and folded her arms.

'What if he does it again? What if he thinks he can get away with it and torments another woman?'

'I don't want to report it,' Anna said firmly.

Harry hesitated and then moved forward, engulfing her in his arms. At their feet the two kittens jumped and rolled, vying for her attention, and with a laugh Harry bent down and scooped them up.

'I can see you two are going to be trouble,' he said, giving both tiny balls of fur a stern look before giving in and stroking them until they purred. 'Do you mind if I take your mama out for a little excursion?'

Anna tidied up the papers on her desk, putting the large accounts book into a drawer and locking it afterwards. Then she gathered her cloak and slipped it on, glancing out the grimy window at the grey sky.

'Don't worry, I have the carriage waiting,' Harry said, following her gaze. 'And it means these two beauties can come along with us.'

The streets were busy as they weaved their way towards Ludgate Hill. Women selling flowers competed with men pushing wheelbarrows and children hurrying along behind governesses, and there was a crush of carriages travelling in all directions.

'What did you name them?' Harry asked as he stroked the kitten that had decided to settle in the crook of his arm, oblivious to the hairs that were already falling on his jacket.

'He's Apollo and this little lady is Artemis.'

'Twin gods. Very apt. I think they'll like Halstead Hall. Lots of curtains for them to get their claws into.'

'They're going to stay with you?' Anna asked, her expression serene.

'I'm sure you'll want to bring them with you when we take up residence.'

'Harry...'

'I'm not rushing you.'

Anna had to suppress a smile. It was hard to resist his easy charm and even harder to remain annoyed at him when he flashed that rather dazzling look. She still felt as though she were in a dream. Ever since their intimacies the night before Anna kept wondering if things were real. She shouldn't want to fall into Harry's arms, agree to everything he was proposing and allow him to sweep her off into the sunset, but she did. Part of her wondered why she was still resisting. She didn't really think Harry was like any of her other husbands. He would never be cruel, never hurt her. Sometimes he liked to make decisions for her, but surely she could work on that. She just wanted to be sure she would be able to maintain her independence if she agreed to this marriage. And that she was almost sure of. Almost.

'We're here,' Harry said, jumping down from the carriage and holding out his hand to Anna. Before she could protest he had handed the two kittens up to the coachman, instructing him to guard them with his life.

Anna allowed Harry to lead her to a shop a few doors down, noting the elegant displays in the window and the fancy lettering above the door. Augustus Grey Jeweller's, it read, and as they pushed opened the door a small man with a clipped moustache and small spectacles halfway down the bridge of his nose rushed forward to greet them.

'Lord Edgerton, what an honour. Please come in and look around. Is there anything in particular I can help you with today?' The words came out in a rush, so much so that Anna had to pause for a moment to separate the sentences.

'I wish to buy an engagement gift for my fiancée,' Harry said.

'May I offer my congratulations to you both,' the jeweller said, giving a funny little bow and flushing with pleasure. 'Please have a look around and if anything catches your eye I will get it out for closer inspection.'

'We're not *really* engaged yet,' Anna whispered to Harry as they began to stroll around the shop.

'I'm hopeful,' Harry said.

Anna tried giving him her sternest glare, but in truth she wasn't in the slightest put out. It was another generous act in a string of generous acts that showed the sort of person Harry was. She'd be a fool to turn down his proposal.

'What would you like?' he asked. 'Perhaps a necklace, or a ring to mark our engagement.'

Anna paused by a beautiful necklace. A string of iridescent pearls of the highest quality, shimmering under the glass. She didn't have much jewellery, only the pieces she'd saved from her adolescence and year as a debutante. Her first husband had gifted her a few pieces, but her second husband had promptly sold them to raise funds before his posting to India. Lord Fortescue had never bought her any jewellery of her own, instead making her wear items that had belonged to his late wife and were certainly never Anna's to keep.

'I can imagine you in pearls,' Harry murmured in her ear. 'Just in pearls.'

Refusing to be embarrassed, Anna moved on, her eyes flitting across the beautiful pieces set out to entice and enthral.

'I don't need anything, Harry,' she said.

'I know, but I would like to get you something all the same. Sometimes it's nice to be spoiled, to have someone buy you a gift.'

Anna stepped up to a case containing multiple beautiful rings, bands of gold and silver all set with different stones. There were some with huge diamonds and rubies, rings that would be noticed and commented on, and one particularly beautiful ring with a perfectly cut emerald, but Anna's eyes focused on something much less ostentatious, much more simple.

'Could I have a look at this one?' she asked.

It had a simple gold band with a green jade stone, unostentatious and beautiful.

The jeweller obligingly took it from the case and offered it to Anna for closer inspection.

'Allow me,' Harry said, taking the ring from her and slipping it on to her finger. It fit perfectly and looked as if it had been made to sit on her hand.

Anna regarded it, trying to suppress the tears that were threatening to form in her eyes. Why couldn't she have met Harry before her father had arranged her first marriage with Lord Humphries? Why couldn't she turn back time and be an eager debutante again, ready to fall in love without all the complications the last six years had added to her life?

'We'll take this one,' Harry said and Anna didn't even bristle at him assuming control of the situation and making the decision for her.

Chapter Twenty-Four

Resisting the urge to twiddle with the ring on her finger, Anna suppressed a smile as she glanced impatiently at the clock. Harry was due to visit and today was the day she was going to accept his proposal. First she was going to gently bring up the subject of her independence and her continuing to run her business, but if that went well she would agree to be his wife.

A bubble of excitement welled up inside her, threatening to burst and make her giggle or clap her hands with joy, but with some difficulty Anna managed to suppress the urge to show how giddy this was making her feel.

She was sitting with her legs underneath her, curled up in the drawing room with her two beautiful kittens frolicking at her feet. Another glance at the clock revealed only a minute had passed since she'd last checked and with a groan of impatience she got to her feet, sidestepping to avoid Apollo and Artemis, and crossed to the piano. Music would make the time pass more quickly.

With an ease that showed her talent at the piano Anna began to play, not bothering to flip through the sheets of music, but instead choosing a piece that was imprinted into her mind. As she played she felt a peculiar sense of contentment. Today she was going to leave her past behind and start to plan her future with the man she loved. Of course she still had a few misgivings, concerns that were only natural for a widow who'd survived three disastrous marriages, but that was not going to stop her from admitting she loved Harry and realising it would only be herself she was hurting if she chose to live her life separate from him.

She kept telling herself that if she went into this marriage making it clear to Harry she would never give up her business, that she would not sit at home organising the domestic matters like most wives, then surely they would have a chance at happiness.

There was a murmur of voices in the entrance hall, inaudible under the piano music, but Anna knew within a few seconds her future husband would be shown into the room. She had butterflies in her stomach as the door opened and couldn't resist the smile that took over her face when Harry walked in.

Just as she was about to stand and fling herself into Harry's arms another man entered the room behind him. Without missing a note Anna continued playing the piano as she assessed the newcomer. He was in his mid-forties, his expression serious, but as Harry leaned in and said something he gave a jovial little laugh.

Anna came to the end of the piece and stood, stepping out from behind the piano and gliding towards Harry, her movements slow and controlled and her expression neutral.

'Lady Fortescue, may I introduce Sir Gregory Hicks.'

Anna inclined her head in greeting before meeting his steely gaze with one of her own.

'Sir Gregory is a magistrate, he's discreet and I trust his judgement.'

'A magistrate,' Anna murmured. 'How interesting.' Pulling Harry to one side, she gave Sir Gregory a polite little smile before turning her back on him so her words were not overheard. 'What is he doing here?'

'Lord Edgerton told me of your little problem,' Sir Gregory interrupted, stepping forward and inserting himself in between her and Harry. 'He thought I may be able to advise you.'

'My little problem?' Anna asked, hardly believing what she was hearing.

'With an overzealous suitor. Malicious letters and packages, following your movements, all in all a very unpleasant episode.'

'Please excuse us for a few minutes, Sir Gregory, I just need to discuss something with Lord Edgerton. Would you care for some tea while you wait?' Anna was so irate she had nearly forgotten to offer the man some refreshments and was glad when he shook his head. It would mean he could be got rid of quicker.

She half-dragged Harry from the drawing room, not trusting herself to speak until they were safely ensconced in her uncle's study, with two doors firmly closed between them and Sir Gregory.

'Explain yourself,' Anna said, her tone clipped and harsh even to her own ears. She was finding it hard not to raise her voice.

'I thought it would be wise to consult a magistrate about how best to proceed with this Maltravers situation.' Harry placed his hand lightly on her shoulder and Anna had the urge to shake it off—instead she focused on maintaining her composure.

'Why?' she asked.

'Why? Because he killed your cat. Because he had been following you and watching you for months. Because he's been threatening you and who knows what he'll do now he's been found out. I want to keep you safe.'

'I asked you not to do anything,' Anna said, shaking his hand off her shoulder and moving away. Her hands were trembling and she felt her breathing becoming quicker and more laboured.

'I know, Anna, but...'

'But what? My opinions don't matter? Is that it?'

'Of course they matter,' Harry said, his voice soothing.

'Clearly they don't. You heard what I said, but just decided to do the opposite anyway.'

'I want to protect you. It's in your best interests.'

Anna let out a short, almost hysterical laugh as she tried to gain control of herself and failed miserably. 'I never asked you to protect me, Harry. I never asked you to do anything except let the matter drop.'

'I wasn't going to just let him get away with all the upset he's caused you.'

'What right have you to make that decision?' Anna asked, her voice rising in volume, but she was helpless to stop it.

'I love you, Anna, I care for you. That gives me the right.'

She shook her head, feeling the anger bubble up and almost close off her throat. Her next words were tight and a little muffled. 'You're just like the rest of them.'

'The rest of who?'

'Men. Thinking you know what's right for me. Making decisions for me.'

'You were just going to let him get away with it. Who knows, he might even have carried on.'

'And that was my decision to make, Harry. It's my life and if I choose to shave off all my hair and disguise myself as a man to join the army, then it is none of your concern. If I choose to give all my money away to the orphans of London, again it is none of your concern. And if I choose to put this matter with Mr Maltravers behind me rather than be tied up in lengthy legal arguments, then it is none of your concern.'

Harry grasped her upper arms and waited until she looked at him.

'I love you, Anna. That means everything you do is my concern.'

As he held her eyes Anna felt herself soften slightly. Perhaps it had all been in her best interests…

Then as suddenly as the thought had entered her mind she felt her resolve stiffen and her jaw clench. His motivations didn't matter. He was still trying to rule her life, to make her decisions for her, and he saw nothing wrong in his actions. Now it might just be an argument over whether to consult a magistrate about Mr Maltravers's persecution, but it would lead to other things. Before she knew it she would be married to a man who didn't see he was taking away her autonomy.

Trying to suppress the tears in her eyes and the sob that threatened to burst from her throat, she pulled the ring from her finger. It had only been there for two days, but already she'd got used to the weight and the feel of it. Her hand felt naked without it, but she couldn't keep it.

'Take it,' she whispered, not trusting her voice to speak any louder.

'No,' Harry said, shaking his head.

'Take it. I was a fool to think this could ever work.'

'Anna, don't.' His voice was firm and authoritative. 'I love you. You love me. This is just a misunderstanding.'

'I can't have a man tell me what to do again. I can't have someone controlling me.'

'I wouldn't try to control you.'

'You already are.'

He took her hand, raising the fingers to his lips. 'I'll send Sir Gregory away. We can talk about it and, if you truly don't want to do anything more, I will never mention Mr Maltravers again.'

With tears running down her cheeks, Anna pulled away. It shouldn't be this hard, doing the right thing. She'd known all along marrying again would only lead to pain, but right now it felt as though her heart was ripping in two.

'I can't marry you, Harry,' she said, wishing it weren't true. 'I can't give up my freedom.'

'Damn it, Anna, I'm not trying to lock you in a room for the next forty years. I want to love you, cherish you, give you the life of happiness you deserve. I'm not going to take away your freedom. I'm not going to try to make your decisions for you.'

But you already are. Anna couldn't bring herself to say the words, instead she reached up and let her fingers trail down Harry's cheek, knowing this would be the last time she saw him. Desperately she tried to imprint every detail of his face into her memory, knowing she would never feel like this about another man.

'Goodbye, Harry,' she said, turning and sweeping from the room. It took a gargantuan effort not to turn and look back, but she knew if she hesitated for even a second she'd run back to his arms and forget all her misgivings.

Chapter Twenty-Five

'Again,' Harry barked, taking up his starting stance and brandishing his sword.

'Take it easy, old chap,' Rifield said, wiping sweat from his brow. Despite his protestations Harry's friend turned and steadied himself, raising his sword and indicating he was ready to begin.

Metal clashed against metal as they began the drill, one of hundreds they'd perfected during their time in the army together. Harry had met Rifield on his very first day after signing away his freedom when they'd been partnered together for training. They'd quickly come to appreciate one another's skill and agility and soon after become good friends.

'I take it she turned you down?' Rifield asked during the next break.

Harry grunted, stalking back to his starting position. It had been three days since he had last seen Anna, three days since she'd told him *good-bye*. In that time he'd tried on numerous occasions to see her, but every time he'd failed. Once he'd even attempted to climb up the outside of the house to her first-floor bedroom, only to find she'd anticipated the move and decamped elsewhere. He'd waited outside her office at the docks for a whole day, but only saw weathered old men going in and out. She'd completely cut him off.

'You knew she was going to be a hard one to convince. What's stopping you now?'

Harry thought of the raw pain in her eyes as she'd told him they couldn't be together. He knew she loved him, that was the worst part. He loved her and she loved him, but she was too scared to let them be happy together. It was entirely understandable after the ordeal she'd endured with her last husband. He'd thought he was breaking down that fear, then he'd gone and brought Sir Gregory into the picture.

When he'd first approached the magistrate he had done it with the best of intentions. There was a deep-seated worry that wouldn't be dismissed inside Harry that Maltravers would continue to watch Anna and perhaps when they were least expecting it he would strike. Harry wasn't sure what he thought Maltravers might do, but he had proved himself to be a malicious and cruel man, and the risk to Anna was significant. So he'd ploughed on despite knowing full well Anna would not like it.

He had underestimated how much value she put on her freedom to make decisions. Many times she'd told him that she didn't want a husband to order her around, to take charge of her business, but he hadn't listened, not properly. He'd thought the main reason she didn't want to marry again was because she was afraid to enter a relationship where she might be mistreated. Of course he would never hurt her, never raise a hand to her, and he thought Anna knew that. Now he was realising that she was more afraid of losing her independence than worrying he might strike her.

'She's refusing to see me,' Harry said, swinging his sword in a practised arc.

'So you're just going to give up?'

Panting hard as he defended himself when Rifield took a few attacking steps, Harry shook his head. No, he wasn't going to just give up.

'No,' Harry said, striking his friend's sword so hard the metal vibrated long after they'd disengaged.

'I need a drink.' Rifield placed his sword in its sheath and laid it on the grass, then disappeared inside the house to find a maid.

Harry allowed his body to slump on to the bench. They were in the garden of Rifield's London town house. It was a tiny patch of grass, barely big enough for their drills, but army life had taught them both to be adaptable and now they were used to fighting in such a confined area.

Rifield was right, of course; he wasn't going to just give up because Anna was refusing to see him.

'This takes me back,' Rifield said as he returned, trailed by a maid carrying two tall glasses of water. 'Practising swordplay while solving the problems of the world.'

Silently Harry gulped down his glass of water.

'Do you remember Blaauwberg?' Rifield asked quietly.

Harry nodded. It had been an unfair fight. Two British infantry brigades against a handful of Batavian troops and some local militia, fought on the side of the Blaauwberg mountain. The British army had taken Cape Town the next day, with surprisingly few casualties.

The Batavian General who had led the defence had retreated inland and Harry had been included in the party to negotiate his surrender. The first round of negotiations had failed, but then they'd tried a different method. Instead of drilling in the facts of the British superiority in numbers of troops, the hopelessness of the situation for the Batavians, Harry had suggested starting the next round of negotiations with a list of the concessions the British were willing to make. Highlighting the good instead of the bad.

As he sat there, remembering the hot lowlands and cool mountains of the Cape an idea began to form in Harry's mind. Rifield was right, he needed to show Anna just how much he was willing to sacrifice to have her in his life.

'You're a very astute man,' Harry murmured, clapping his friend on the back.

'Anything to stop you battering my sword arm. I don't think I can take any more drills with you in such a dark mood.'

Quickly Harry stood, handed over the sword he'd been using and strode towards the door.

'Next time I see you I'll be engaged,' he called over his shoulder. 'Properly engaged.'

Sacrifices, that was what he needed to highlight. Show Anna exactly what he was prepared to do for her, how he would protect her, even against himself.

* * *

Leaning back in the comfortable leather chair Harry declined the offer of a drink from the solicitor's assistant with a shake of his head.

'This is most irregular, Lord Edgerton,' Mr Crosby said. He was a tall man with a hawk-like nose and small eyes, giving his face a predatory appearance.

'I am aware how unusual my request is,' Harry said, smiling at the man in front of him, 'but all I want to know is can you do it?'

'Well of course, it is just a matter of the right paperwork signed in front of witnesses, but I must caution you against this. Have you sought advice from anyone?'

'I do not need advice, Mr Crosby. My mind is quite made up.'

'And what do your family think of your proposal?'

Harry gave the solicitor a hard stare. 'I hardly think that is any of your concern. Now will you do as I ask or shall I take my business elsewhere?'

'As you wish, Lord Edgerton. The papers will be ready to sign in three days.'

Harry stood, holding out his hand for Mr Crosby to shake, then left the office with a spring in his steps and a whistle on his lips.

* * *

Anna sat stroking Apollo while Artemis frol-
icked around her feet. Morosely she stared out the
window, half-hoping Harry would appear around
the corner with a grin on his face and hard per-
severance in his eyes. She'd done the right thing,
sending him away, but that didn't mean it hadn't
hurt. Even now, six days later she had a deep ache
in her chest and a longing that seemed to come
from her very soul.

'You're moping,' Beatrice announced as she
twirled into the room.

Anna gave her cousin a weak smile but couldn't
summon the energy to argue. She *was* moping.

'We've got a ball to go to this evening,' she said,
running her critical gaze over Anna's red-rimmed
eyes and flushed cheeks.

'I'm not going,' Anna said.

'Yes, you are.'

'Your father has sent a note to Mrs Towertrap,
letting her know I am unwell and asking if she
will be so kind as to chaperon you tonight.' The
Towertrap girls were good friends with Beatrice
and their mother had chaperoned her on numerous other occasions.

'I know. I sent one half an hour later saying I

no longer needed a chaperon as you were feeling much improved.'

Anna blinked in surprise. 'Why?'

'Otherwise you'll sit around here moping for ever.'

'Is this one of Harry's schemes?' Anna asked. 'Has he told you to ensure I go to the ball so he can ambush me there?'

'No. Although I think you are being an utter fool, I wouldn't force you to see Lord Edgerton. Not when you're hurting so much.'

'Then why do you want me to go so badly tonight?'

Beatrice sighed a sigh of a much more mature woman. 'You're miserable, you're dwelling on whatever it is that's happened with Lord Edgerton, and sitting here by yourself is just making everything worse. Come to the ball with me. You might not have fun, but at least there will be something to distract you.'

Opening her mouth to refuse once and for all, Anna paused. She didn't want to go out. In truth, right now she didn't feel like she'd ever want to venture out of the safety of her uncle's house ever again, but there was a matter she needed to see to. In the eyes of the world she and Harry were still engaged. It would make the whole matter neater, more final, if she openly broke off the engagement.

It would have to be her to do it. Harry still thought he would be able to persuade her she'd made a mistake so he wasn't going to go around announcing to the world that they'd decided to go separate ways. No, she had to be the one to end things and the sooner she did it the easier it would be to move on.

Tears welled up in her eyes at the thought of never dancing with Harry again, never taking a stroll through the park or never hearing him bound up the rickety stairs to her little office at the docks.

'What time are we leaving?' Anna asked, summoning a little smile for Beatrice.

'Eight.'

Anna nodded, trying to keep her expression unreadable as her cousin scrutinised her. Tonight she would attend the ball and she would ensure the whole of society knew her and Harry's engagement was broken. Of course she would have to do it in such a way that cast Harry in the role of the injured party. He still had a chance at a happy future, a respectable wife. She had turned down the only man who could ever make her truly happy, so what did a little more malicious gossip about her matter.

Chapter Twenty-Six

Steeling herself for the unpleasant task ahead, Anna smiled warmly at the middle-aged gentleman in front of her. His name was Mr Warner and he had propositioned Anna on a few occasions in the past, mainly after she was widowed for a second time before she became Lady Fortescue. He was good-looking, well connected and likely the most arrogant man Anna had ever met. Their encounters in the past had consisted of Mr Warner paying her a few tepid compliments, talking about himself for a good long while, then suggesting they retire somewhere a little more private.

Anna hadn't seen the man for a couple of years, but he was perfect for what she had to do this evening.

'Of course I reminded the man of the penalty for trespassing and then had a quiet word with the magistrate.'

'What else could you do?' Anna murmured, laying a feather-light touch on Mr Warner's arm.

'Exactly. These riff-raff need to be reminded of the social order and their need to respect their betters.'

Anna suppressed the urge to tell Mr Warner exactly what she thought of his view on society and instead gave him an encouraging look, then dropping her eyes and biting her lip.

'Perhaps you would like a breath of fresh air,' Mr Warner suggested.

'It is rather warm…'

She allowed him to lead her out on to the terrace, shuddering as he placed a hand in the small of her back to guide her. For a moment she wondered if she could abandon her plan and just announce to the assembled guests that she and Lord Edgerton had called off the engagement. The idea of allowing Mr Warner's hands to roam over her body, his lips to meet hers, disgusted her, but she knew it was the only way to cause enough scandal and make Harry out as the victim. Then he would be free to marry someone respectable, someone who could give him the trust there should be between a husband and wife.

They strolled outside and Anna felt the chill of the evening air on her skin. It was a typical spring evening, overcast and threatening rain, but it did mean they had relative privacy on the terrace. Just as long as someone appropriate came out and caught them mid-kiss.

'I understood you were engaged to Lord Edgerton,' Mr Warner said as they paused at the edge of the terrace.

'A passing fancy, nothing more. We have decided to break the engagement,' Anna said, the words almost catching in her throat.

'Sensible decision. There was some big scandal with the family last year, something to do with Edgerton's sister...' he paused and brought her hand up to his lips '...and I am most pleased you are free to do as you wish. With whoever you wish.'

Anna watched as he glanced over his shoulder to ensure no one was observing them and then pulled her around the corner away from the lines of sight of the ballroom. Now if anyone exited through the doors on to the terrace they would have to step right up to the stone wall to catch a glimpse of her and Mr Warner.

'Perhaps we can come to some sort of arrangement,' Mr Warner said as he looped one arm around her waist and pulled her closer to him.

Anna worked hard to keep her expression impassive, not wanting to let him catch a glimpse of how repulsive she was finding the whole situation.

'Take your hands off my fiancée,' a low voice growled from somewhere in the shadows.

Guiltily Mr Warner and Anna jumped apart, both looking round for the source of the voice.

'Harry,' Anna whispered. He was standing behind her, half-hidden in the darkness, his hands bunched into fists.

'I thought…she said…' Mr Warner stuttered, his normally arrogant posturing replaced by meekness in the face of Harry's hostility. 'She said you were no longer engaged,' he managed eventually.

'Lady Fortescue is mistaken. We are still engaged. So I suggest you leave me and my fiancée in peace.'

Mr Warner glanced at Anna and then shrugged, as if it were too much bother to protest.

'Harry, it's not what it looks like,' Anna said, feeling the tears welling up in her eyes. The whole point of this little escapade was to be discovered, but she hadn't wanted Harry to be there when it happened.

He stepped towards her, emerging from the shadows like a predator stalking his prey. Anna felt an instant thrum of desire and knew that this reaction to him would never fade. That was why she'd been so keen to make him hate her. She couldn't bear to see him at social events and if he hated her then he might keep away.

Now she could see that her plan had been flawed. She didn't want him to hate her, couldn't bear the thought of him thinking she could be so fickle in her feelings.

'It looks like you were trying to seduce Mr Warner to create a scandal and publicly end our engagement, leaving me as the victim and free to marry some nice, respectable, dull young woman.'

Anna opened her mouth to protest, but realised he was pretty much right in every detail.

'I never thought she had to be dull,' she mumbled eventually.

'Praise be!' Harry exclaimed. 'For the woman I'm going to marry is anything but dull.'

She felt all her resolve slipping away as he reached out and took her hand.

'Harry...'

'Come here,' he said, his voice soft but authoritative. Anna felt her body sway towards him and before she could stop herself her lips were meeting his. He kissed her deeply, passionately, and for a long moment Anna forgot all the reasons they couldn't be together and lost herself in his embrace.

'Well, I never! The disgrace!' A voice came from behind them.

Slowly they broke apart, turning to see Mrs Winter, the middle-aged woman who had discovered them together all those weeks ago at the Prendersons' ball, glaring at them indignantly.

'Go away, Mrs Winter. I'm having a private moment with the woman I'm going to marry,' Harry said, turning away and taking Anna back into his arms. Anna had to suppress a giggle as she heard Mrs Winter huff in indignation. 'Where were we?' he murmured, and kissed her again.

'Harry…' Anna said as he pulled away after a few minutes.

'Hush. I know you're worried about marrying again and giving up your independence, your freedom to make all your own decisions.'

'I know you wouldn't treat me badly, Harry, it's not that.'

'I know, my love. I understand how few choices you were allowed to make in your last marriage and how hard you have fought to become independent now.'

'I can't give that up,' Anna said, her voice quavering.

'Do you trust me?'

Without any hesitation Anna nodded her head.

'Then I have something to show you.'

He took her by the hand and led her back along the terrace and into the ballroom. All eyes turned to them as they entered and Mrs Winter was talking loudly with her group of indignant friends.

They didn't stop to talk to anyone, just marched straight through the ballroom and out the front door.

'I'm meant to be chaperoning Beatrice,' Anna said, hesitating as Harry helped her up into his carriage.

He laughed. 'You must be the worst chaperon in London.'

He wasn't wrong. The number of times she'd left early or abandoned Beatrice in the middle of a ball and it wasn't as though she was setting a good example to her younger cousin either.

'I'll let you into a little secret,' Harry said. 'Your cousin helped me to get you here this evening. She knew you'd be leaving early and has made arrangements to stay under the watchful eye of Mrs Towertrap for the duration of the ball.'

'The sly little—' Anna started, cut off by Harry's deep laugh. 'She assured me she wasn't scheming with you to get me to go to the ball.'

'She lied. She's very good at lying, I think.'

The carriage started moving, weaving slowly in and out of the rows of other waiting coaches, picking up speed a little as it got away from the house.

'I'm sorry about how I tried to end everything,' Anna said after a few minutes of silence, 'but nothing has changed, Harry. We still don't have a future together.'

'Give me ten minutes. Let me show you how much I care for you. And how much I respect you.'

Anna nodded. It was the least she could do after her antics of the evening, but she knew whatever it was Harry wanted to show her, whatever grand gesture he had made, it wouldn't be enough. Nothing could be.

They travelled in silence the rest of the journey to Harry's town house, sitting side by side, Anna's small hand engulfed by Harry's larger one. As they slowed to a halt he jumped down, helping her from the carriage before pulling her up the steps. Anna could see how eager he was to get inside.

'This way.' Once inside the house he led her to his study, a large, airy room filled with books and with a desk at one end. He led her to the desk and motioned for her to take a seat.

Lamps were burning, giving the room a warm glow, and several candles were dotted around in various nooks, meaning the documents on Harry's desk were well illuminated.

'I went to see my solicitor,' Harry said without any preamble. 'I explained our little impasse when it comes to the subject of marriage, and discussed how to get around it.'

'With your solicitor?'

Harry grimaced. 'He wasn't the most supportive, but he drew up the documents I asked him to nonetheless. Everything I show you tonight is legal and binding once we obtain your signature in the presence of a witness. I have already signed both documents.'

'Harry, what are you talking about?'

'This first document states that when we marry I will have no claim over the Trevels Shipping Company. I cannot make any decisions pertaining to it, withdraw any money from it or borrow against it. It will remain completely yours.'

Anna's eyes flitted over the legal document. It was written in complicated legal terms, but in her year running the shipping company she had become used to decoding difficult papers. Laid out on the three sheets of paper was the agreement that the Shipping Company and any profits from it were to remain solely Anna's property and Harry would never have any rights over them.

She glanced at Harry, trying to swallow over the lump that was forming in her throat. It was a lovely gesture, probably the most thoughtful and sincere thing anyone had ever done.

'Wait,' Harry said, 'there's more.'

He took a second set of papers from the pile and laid them in front of her.

'This document will be kept with a solicitor of your choice. You do not have to tell me where or who. It is a document that agrees to a divorce between us at any point in the future. It states you do not need to give a reason for the divorce, you do not need to prove adultery or anything similar. It gives you equal rights to any children we have during our married life together.'

Anna was frowning. She couldn't quite believe everything Harry was saying. Surely such a thing wasn't possible.

'It safeguards you entirely, Anna. It means we can marry without you worrying about becoming unhappy in the future. If I ever raised a hand to you, if I ever belittled and abused you, you could get out of the marriage without any difficulty.'

'Is it legal?' Anna asked.

'It is.'

She shook her head, her eyes flitting over the words. 'Why? Why would you do this?'

'I want to marry you, Anna. I want to love and protect you, and most of all I want to make you happy. This was the only way I could think of to make you see I will not take away your independence. We will be equal partners in everything, and if in a year you find you are unhappy, then I wouldn't want you to remain tied to me for ever. I would never deny you a divorce if you asked for it, but this document just gives you that extra reassurance that you will never suffer by being married to me.'

'It's not possible.'

'My solicitor advises me that it is. Highly irregular, but possible.'

She ran her hands over the two sets of documents, trying to process what had just occurred. In one swoop Harry had removed all the obstacles to them being together.

'If we married,' Anna said slowly, trying to ignore the giant smile on Harry's face, 'I would be free to carry on running the business? Free to make my own decisions?'

'I hope you'll run it, because I'm not allowed to.'

Anna stood abruptly and flung herself into Harry's arms.

'Yes, yes, yes,' she said, her voice muffled by the fabric of his jacket.

'I love you,' he said, dropping a kiss on the top of her head. 'And I promise every day I will strive to make you feel safe and loved.'

Reaching into his jacket pocket, he withdrew the ring she'd given back only a few days earlier and slipped it on to her finger.

'Is this really possible?' Anna asked, pulling away slightly to look up into Harry's face.

'It's not just possible. We're going to be married and within the month if I have my way.'

Nestling her head back into his chest, Anna glanced at the documents on the desk, wondering if she should just tear them up. A man who was willing to do so much for her wasn't going to try to stifle her independence. He loved her and she believed he would support her to do whatever was important to her.

She felt his fingers on her chin, tilting her face up for a kiss. Suddenly all thoughts of legal documents were wiped from her mind as she kissed the man she loved, the man who was going to become her fourth, and final, husband.

Epilogue

Hitching up the beautiful gold silks of her gown, Anna ignored the shouts from her cousin and ran down the length of the docks. Today was her wedding day and, despite her protestations that she didn't need a grand affair, Harry had insisted they celebrate their union in appropriate splendour.

The ceremony was to take place in less than an hour in the drawing room of her uncle's house. Harry had insisted on obtaining a special licence so they could enjoy their wedding in private, with just a few select guests attending.

Scanning the horizon, her eyes flitting over the ships sailing to and from London, she knew she should listen to Beatrice and return home. There was no excuse to be late to her own wedding.

'Thinking of hopping on a ship and sailing for Australia?' a low voice said into her ear, making her jump.

She spun around, allowing the surprise to register on her face as she looked into Harry's eyes.

'What are you doing here?' she asked.

'I could ask you the same. You should be spending your last minutes as an unmarried woman preparing for married life and instead I find you down at the docks, mixing with rowdy sailors.'

'Hardly rowdy,' Anna said, looking around. It wasn't yet ten o'clock and most of the sailors currently ashore hadn't slept off the excesses of the night before.

'Hardly respectable.'

'If you'd wanted respectable, you should have married Miss Wright.'

Harry dropped a kiss on her lips as he pulled her towards him. 'Perhaps I'll admit I like chasing you, never knowing where you're going to end up next.'

Anna turned back to the docks and motioned to the ship that had just appeared in the distance. 'The *Lady Magdalene*,' she said, a smile crossing her face. 'The ship I told you about, the one we nearly lost in the storm off the coast of Portugal.'

They watched as the sailors busied themselves on deck, shouting orders and scuttling about as the ship came in to dock.

'All the crew survived?' Harry asked.

Anna nodded her head. Since taking over the running of the Trevels Shipping Company they'd only had three fatalities among the crews of the various ships, much better than almost every other shipping company Anna knew, but still not as good as she wished their safety record to be. Still, she was making improvements all the time, and with the extra money she now had available from the settlements she'd been due from the late Lord Fortescue's will the company was going from strength to strength.

Marrying an earl did have its advantages, Anna had to admit. Harry had taken a few key people aside and murmured in their ears about the difficulties Anna was facing with the Fortescue children denying her the settlements that were due. Suddenly Anna's stepchildren had capitulated and the money was paid almost immediately.

'Let's go,' Anna said, taking Harry's arm.

'You don't want to stay and greet the captain?'

Anna shook her head, motioning to the middle-aged woman a hundred feet away.

'The captain will be more interested in seeing his wife. Perhaps we could come back after the ceremony, before we leave for our honeymoon.'

'Whatever you wish, my dear.'

They walked arm in arm back towards Beatrice, who was tapping her foot impatiently as she waited next to the carriage that had brought her and Anna to the docks. A few feet further away was Harry's own carriage.

'She's impossible,' Beatrice declared, addressing herself directly to Harry. 'Who runs off to the docks on their wedding day?'

'I wanted to see the *Lady Magdalene* returned safely.'

Beatrice shook her head in disbelief. 'And now I suppose you two are going to ride back into town together.' She held up her hand before either of them could say anything. 'No, I don't want to know any more. I'll stop the carriage around the corner so you can at least *appear* to arrive separately.'

Anna silently kissed her cousin on the cheek, watching as the younger woman hopped up into the carriage and instructed the driver to leave.

'Shall we get to our wedding, Lady Edgerton?' Harry asked, helping Anna up into his carriage.

'You're not having doubts?'

'No doubts at all. You?'

'Oh, lots,' she said breezily, 'but none that are going to stop me from marrying you.'

'I'm glad to hear it. Otherwise I might just have

to kidnap you and whisk you away in the biggest scandal London society had seen in a decade.'

'I'll come quietly,' Anna said, leaning in to Harry and feeling the warmth spread through her as he placed his arm around her shoulder.

The carriage weaved its way through the docks, dodging the seamen and traders as they unloaded the cargo ships and whisked the goods away to the local warehouses. Anna looked back at the spot reserved for the *Lady Magdalene*, watching with contentment as the large ship docked and the sailors threw the ropes to the waiting men, ready to secure the storm-battered ship for unloading.

As they lurched forward, swerving to avoid a stray dog that dashed in front of the horses, Anna felt a swell of nausea in her stomach and had to close her eyes for just a minute. Placing one hand on her lower abdomen, she took a deep breath, steadying herself before opening her eyes again. It was another little sign, another little ray of hope. The nausea had been coming for four weeks now, never bad enough to make her vomit, but an almost constant disequilibrium that made her wonder if she might just be growing a little life inside her.

It was possible. She and Harry hadn't exactly had a chaste engagement. There had been that time before her uncle's dinner party when she and Harry had first been intimate. And then the time they'd been a little overcome with passion in the carriage…twice. And of course the time she had visited Harry's town house with the expectation of taking Lydia shopping, but had been cornered by her husband-to-be and they'd spent a wonderful afternoon in his rather masculine bedroom.

So a pregnancy was possible, it was just not something Anna had ever dared to hope for. Three marriages and no hint of a child, she'd assumed she was the one who was barren. Admittedly Lord Humphries had been quite elderly and Mr Trevels was barely in the country during their marriage. And Lord Fortescue hadn't been able to consummate their union, but still she'd assumed she had been the one unable to conceive.

She glanced at Harry. Soon she would tell him, but not yet. She barely dared to hope it might be true, so she didn't want to speak the words out loud. Instead she closed her eyes and leaned back into the strong arms of her husband-to-be.

Harry was whistling softly, stroking her arm and dropping the occasional kiss on her head. It would only be half an hour until they were home and the small number of guests would be gathered to watch them say their vows. The start of a new life.

'What happened to Mr Maltravers?' Anna asked quietly. Their carriage was just passing his office as she asked the question, keeping her demeanour calm and non-accusatory.

'I heard he decided to work on expanding his business on the Continent,' Harry said mildly.

'Did he have any help making that decision?'

'Will you still marry me if I say yes?'

Anna regarded him for a few seconds, searching his honest, open face and realising there wasn't much he could say to stop her from wanting to marry him.

'Yes.'

'I challenged Mr Maltravers to a duel,' Harry confessed.

Straightening, Anna turned to her fiancée and shook her head in disbelief.

'I challenged him to a duel. He refused. I told him I would seek justice for his crimes, that he'd better remain vigilant at all times.'

'He believed you?' Anna asked, trying to suppress the smile forming on her face.

'He believed me.'

She supposed if you didn't know Harry well he *might* be able to convince someone he was a violent man. And an earl was a powerful enemy to make.

'I suggested he take a long trip to Europe and while he was there forget he ever knew you.'

'Thank you,' Anna said quietly. Despite her reluctance to involve a magistrate in the matter she had dwelled on what might happen in the future with Mr Maltravers. The idea of bumping into him in the docks or hearing his heavy footfalls ascending the staircase to her office had preyed on her mind, and now Harry had quietly and efficiently resolved everything. It was rather refreshing to have a husband who actually cared about her.

'I hear there are bookmakers in London taking bets as to how long before you dispose of me, now you're Lady Edgerton,' Harry murmured into Anna's ear, dodging the hand that swatted at him.

'How long do you think you've got?' Anna asked.

'I believe I can keep you interested for at least a few months.'

Anna regarded him seriously, looking over every inch of him with her businesswoman's eye.

'Perhaps a month or two, and then you'll have to go,' she said, her serious façade cracking as

Harry nodded in agreement. 'Or perhaps I'll keep you for eternity.'

'Four husbands is quite enough,' Harry agreed. 'Any more would be greedy.'

'I wouldn't want to be greedy.'

'That's settled then, you'll remain Lady Edgerton for ever.'

They were sitting at the dining table, having a late wedding breakfast with their assembled guests. The ceremony had been a private affair, with only four guests, who were all sitting around the table talking amiably. Harry's mother hadn't been persuaded to leave the safety of Halstead Hall for the wedding, but Harry had his sister and Rifield as his guests. Rifield was deep in discussion with Anna's uncle, leaving the two young girls, Lydia and Beatrice, free to discuss whatever young women of eighteen talked about.

Harry ran a critical eye over his sister. She looked happy today, at least as happy as he'd seen her in a long time. She'd been with Anna to purchase a new dress and had allowed the maids to style her hair in the latest fashion. She didn't smile as much as Anna's cousin, or laugh in the same carefree way, but slowly he was starting to see flashes of the old Lydia returning. She was engaging a little more with the world now, seemed to spend less time inside her own head and more time experiencing what was going on around her. Slowly, Harry could see progress.

'She'll find her way back,' Anna said softly, nodding towards Lydia.

A few months ago Harry would have overanalysed a comment like that, wondering if it was possible, wondering if he was doing everything he could, but now he just nodded. He believed she *would* find her way back. It might take longer than he liked and she probably wouldn't be the same person as she had been two years ago, but that wasn't the end of the world either. Together they would make it through and one day he would be able to look back on these past couple of years and realise what a small part of their lives they had been.

'I would like to propose a toast,' Rifield said, standing and raising his glass. 'To the happy couple, Lord and Lady Edgerton.'

Everyone around the table stood and raised their glasses and Harry felt a moment of complete happiness. He had just married the woman he loved and was surrounded by people who cared about them both. What more could a man ask for?

'No killing this one off until we've had a rematch,' Rifield said to Anna. 'The last time we went through our sword drills he made me look like a beefy drunkard and that's not how I want to remember our friendship.'

'Slander my wife one more time, Rifield, and I'll make you look worse than a beefy drunkard,' Harry said with a grin.

'Forgive me, Lady Edgerton. I was wrong,' Rifield said with a little bow. 'Dispose of him as soon as you see fit, perhaps even before you leave for your honeymoon.'

Harry felt Anna's hand take his own, her fingers lacing in between his.

'The *ton* will have to find someone else to gossip about,' Anna said serenely. 'From now on I'm going to be the perfect embodiment of respectability.'

Unable to resist, Harry leaned down and whispered in his new wife's ear, 'We'd better hope our baby isn't born *too* early then, otherwise the gossips will be talking again.'

The hand that flew to her lower abdomen confirmed what Harry had suspected for the past week. Anna was carrying his child. The bouts of nausea, the subtle changes in her body, the lack of her monthly courses, all had made Harry suspect, but now he knew. Soon there would be another addition to their family.

'I'm not sure,' Anna said quietly.

'I am.'

'I don't know if I can...'

'You can. You were just waiting for the right time. The right husband.'

'And that's you?' There was a twinkle of humour in her eyes.

'That's me.'

* * * * *

LET'S TALK
Romance

For exclusive extracts, competitions
and special offers, find us online:

- facebook.com/millsandboon
- @millsandboonuk
- @millsandboon

Or get in touch on 0844 844 1351*

For all the latest titles coming soon,
visit millsandboon.co.uk/nextmonth

*Calls cost 7p per minute plus your phone company's price per
minute access charge

Want even more
ROMANCE?

Join our bookclub today!

'Mills & Boon books, the perfect way to escape for an hour or so.'

Miss W. Dyer

'Excellent service, promptly delivered and very good subscription choices.'

Miss A. Pearson

'You get fantastic special offers and the chance to get books before they hit the shops'

Mrs V. Hall

Visit millsandbook.co.uk/Bookclub and save on brand new books.

MILLS & BOON